The Other Mother

J.A. Baker

D1621771

Print ISBN 978-1-912175-80-2

Praise for Undercurrent

'I struggle to believe that this is actually a debut novelist, the story is written with such assurity and fluidity that it has the feel of a more seasoned writer.'
Sarah Kenny - The Great Bristish Book Off

'An extremely gripping read that was bound in mystery and atmosphere.' **Alexina Golding - Bookstormer**

'From the haunting throwbacks to the past, to the tense and suffocating atmosphere in the present, this harrowing tale sweeps easily and effortlessly from start to finish...'
Linda Green - Books Of All Kinds

'This is a super book with only a small cast of characters that gets smaller the more you read. Fantastic!'
Susan Hampson - Books From Dusk Till Dawn

'In terms of the writing, Baker has a gift, a wonderful gift and I am so pleased that she has put pen to paper and delivered such a bloody impressive debut.'
Emma Mitchell - Emma The Little Book Worm

'This is an enjoyable debut with a fabulous prologue that really creates a desire to invest yourself fully in the plot as it unfolds.'
Joanne Robertson - My Chestnut Reading Tree

Praise for Her Dark Retreat

"I found this book so addictive, it grabbed me from the first page and didn't let me go!" **Lorna Cassidy - On The Shelf Reviews**

"I just can't wait to have another taste of this author's crisp, clear, evocative writing." **Joseph Calleja - Relax And Read Reviews**

"An addictive story that will play on your darkest fears!"
Rachel Broughton - Rae Reads

"Her Dark Retreat is another excellent edge-of-your-seat psychological thriller from J.A. Baker."
Michelle Ryles - The Book Magnet

"I highly recommend this dark chilling thriller, it is perfect for these dark cold autumn nights." **Juliet Butler - Bookliterati**

To my muse and inspiration.
You know who you are...

Weak people revenge
Strong people forgive
Intelligent people ignore
Anon.

AFTERWARDS

I hold the knife aloft, fury splitting my veins, pulsing through me, burning my flesh as it traverses round my body. A furnace of anger driving me on making me do it. I take a shuddering breath and stop, poised, thinking about everything that has happened. I stare at the face beneath me; see how the features are contorted with terror. The knife trembles in my hands. I grip it tighter as it slips about in my palm. It feels alien against my hot skin, the metal smooth and cool, the blade glinting as it sways about. I gasp. This isn't me, not the real me.

'Don't do this. Put it down. Please, just put the knife down.'

I shake my head. The room seems to move. Images rush past me, a blur of colours merging and fusing, seeping into my brain, making me dizzy. I grip the handle tighter.

'Let me go and I won't tell anybody about this, I promise.'

I try to speak but the words won't come. They stick in my throat, hot and clunky, no way to escape. Trapped. I widen my eyes and a trickle of saliva escapes from my mouth and runs down the side of my face.

A small whimper, 'Come on, you know this is wrong. Just let me go. Please ... LET ME GO!'

The knife wobbles in my hand. It's heavy, a deadweight. I hold on to it. I must go ahead with this. All I need to do is push; place all my weight on it and drive it home. That's all I have to do.

The air is thick with fear, the smell of it filling my nostrils; an acrid, pungent stench ripping through me, over me. Great waves of terror gliding across wet skin.

Outside, birds sing, cars drive past, life rolls on. The mundane continues. Just as it did all those years ago and as it always will.

People everywhere; eating, sleeping, going about their lives while others kill and die and grieve. Life offers no compassion. It is a cold, hard mistress and we are all its victims. I stand here ready to do it, to finally bring an end to it all.

A noise close by alerts me. My heart thumps even faster. I keep my back to it. No time to reconsider. My mind is made up; it has been for a long time now.

'Put it down,' the voice calls from behind me, a gentle beckoning for me to stop.

I bring the blade up, hold it high above my head and stand with my legs apart, ready. It wasn't meant to be like this. Everything is different, wrong, spoiled. Nothing is as it should be.

'Please,' the voice in front of me begs, 'please put it down. I'm sorry. I'm so sorry.'

'We're all sorry,' I murmur before everything goes black …

CHILD A

*T*he moon cast an eerie glow, silvering the room, bathing everything in a soft metallic haze. Her skin was clammy as she sat immobile, jaw clenched tight. It was insistent, urgent—the relentless howling that filtered down from the room overhead. She drew her hands into tight fists, knuckles taut and white as she waited for it to stop, silently pleading for it to come to an end. She wasn't sure how much longer she could bear to listen to it – that noise – the endless screaming that tugged at her nerve endings and clawed at her senses. She was at her wits' end. Unfurling her hands and placing her bony fingers over her ears, she began to rock backwards and forwards. Humming loudly, her voice was a continuous, guttural drone; a feeble attempt to block it all out. The noise was unrelenting, knocking against her skull; a hammer bashing at her brain. It was useless. The screaming was still there, worming its way into her head. With a half shriek, she released her hands, her fingers springing free, flapping through the still evening air.

She looked around, her eyes desperately scanning the room, hoping for inspiration, hoping to find something, anything that would take her mind off the incessant caterwauling from above. A book, a magazine, the daily newspaper. Her gaze swept over the grey shadows stretched across the furniture, their familiarity providing no answers, no easy way out. She bit at her nails, already ragged and filthy, gnawed down to the bone, and didn't know which was the most difficult to contend with – the screaming toddler above her, or keeping her thoughts in check, doing what she could to stop them from escaping, to stop them from creeping out into the open where she couldn't possibly control them, where they would do what they always *do. She shook her head and moaned as she thought about the incident at school.*

Five minutes, that's all she would give him. Just five more minutes to stop his awful, dreadful whining and then she would go up there and sort him out.

It couldn't go on much longer, could it? Surely, he would cry himself out, fall asleep a sodden mess of snot and tears.

Pulling a chunk of coarse wool off one of the cushions and rubbing at it fitfully, holding it between her pale, thin fingers, she stared ahead, her gaze listless. She had been tricked into coming here. It wasn't meant to be like this. She had only agreed to do it because it was better than being at home. She shivered. Anything was better than being at home.

He had been so excitable all evening, this toddler who now seemed intent on disturbing the entire neighbourhood. And at first it was cute, seeing him run around, listening to his giggles every time she pulled a silly face, but then it had all gotten too much for her. He kept wanting more. Shouting at her to do it again and again until her eyes were gritty and her head ached. That was why she had put him to bed, she couldn't stand it any longer, having to put up with his constant demands for attention and big, fat snotty tears if she didn't play with him all the time. He had climbed all over her, tugging at her hair and shoving his sticky fingers in her face, even pulling her eyelids open when she had pretended to be asleep. Even his chunky little legs and the way they wobbled when he ran; his bright blue eyes, pink rimmed and glassy from crying all the time; his lisp and the way his tongue poked through his lips every time he spoke; they had all begun to get under her skin. By the time she had put him to bed, everything about him had started to put her on edge, made her want to gnash her teeth and tear at her skin with her ragged fingernails until the blood came. And she didn't like feeling that way, she really didn't but she had no idea how to stop it. It just took over her entire being, like a possession, as if an entity had crawled under her skin and was ripping her sanity to shreds, tearing it apart bit by bit by bit. That happened sometimes, uncontrollable rages that howled at her brain, told her to do things terrible things. Occurrences where she wanted to just bash things up, break whatever she could get her hands on; ornaments, clothing, people ...

She squinted and stared longingly at the clock, wishing her friend would hurry back. She was only supposed to have gone out for a few minutes; a quick dash to the corner shop for two cans of coke she had said. She would be back shortly she had said. That was ages ago. More than an hour, probably nearer two. She was supposed to be here with her looking after him and instead she was out there somewhere, doing God knows what with God knows who. She always was quite the liar. And now here she was, all alone in this house, with that child. That child and his incessant crying and sobbing that just went on and on and on. A screeching, clingy toddler whose neediness was becoming just too much for her.

The howling from upstairs grew louder, making her head buzz, augmenting her fury and resentment. It crept over her, within her — the anger; hot, bubbling bitumen slithering around her body, coating her pale flesh and blackening her soul. Her skin burned and her eyes began to water. That sound. That high-pitched, endless shriek. It made her stomach clench involuntarily; turned her insides to water. Why wouldn't he stop? Sometimes, when she was at home, alone in her bedroom, she cried like that, but not for long and only when she was sure she wouldn't be heard. Never around other people. Never. It was strictly forbidden. Crying is for soft people, for babies, her father would say. And she wasn't a baby. Even when the sharp, metal buckle on his leather belt made an imprint on her back so deep she could fit her fingers in there, she didn't cry. She refused to let the tears fall, keeping them carefully tucked away out of sight. Easier that way. Safer. And he was right. Crying was definitely for babies. Crying just brought on more of his anger.

She narrowed her eyes and stared at the pattern on the multi-coloured rug, then squinted hard and counted the red stripes that were woven in with the cream dots, looking closely at the brown and beige curves wondering who would design such a ghastly pattern. If she focused her eyes for long enough she could see shapes of things, people's *faces, animals, aeroplanes. Anything to keep her mind occupied, to stop the images galloping and rampaging through her head.*

Biting her lip, she flung herself back on the sofa and thought about the incident a few months back. For some reason, it made her go hot and filled her with a mixture of emotions that she didn't quite understand. Feelings that caught her by surprise. Sometimes they made her feel queasy and then other times a shiver of excitement bolted through her. It was wrong to feel that way, she knew it. Very, very wrong but it didn't stop the electricity from coursing through her veins every time that small face came into her head. Sometimes she was filled with horror at what had gone on and other times ... well, other times it set her entire body alight.

It was an accident. Of course, it was. She wasn't a monster. It just kind of happened. But then afterwards, she clung onto it, enjoyed the residual, lingering sensation of power and secrecy that it gave her. Like scratching an itch after waiting for so long and savouring the wonderful, tingling feeling it left on your skin. It had filled her with a warm glow, all the attention that terrible event had brought her. She had never known such interest, or been spoken to with such consideration before. People everywhere, initially cross with her but then sympathetic. Even her parents were attentive. For a short while, anyway. Then it was soon forgotten, that day, buried amidst the chaos that was their everyday life. Hidden amongst the heartache and horror that was her existence for as long as she could remember.

LISSY

'C'mon, c'mon! Up you get.' The room smells like an old sock. I let out an exaggerated sigh as I stand at the bedroom door and wait for Rosie to rouse herself. An array of tangled tights and discarded clothes are strewn all over the floor. Pointless nagging her about it, the poor kid has enough on her plate at the minute. I stride in and lean over her. My hair hangs over my eyes as I shake her awake. She stretches and yawns, her mouth a wide cavern of exhaustion. Her breath hits mine; small, sweet pockets of warm air meeting and merging, curling together in a concentrated, invisible cloud of moisture.

'Rosie, time to get up or you'll be late,' I whisper softly, my voice thin and reedy after too many glasses of wine last night. I don't always drink midweek but every so often I feel the need to partake in a few. Just enough to blot it all out. Just enough to help me through the crushing darkness.

She blinks and pushes me away.

'Stop it, Mum. Told you yesterday, I'm not going.' Her face is creased from where she has lain on the crumpled sheets all night. A red welt runs the length of her cheek, out of place and brutal against her soft, pale skin.

'Sorry, sweetheart, but you have to go.' I step away and flick the light on. She squawks and covers her eyes with her arm before slinking back down under the covers.

'You've got half an hour before it's time to leave,' I say lightly, 'and your breakfast is already on the table. Scrambled eggs, with a light dusting of pepper just how you like them.'

No response. I stand and watch her for a while, noticing how quickly she falls back into a deep sleep, how perfect her dark hair is, how softly she breathes as she exhales through slightly parted lips. I stare and wonder, as I often do, how I managed to create such a vision of perfection. I realise I am biased but I think she is the most beautiful creature I have ever seen.

I clap my hands lightly, just loud enough to stir her once again. She jumps up startled and stares at me, a flash of deep annoyance in her expression.

'For God's sake!' she barks. 'You're giving me a headache.'

'Up!' I shout again. 'You now have only twenty-five minutes.'

An exaggerated eye roll as she enunciates every syllable, her voice crystal, ringing throughout the room, 'Told you already. I am not going.'

'Told you last night, you are,' I reply in my best sing-song voice.

I try to keep my face composed as I observe her trembling chin. Got to stay determined. She has to do this. Opting out of everyday life isn't possible. It is not going to happen. Not if I have a say in it.

'I hate it there, Mum. They all loathe me,' she says, her voice thick with tears.

'Nobody loathes you, sweetheart,' I murmur, hoping to God what I am saying is true. 'You're just a new face that's all. You'll have a stack of friends in no time at all.'

'And what if I don't?' she whines, her voice nasally and child-like. 'What if I continue sitting there on my own, day after day? What then?'

I stride back into the room and perch on the edge of the bed. Rosie shrinks away from me and I feel myself begin to shut down. I can't allow any gaps to open between us. She is my life. She is all I have.

'That simply won't happen.' The mattress creaks under my weight as I shift about to get comfortable.

'You don't know that,' she replies curtly.

I suppress a sigh and run a hand through my knotted hair. 'These things take time, sweetheart. You just need to be patient.'

Reaching over I attempt to stroke her face, to soothe the lines of worry that are etched across her forehead, but am thwarted as she flings the covers back and sits bolt upright. She is ramrod straight as she turns to frown at me, her eyes full of scorn and disdain.

'This is all your fault, anyway,' she barks. 'I wouldn't have to go through any of this if it wasn't for you.'

A spike of ice traces its way down my spine. This, again.

'Come on, Rosie,' I say, trying to keep the edge out of my voice, 'we can have this conversation another time. Right now, you need to get moving or you'll be late.'

She is resolute, her voice laced with rancour and bitterness as she turns to face me. 'You haven't tried to deny it, have you?'

Ignoring her accusatory tone, I move away and head out of her room. I don't have time for this. Not this morning. Not any morning. I have too much on my mind, too much to do; lots of tasks to be getting on with. A life to live.

'Your twenty-five minutes just dwindled away to twenty,' I shout over my shoulder as I make my way downstairs, hoping she doesn't spot the tremor in my voice. No cracks in my facade. I won't allow it. I'm the strong one here, the backbone of our tiny family. Damage or remove me and the whole thing collapses around us like a pack of cards.

I busy myself with minor chores while she is getting ready, emptying the dishwasher and sorting the laundry out into small piles. I step outside to water a few plants in the front garden and listen to the occasional hum of a passing engine, a reminder of how fortunate I am to not have to be part of the rat race; to not be stuck on the treadmill of life.

I am preparing my paints in the studio when I finally hear Rosie thump her way down the stairs. She is full of hell. Her footsteps are a great indicator of her mood. Rarely does she float through the house like a whisper on the wind; deep thuds accompany my daughter on most of her journeys these days to let me know that her current predicament is all my doing. Her misery and angst are all down to me.

'Your eggs are cold,' I shout after her, but am met with a wall of silence as she unlocks the door, steps outside, and slams it loudly behind her, the walls vibrating with the force of her fury.

A headache begins to creep its way up over my skull, a thick ribbon of pain that wraps itself tighter and tighter around my head until I am left with no option other than to down tools and grab a couple of painkillers which I wash down with a glass of cold water. I had hoped she would adapt, take it all in her stride, but it would appear that just lately, anything can upset the delicate balance in Rosie's world. And it is difficult for her. I can see that, I really can. But she has to put her best foot forward and forge ahead with her new life. We have no other option. We are here now. What's done is done.

I stare out of the window, my hands resting on the work surface, and admire the view. We were very lucky with this cottage, with it coming up for sale at the exact same time I chose to move. Otherwise, we would be renting somewhere right now, living in a hiatus with no secure place to call our own, and no roots to bind us. Not that ours go down very deep anyway. But Peartree Lodge already feels like home to me. Perhaps not to Rosie but that will come in time. This will be our last move, our final one. I have made that promise to myself and I will damn well keep it. No amount of worrying or sleepless nights will alter my thinking. This time, our home, this tiny hamlet we now live in, set in the wilds of North Yorkshire, is for keeps. Nothing, not even Rosie's deteriorating temperament, will force me out of this house. This is our forever home. Come hell or high water, Rosie and I are here to stay.

BEVERLEY

Today, life feels good. I am happy. I say the words, softly at first, murmuring them slowly and deliciously; whispering them to myself before chanting them over and over like a mantra in my head, a stream of sounds churning, spinning, making me dizzy. So exciting and full of promise. Good days are few and far between in my life. That's just how it is, so when I do have them, I feel the need to cling on to the thought, clutch it to my chest; shout out to the world that for once, I am content. Even my weekly visit to my mother's house will not dent this feeling. The sound of her voice, the sarcastic, cutting words that tumble out of her mouth every time she speaks won't bother me. I won't let it. I will rise above her caustic comments and phrases that are designed to cut me down and hurt me. I will ignore it all because my life is now on the up and up. So much to look forward to. A shiver of satisfaction runs through me.

I pick up my phone and read Warren's message. He is concerned about me. Warren is always concerned. He has spent his entire adult life worrying about me. I reply to his message, assuring him that I am fine. I tell him that my week went well and that the new position that I have recently landed has worked out brilliantly. It is my dream job. He won't believe me and I will have to spend an inordinate amount of time convincing him that it's true. Because it is. Admittedly there have been times in the past when I have lied, told him I am fine when I am anything but; however, this time it is different. This time I have a reason for smiling.

Slipping my phone into my bag, I snatch up my car keys and head out into the sweet summer air. The chirrup of birdsong further elevates my mood. I stop and watch, mesmerised, as a blackbird tugs a worm out of the lawn and flies away with its prey tucked firmly between its beak. The worm wriggles and battles against its attacker, its vain attempts to free itself pointless, as the bird tips its head back and swallows it whole. I shudder and remind myself that everything dies at some point. *Everyone.* All living things have an expiry date.

I inhale deeply. The musky aroma of the lilac trees takes my breath away, deep and heady. Everything is in full bloom. Winter has passed; now only a lingering memory of a time when the shortest days seemed to drag on and on; an endless stream of hours filled with swathes of grey. But now summer is here and the darkness is behind us. I hum softly as I unlock the car and slide in. The world is suddenly a brighter place.

The usual feelings of apprehension and gloom that accompany me on my journey whenever I visit my mother are conspicuously absent today. I will not let her get to me or tear me down. Her words will wash over me like liquid mercury, slipping off my skin, leaving no trace.

As expected, she starts the minute I arrive.

'You're late,' she says as I stroll into the living room and drop my keys into the old wicker basket on the window ledge that she uses to keep all her bills and receipts in.

She's been smoking again. The stale scent of tobacco is everywhere, lingering in the air; an invisible haze of addiction. She has tried to mask it with room sprays but it's there. An obvious sign that she has lapsed. If she is smoking then she is drinking again as well. The two are inextricably linked and an inescapable part of who she is; interwoven into her psyche and DNA, like the colour of her eyes or the texture of her skin. There are times when I despair at her behaviour and want to shake her and scream at her that she needs to stop it, but then I often wonder how she has made it thus far without collapsing in a heap. How she has managed to stagger through her life and remain relatively sane after what happened to her, what I put her through. So, as much as I dread these visits, I will continue to make them for as long as she is alive. I owe her that much.

'And you've had a fag or two,' I reply, sticking my nose forward and sniffing the air dramatically.

She shrugs nonchalantly and turns to stare out of the window.

'I brought you some oranges and apples and the other things you asked for.'

We don't need to voice it out loud, what those other things are. I place her incontinence pads in the bathroom, wondering how much longer we can keep up with this pretence, how much longer she can remain here, on her own, with her ailing body and half-ravaged mind, her bouts of depression, her inability to move on. I blank it out. No time for such worries. We will keep on like this for as long as we possibly can and will cross that bridge when we come to it. Right now, I have other things to be thinking about, other important things I need to do.

She nods and fiddles with a strand of hair. 'She came to see me the other day.'

I freeze at her words and continue to busy myself rearranging dying flowers and sorting out the rotten fruit which is beginning to wrinkle and bruise. I know what is coming next and I am never fond of where these conversations lead us. I remain mute, more than a little reticent to answer. Any show of interest from me will only encourage her, set her off down a route I don't want to revisit, a route that will drag a heavy mantle of misery over my day. And I will not allow that to happen. I refuse to let her blacken my mood.

'I'm going to throw some of this out, Mum,' I say just a little too cheerily as I manhandle the collection of mouldy, powdery tangerines and apples that are so soft they practically fall apart in my hands.

'Do whatever you must,' she says in a tone I recognise all too well, a tone that is indicative of her simmering anger towards me.

I sing softly and quietly as I sort it all out, careful not to poke my fingers through the skin of the decaying fruit, a sight and sensation that reminds me of touching rotting human flesh.

'I love my new job,' I say over my shoulder, knowing she doesn't really give a flying fig how I spend my days.

I do this a lot when I am here; make small talk about things neither of us cares about. It's all rather cathartic this dodging and weaving, overlooking the obvious, talking only about the mundane, ignoring the elephant in the room, the one we haven't spoken about for as long as I can remember.

'The secretarial job?' she mutters quietly.

'That's right!' I exclaim, hugely surprised and rather flattered that she has remembered.

It's been a week since I told her I was starting an administration job and a week is a long time in my mother's tiny, insular world. I feel privileged that she has given it any thought at all. Privileged and secretly delighted. Her hatred and resentment towards me isn't as deep rooted as I imagined it to be. At least at some point I have figured in her thoughts. That is enough to give me a warm glow as I finish the menial task of fruit sorting in my mother's dated kitchen; the one she refuses to have modernised despite our offers of money to assist her.

'With your qualifications, I would have thought you could have achieved better,' she barks as I drop the rotten fruit into the bin. They land with a thump and for a brief moment I picture their exploding skin as my mother's face. I quickly brush the image aside. Cruel and unnecessary. This isn't why I'm here. I came to help her, to do my duty as her daughter; the only child mother has who functions as she should.

'I'm enjoying it there,' I reply gently as I walk back into the living room, 'and I don't do it for the money. We don't need more money. I do it because I want to get out and meet people.'

She shrugs her shoulders and I take this as an indicator that she is no longer interested in discussing this subject. It is dead in the water.

'Mrs Lovett came to see me the other day,' she says, her voice shaky as she speaks.

I watch and wait for any kind of breakdown in her composure as her words flow towards me. Any sudden movements or facial tics, but there is nothing. She sits upright, her ageing hands placed gracefully in her lap.

'I haven't seen her for some time,' I say through gritted teeth, determined to stay calm and not get dragged into any of this. This is what she does, my mother, to get back at me. She uses subtle ways to rake it all up again, to dredge to the surface what should be left well alone. The sediment of our lives brought out in the open; all our dirt and filth on display for the entire world to see.

'Yes, she was asking after you. Her daughter is still living in London. And still married to a banker chappie. Quite high up in the city, apparently. She was telling me that they have a house worth nearly a million pounds. I mean, a million pounds! Can you imagine that?'

I wince. I have no doubts that Celia Lovett's daughter has a nice life. My life is far from perfect but no amount of my mother's scathing comments will rile me or give me cause to respond, to become embroiled in this this *game* of hers that she plays every time I visit. Using other people's purported high-flying lives and flourishing careers to blame me for her miserable existence. Does she not think I've suffered enough over the years? Is it not obvious to her that I have been punished a million times over?

I take a deep breath and head back into the kitchen where I stand and stare out of the grimy looking window into the garden beyond. I stop for a while to control my rising anger before I fill the kettle and get the cups ready, giving myself time to regain my poise.

'Sugar?' My voice feels thick in my throat, as if it is coated in molasses. A bitter taste floods my mouth. I swallow and grip the spoon tightly.

'Two,' she replies in her birdlike tone; a soft, sibilant chirp that echoes throughout the unnatural quiet of the room. This is another of the games we play every week. I know exactly how she likes her tea and she knows that I know. Neither of us ever falters though. We rehearse our lines and play them out faultlessly. It's all we have left, this painful and awkward routine; it's the tie that binds us. Without this we are nothing.

I scoop up a handful of biscuits and plop them on to a plate, her favourite lemon-coloured china one, the one with the tiny flowers round the rim and place it all on a tray. Clinking as I make my way back in, I carefully lay it down in front of her and watch her face as she scrutinises it, making sure the biscuits are arranged properly and the tea is the right shade of amber. When she has finally decided it is acceptable and worthy of consumption she picks up the cup and sips at it, her lips pursed against the heat.

'Theresa was asking after you, as well.'

There. She has said it. I feel a small shudder take hold in my jaw as I try to speak and feel my voice quiver as it threatens to fail me. I cough and allow myself a few seconds to gather my thoughts, and to make sure the words that come out of my mouth are the intended ones, and not a stream of garbled obscenities; a rapid release of years of pent up anger and hurt and bitterness.

'I hope she is well,' I mumble as I lower my eyes and focus on drinking my tea. I am all too aware that my stilted phraseology sounds like something you would write in a card to someone you barely know, not the sort of warm, convivial greeting a sibling should use when enquiring about her sister's well-being.

'She's put on weight. Not skin and bone any more.'

I nod to convey my satisfaction at this comment. I have no idea what else to say or do.

'And she's moved again.'

I stay completely still, my thumping heart the only movement in my rigid body. This doesn't surprise me; her move. She has lived her adult life shifting from one hostel to another. Slip sliding her way through life, a desolate being who staggers from one crisis to another, completely removed from the rest of society. I remain silent, unable to choose the right words; words that will say nothing but mean everything.

'I'm sure she will …' I stop speaking, not entirely certain what it was I was going to say anyhow. She will what, stop drinking? Stop injecting herself with heroin and live a normal life? None of those things are likely to happen, which is why I am stuck for the right thing to say. There are no words to explain my sister's life path and her choices. Nothing seems to fit. Except, of course, that I drove her to it. My actions caused her life to shrink to the sort of dreadful existence that she now has. That's what everyone thinks. Nobody has said it. They don't need to. Sometimes silence is worse than anger and rage. Sometimes the unspoken says more than words ever will.

I look over at my mother. She is staring out of the window, already losing interest in what it was I was going to say. My thoughts won't be missed.

'Is there anything else you need?' I ask, keen to fill the silence and inject a noise into the painful emptiness that sits between us.

Her eyes flicker and narrow, a contemplative glaze behind the rheumy film covering her dulled irises as she considers my request. 'Which way are you going home?'

I feel my stomach sink and fight against the sense of panic and dread that is clawing its way up my chest and burrowing into my head. I'm almost certain she is doing this deliberately, trying to knock me off-kilter. I know exactly what she is going to ask and will do anything to avoid it.

'I'm calling into the library then going to see a friend in Osmotherley,' I say, a little too quickly. This isn't strictly true. She probably knows this by the way I babble it out. I am planning on visiting a friend but not until this evening, and as for the library; I have no idea where that one came from. Just goes to show the sort of things that are stored in my head, ready to make an appearance unbidden. Quite scary really, isn't it?

'Oh.' Is all she says in return and then I am wracked with guilt as I watch her chin tremble and her skin pucker slightly as a small frown sits between her eyes. I should go. I know I should pay a visit, do what she wants, but I simply cannot face it. Perhaps another time, but definitely not today.

There is a long drawn out silence. I feel like a small child once more, wrong footed, unsure how to put right the terrible atrocity I have committed, to be absolved of my sins.

'Next week,' I murmur and turn to stare out of the window. 'I'll go next week.' I say this knowing it's not true. I won't go next week. Or even the week after. I dread going there and always put it off for as long as I can, coming out with one lame excuse after another.

'Well, somebody will have to,' she says, her voice brittle with disdain, 'because nobody has been for ages. And that can't be right, can it?'

I remain quiet, the sound of my own breathing a pulsating, throaty rumble in my ears. Why is it I can never find the right words to say? Even after all these years, after all the heartache and tears, I am somehow supposed to make it all better. If only I could. If only …

'Tell Mrs Lovett I was here and to give my best to her daughter.' *Her only remaining child.* The words roll around my head, crashing and banging into my skull. My mother doesn't reply but then I don't really expect her to. I was just making small talk, helping to move the moment along, to rid us of the awkwardness that has settled. She nods instead, her body half turned away from me as she stares at the goings-on in the street outside; children playing, neighbours chatting, the entire world continuing to rotate when ours grounded to a juddering halt all those years ago. We have lived our lives in a state of suspended disquietude ever since. I have a friend who is constantly on edge, waiting for bad things to happen, waiting for that metaphorical hammer to fall. Ours fell years ago and we have never recovered from it. Our lives remain crushed beyond repair.

I bid my goodbyes, kissing my mother on both cheeks, her skin papery thin, her face cold to the touch. She doesn't respond. But then what do I expect from her? She is not a tactile lady and her feelings towards me are as delicate as her ageing body; fragile and always on the cusp of fracture.

Only when I am safely seated behind the wheel of my car do I let it all out – the tears and unspent misery that these visits cause. No matter how many promises I make to myself that I will not let her get to me, she always does. She constantly manages to have the upper hand and pull those invisible strings, jerking me around frantically, pushing my emotions into overdrive with her silent, festering rage.

I drive away, wiping the tears from my face with angry, tight fists, vowing that next week I will be stronger. Next week I will *not* let her pointed comments and thinly veiled jibes drag me down. Next week I will be impervious to it all. Because by then, things will have been set in motion. I will soon be absolved of my sins. My wrongdoings will be a dim and distant memory.

LISSY

I find it hard to concentrate. The paint refuses to go where I want it to and my arm aches from the effort of trying to get it right. Eventually, after a stream of expletives and stomping around the room, I clean my brushes and give up. There's no point in forcing it. I can spend the rest of the day tidying Rosie's room and catching up with housework. The ever-growing pile of ironing that has been sitting in the spare room for the past two weeks needs doing. There are plenty of things I can occupy myself with. I'm almost certain there are some boxes in the attic that still haven't been unpacked since moving in. Lots to be getting on with. Plenty of things for me to do.

I leave my studio and close the door behind me, thinking about Rosie's exit this morning. My head is full of images of her sitting in class, miserable and alone, a sea of chattering faces around her, none of them speaking to, or including her. I quash them. Got to be positive. I really hope she is having as good a time there as she can. She is a bright girl, very skilled emotionally; certainly a damn sight better than me. I just know that if she gives it a chance she will soon have an army of friends at her side. It takes time, that's all. She just needs to be patient.

A tractor rumbles past outside, a low, slightly metrical sound that echoes throughout the house, accentuating how quiet it is here. Perfect. Better than living in the town. Fewer neighbours, fewer intrusions. We are one of only four houses a hamlet set up on a hill, six miles out of town. A life away from the living. I need solitude while I am painting. I sigh softly. I need solitude all the time. Rosie is constantly nagging me to get out more, to make friends, and get some kind of life for myself. I'm happy as I am, though. I don't need other people. Other people are volatile and unpredictable, not to be trusted. I had a friend once and she let me down. I'm not about to make that mistake again. The memory of her is buried now. She is part of the past; a past I must never revisit. She was meant to be my friend, the first and only person I have ever trusted and she did the unthinkable. Never again. I am better off being alone. That's just how it is. Rosie doesn't understand it at all but then I don't expect her to. I don't expect anyone to, which is why I prefer being on my own. Much easier that way.

The thump drags me out of my thoughts, sending a pulse of electricity across my skin. My head buzzes, a small throb of anxiety rattles through my veins as I make my way towards the source of the noise. The living area. I am almost certain it came from in there. I hesitate before stepping into the room. There's nobody here. I know that. Every door is locked, every window sealed shut, yet still I feel that overwhelming sense of dread as I walk in, every muscle in my body clenched in anticipation.

As my eyes scan the room, I let out the breath I have been holding in. Nothing. It is exactly as I left it an hour ago. Every cushion is strategically perched in place, each and every tassel on the rug flat and unruffled. Everything in order, just how I like it. I do another quick sweep of the room and smile. Relief floods through me. How silly to think something was amiss. This is a secure environment. Nobody can get to me. This is my home, my sanctuary. I am completely safe here.

I head back out into the hallway and stop at the door. Something looks different but I can't quite work out what it is. Standing for a few seconds, I survey the immediate floor space and scan the walls and corners, leaving no crevice or dark corner untouched by my close scrutiny. And then I spot it. There is a mark on the panel of the door. A large, grey smudge is spread across the pattern on the glass. I move forward and reach out to touch it. The clean glass squeaks beneath my fingers as I drag them over the surface. The mark is on the outside. Of course it is. How could it be on the inside of the door? There is nobody here but me. My heart begins to pitter patter in my chest as I unlock the door and turn the handle to open it, a small arrow of fear stabbing at me as I do so. My stomach lurches when I see it lying there. Lifting my foot, I carefully step over the pigeon that is curled up on my doorstep, its wing sticking out at an unnatural angle. I kneel down to see if it is still alive and feel my body turn to stone when I hear the voice.

'They do it all the time. One of the joys of living round these parts, I'm afraid.'

I look up to see a man at the end of the drive. He is shaking his head wistfully and looking at the bird on my doorstep. He is probably in his forties, quite close to my age, and is staring straight over at me. Everything else is a blur – his features, the timbre of his voice, what he is wearing – it all becomes unimportant as I scramble to my feet and slip back into the doorway. I am about to dart back into the house, to make my hasty retreat and lock myself in, when I think of the poor creature on my doorstep. I can't just leave it there. I will have hordes of scavengers around it if I don't move it. I need to do something. Somehow, I need to dispose of it. I lean down, my insides churning, and am about to pick it up when he shouts over again.

'Do you want me to help you?'

Something about his voice, his stance, his casual manner, makes me turn to face him, allows me to relax my composure and let my guard down. He sounds friendly, non-menacing, helpful. And right now, I need some help.

'I – I think it's dead,' I call back, my voice croaky with apprehension.

'Not to worry,' he says and starts to walk up the drive towards me. I suddenly wish I hadn't spoken and had grabbed the dead bird and closed the door. I am unsure what to do and feel my breath catch in my chest as he comes into focus. He is in front of me, his body just feet from mine before I have a chance to do or say anything in protest, to tell him to leave and that I am too busy to chat or make small talk with neighbours.

Only when he stoops to inspect the creature do I take the time to notice his appearance. He has dark hair and a tanned complexion. I suppose he could be considered handsome in a conventional way. It's been that long since I have thought about what constitutes attractive, I'm not even sure I'm qualified to make such a judgement. I watch the muscles on his shoulders flex slightly as he moves and scoops the bird up in his hands. Its head flops to one side making me feel slightly sick.

'I'll just go and dispose of it. You'll find this happens quite a lot round this neck of the woods. The birds get disorientated and fly low, and with us being high up here they slam right into …' he stops and looks away, suddenly embarrassed by it all, aware of his choice of words, aware of the look of horror on my face. 'Well anyway, I'll just go and get rid of it for you.'

I nod politely and watch as he walks off, his feet crunching on the gravel. It's only then that I notice him properly. He is tall and broad across his shoulders. His hair is slightly longer at the back and flecked with grey.

At the bottom of the drive, he turns and heads up towards the property on my right. If I crane my neck I can just about see over the top of the conifers to what I assume is his house. I have been here for over a month now and haven't heard or seen anyone there, which has suited me just fine. For some reason, I presumed it was inhabited by an older person, somebody immobile or incapacitated. Not by a younger person. Not by him.

I am about to close the door when I remember I haven't thanked him properly for helping me out. It's the least I can do, isn't it? I move towards the hedge that separates our houses and stand on my tiptoes to see over the top. He is wrapping the bird in a plastic bag as I shout over to him.

'Thank you for this. I very much appreciate it.' My words sound so formal and cold, lacking in any real emotion. That's just how I am. Any emotions that I do have, I usually pour into my paintings; inanimate objects that can't hurt me. Even Rosie finds me aloof, unreachable. Damaged goods.

He looks up, seemingly startled by my sudden presence; a pathetic face peering through a forest of green needles. He smiles and I feel a hot flush spread over my neck and curl its way up into my cheeks.

'You're welcome,' he replies, 'anytime.'

I step back as I watch him drop the dead pigeon into the bin. It hits the bottom with a dull thump, sending a jolt through me. Reminding myself of the chores I have waiting inside, I back away. I am halfway across the lawn when his voice sends a prickle of alarm up my spine.

'Would you like to come in for a coffee? I mean, I just thought …' He stops, suddenly conscious of how absurd this all is. I don't even know him. We are strangers. He could be anybody; anybody at all. I shut my eyes and clench my fists tightly then take a deep breath before opening my eyes again, the sudden reappearance of the sun causing me to blink repeatedly against its harsh glare.

'Sorry,' he continues, 'I realise how that sounded. All I meant was …' He stops again and clears his throat. Turning around I let out a small shriek as I see him peering over the top of the hedge. He is standing on the fence and has his arms splayed over the top of the conifers.

'I'm not doing very well here, am I?' he laughs and once again I feel my face burn as he reveals a row of perfectly white teeth. His eyes twinkle at me and my gut instinct is to run inside and bolt the door behind me. No intrusions, complete privacy, that's how I operate. But there is something about him that I feel drawn to; a connection, something I can't quite put my finger on. A sensation I haven't felt for so many years stirs somewhere deep down in my gut.

'How about we have that coffee in my back garden?' I offer. The words are out before I have a chance to stop them. My house overlooks a field at the back. There is a low fence. A place to escape should things take a turn for the worse. Not that they will. In fact, the chances of that happening are so slim they are probably non-existent. But still … I bite at the side of my mouth and feel my fingers begin to twitch. They hang at my sides, fearful, and impotent. I know that I have to stop doing this. I need to remind myself that the world isn't full of bad people but I can't seem to bring an end to it. He nods appreciatively and before I have a chance to change my mind, he is back on my driveway. His hands are slung deep in his pockets, giving him the look of somebody much younger, somebody who doesn't have a care in the world. How little we have in common.

I lead him around the side of the house and into the garden where I drag the chairs over to the table and motion for him to take a seat. He slips into it effortlessly and stares around at the foliage and spread of colour. 'Lovely garden you have here,' he murmurs, taking in every aspect of it, his eyes roving greedily over the lawn and rows of flowers.

'I wish I could take credit for it,' I say quietly, 'but as you know, we've not lived here for very long.'

Reaching into my pocket I pull out the keys I always have a set of keys on me, just in case then leave him sitting there as I head towards the back door and let myself in. It's not that I enjoy living in a fortress; it's simply a habit of old that I can't seem to shake. From the safety of my kitchen I observe my visitor while I'm making coffee. He is undoubtedly good looking and charismatic, which leads me to a question I don't have the answer to: what does he want with *me*? I remove the filter from the pot and empty it, then shake my head, cross with myself for thinking such thoughts. We're just neighbours. He is simply being friendly, nothing more. I brush my suspicions aside, finish making the coffee and then head back outside into the warmth of the garden where shadows stretch over the lawn like dancing silhouettes.

'Oh, that looks amazing. Thank you very much!' He gently grasps the cup and takes a good, long gulp. 'This is most welcome. I only arrived home a couple of hours ago. Been travelling most of the night.'

I raise an eyebrow to indicate my puzzlement. I won't ask. I refuse to. Neighbours, that's all we are. Maintaining a safe, healthy distance is a necessity I have to bear. I get close to people at my peril.

'I work in Aberdeen and only got back a few hours ago,' he says quietly as he takes another sip of scalding hot coffee. I nod and we sit for a while, the silence between us effortless and comfortable. He doesn't explain and I don't ask.

'I'm Rupert, by the way,' he says, in that easy manner of his that I am rapidly becoming accustomed to. I smile and roll my eyes to indicate I am a fool for forgetting to introduce myself.

'Hi, Rupert. I'm Lissy,' I say and despite myself, I take the hand that he has proffered and shake it vigorously. My sleeve pulls back and I drag my fingers away as if burnt, but not before I notice his expression, see his eyes scan my arm and watch how he blinks rapidly and colours up at this minor indiscretion. I hear the small, still voice inside my head telling me this was going to happen. This is why I need to stay away, to be a loner, to live in my own enclave of anonymity. People can't be trusted, you see. Even the ones you think you know really well. We all have our dark secrets, don't we? And everyone has emotions they can't always keep in check. I put my trust in people in the past and they let me down. I won't do it again.

From inside the house, I hear the phone ringing and feel my skin ripple with apprehension. I am quite literally being saved by the bell. I stand up quickly and wait for him to do the same. He continues to stay seated so I stride off into the house feeling rather aggrieved at his resistance to leave.

When I come back out five minutes later he is still in the same position. His cup is empty and he is smiling at me.

'Sorry, Rupert,' I say, trying to keep the edge out of my voice, 'but that was my daughter's school calling me. I need to go and collect her as soon as I can.'

Still, he doesn't move, although a look of concern flashes over his face.

'Oh, I'm sorry to hear that. Is she ill?'

I realise he is only trying to show some compassion but I start to feel irritated. He needs to leave. *I* need to leave and I need to do it now.

'No, she's not ill but I'm afraid I must get down there as soon as I can ...' I leave it hanging there and wait for him to move, to get up and go. Very slowly, he rises from his seat but not before I see him cast another glance down at my arms. I suddenly feel vulnerable and naked. I want to be away from here from *him*. What was I thinking of inviting him round for God's sake? I should have known, really. It's not as if my own instincts can be trusted. I really, really should have known ...

'Right, well, good luck with whatever the problem is,' he says as he sets his cup down and stares over at me.

'Thank you,' I reply, unable and unwilling to elaborate any further. This is my business, my problem. Rosie and I, in it together. A team.

I clench my teeth as I watch him walk off, silently chastising myself for being too relaxed. From now on I will be more vigilant, more measured when allowing people into my life. I can't afford to be let down again. As long as I keep it in mind that I will always be on my own, with nobody to help me sort through life's difficulties, then everything will be just fine.

CHILD A

She had no idea what to do with him. He stared up at her with his huge blue eyes, the ghastliest sound escaping from the back of his throat. He reminded her of a wild animal stuck in a trap, its limbs being severed by metal teeth that were slowly ripping into its body. The shrieking made her skin crawl. Standing over the cot she shook a cuddly toy at him, making silly baby sounds, trying her best to make him giggle. Nothing worked. The screams grew louder. Reaching down, she touched his skin and recoiled slightly. He was cold; really cold, despite his screaming and howling, despite his face being red with fury and despair. It was hardly surprising, though. She pulled her own sweater tighter around her body the room was freezing. She touched the cot lightly and rubbed her fingers over the thin sheet that was covering him. More blankets, that was what he needed. If she could cover him up, he would stop crying. Racing around the bedroom, she flung cupboards open, searching for something, anything to put over him to warm him up. That would stop him, wouldn't it? Toddlers cried for a reason, that much she did know. She just needed to work out what was wrong with him, that's all it was, and if the extra warmth stopped him from crying and screaming then she will have sorted it, won't she? She was desperate for the noise to stop.

A tall cupboard in the corner of the room contained a pile of woollen sheets. She wanted to howl with relief as she stood there staring at them, a bundle of checked blankets folded into neat squares. The answer to her prayers. With trembling hands, she tugged hard, pulling them down one by one, watching as they fell in great waves and lay sprawled at her feet. Scooping them up, she grabbed an armful and covered him up, pushing each sheet tightly down the side of the mattress, his cries muffled and smothered under the layers of fabric.

She shivered. The room was freezing. There wasn't any heating on. She remembered her friend once telling her about how tight her parents were, how they limited the food she could eat and the amount of television she was allowed to watch. Well, they obviously had enough money go for a night out and leave this poor kid here to freeze half to death. Grabbing more sheets, she stuffed them into the tiny bed and tucked them down each side of the cot, watching as his little head disappeared amongst the yards of material. Suddenly there was nothing. No more crying, no more sobbing. An unexpected hush filled the room. He had stopped. The noise was gone. No sounds at all. That was a good thing, wasn't it? He was warm now and the yelling had ceased. That was all she had wanted, for the screaming to stop. She hated the sound, the very idea of people sobbing. Nobody likes it when people cry. Her dad said it to her all the time. STOP CRYING! He would scream at her again and again and again if she ever dared to let her chin wobble in protest at something he had done or said to her. She stored her anguish, kept it safely tucked away until her eyes burned with unspent tears and the lump in her throat was the size of a plum stone. She clung on to it, that ever-growing lump that was lodged in her aching gullet and swallowed it down, never letting the tears flow. Tears were a sign of weakness. Tears meant another beating. From both of them. First from her dad for simply crying, then another from her mother for causing his anger. Because once his anger was unleashed, there was no telling what he would do.

She stared down at the small bump under the sheets and bit at her stubby fingernails, chewing and spitting, chewing and spitting until there was nothing left to go at. She hoped he was OK now. He had gone really quiet. She stared at his back and softened. She didn't really hate him. He was just a kid after all. It was just that she got so angry sometimes, like a thick, black cloak had dropped on her, smothering her, choking the very life out of her. She was only a child herself, barely thirteen. Anyway, she shouldn't have to put up with this, should she?

Here, babysitting on her own. It wasn't even her house. This was her friend's responsibility. He was her little brother after all. She shouldn't have left her here on her own. It should be her friend, up here looking for blankets, trying to stop the crying, not her, somebody this kid barely knows. And her so-called friend still wasn't back. She had been gone for an age. She tore at more of her fingernails, a strip of blood appearing as she bit at a loose flap of skin and ground it between her teeth. Where the fuck was her friend?

A noise downstairs disturbed her, made the hairs on the back of her neck stand up in alarm. Had her friend returned? It sounded like her. Not before time either. This whole thing was beyond a joke.

Closing her eyes tight, she pushed the blankets down a bit more. He was warm now. He had stopped crying. She had made it all better. She had kept her temper in check. Or at least she hoped she had. With all the worrying and fretting, it had been hard to remember everything, but she was pretty sure she had done the right thing.

She stood for a while, watching for some movement. Nothing. He was as still as the grave. A tiny sliver of trepidation slithered up her backbone. The other child's face crept into her thoughts as she began to tremble. She had stayed calm, hadn't she? Kept her cool, warmed him up with blankets and sheets. She hadn't meant to do anything wrong. She can't recall doing anything bad. Her legs began to weaken. This wasn't her fault.

She reached down and prodded him with her outstretched finger. Still no movement. Her insides knotted together. The room swayed. She began to feel sick.

The sound of the fridge door slamming downstairs punctured her thoughts. It was definitely her friend. She had come home. The absent friend had finally returned. She had been gone for far too long. Where the hell had she been anyway?

Taking the stairs two at a time, she half flung herself into the kitchen where the other girl was standing, head tipped back as she drained the contents of her Coca-Cola tin.

'Where the fuck have you been?' Her voice was croaky, riddled with panic.

'Told you,' the other girl replied, 'out to the corner shop for a drink.'

'You've been gone for ages!' Her voice was rising in pitch, her growing fury and resentment a palpable wall between them.

The other girl shrugged, unperturbed by her friend's anxiety. 'So? Back now aren't I? What's your problem?'

'What's happened to your clothes?' she asked her as she watched a line of muddy coloured Coca-Cola trail its way down her chin and drip on to her neck, resting in her clavicle a tiny pool of frothy liquid, bubbling and spurting against her skin. Her jeans were caked in mud and her T-Shirt had a rip down the back. She smiled and shrugged casually before speaking.

'Met someone on the way, didn't I?' Her eyes danced mischievously, her lips parted with a knowing smile.

'Daryl?' she squealed, furious at the thought of it, the thought of her out there, cavorting and giggling while she had been stuck in here trying to calm her little brother down.

'Might have been,' she replied and stalked off into the living room.

'Where did you go? Fucking Timbuktu?' she cried, racing after her, her heart beating furiously, her neck taut with anger.

'Ha!' her friend laughed as she turned the TV on and watched the screen fizzle into life.

Her blood boiled at the sound of her voice. It wasn't meant to be a joke.

'We went to the park,' she continued, 'rolled down hills and stuff. Had a few snogs … if you know what I mean.' She tapped the side of her nose and smiled, making ridiculous faces as she flopped into the armchair, a smug expression on her face.

'Well, you left me here on my own!' Her voice was in full throttle now as she stared at her friend incredulously, her back rigid with anger.

'Ah yeah. How's he been? Asleep upstairs?'

She felt her heart begin to thrash its way round her chest. This was her chance. She could lie, tell her everything's been fine, say he's been really quiet all night. Make out as if they'd had a great night *together, singing nursery rhymes and telling stories. But they hadn't. It hadn't been like that at all. It had been absolute torture, putting up with the screaming, trying to work out what was wrong with him, trying to keep her temper in check …*

'Suppose I'd better go and have a look in on him, hadn't I?'

Fear suddenly gripped her. It was silent up there. Why wasn't he crying any more? Had she done something to him and not realised? It had happened in the past. She had blackouts, occasions when everything became a blur and then memories gradually came back to her bit by bit. Like the time Justine White had called her a skinny freak, and so she had barged into Justine as they were leaving the classroom. She couldn't remember doing it but did recall feeling furious, as if her entire body was going to combust. Afterwards, her father had done the same to her, pulling her around the room, asking her why she had done it, why she had punched a schoolmate and pushed her over causing her to bang her head on the corner of the desk. She paid dearly for that particular blackout, the imprint of her father's hand on her back for days afterwards, a reminder of what she had done.

She waited while her friend sauntered upstairs, hoping a peek around the bedroom door would suffice, hoping for a miracle. The silence was deafening. She tried to picture her friend's face; unassuming, expectant, seeing him there, swamped under a pile of heavy blankets. There was nothing. No response. She listened and heard the flush of a toilet. Dread and horror crawled up her spine. She hadn't been in the room yet. She hadn't seen him. There was still time to escape, to get out. She could leave right now, run away. She knew where her mum and dad kept their cash. Stashes of it all over the house. It would be so easy to grab it, sling some essentials in a bag and just get the fuck out of there. Leave all this shit behind her; all the fear and beatings and the worry. Just pack up and go.

Time dragged on, an endless moment where everything was suspended; the world in a lull. The footsteps above her made her heart pound even harder. She looked up and traced their movement out of the bedroom, across the landing, and back down the stairs. Her skin felt as if it were on fire. Blood rushed through her ears, a gushing, rhythmic torrent making her dizzy as it tore its way around her body.

'He's asleep,' came the voice from behind her as her friend sailed back into the living room, her slim frame a grey shadow in her peripheral vision. Like a ghost lodged in her memory.

'Asleep,' she found herself murmuring in reply.

'Yeah. Quite cute, really. He had his head shoved under the covers. He does that sometimes when he says he's hiding from the monsters. I gave him a kiss and left.'

Gave him a kiss? Perhaps she had imagined it all. Or maybe her friend was lying. It wouldn't be the first time. It was all too much, the worry of it. She felt herself begin to burn up. Beads of sweat ran down her back coating her skin in seconds. She had to get out. Her vision was blurred and her head pounded as she made a feeble excuse about not feeling well and having to leave, and being sorry and all that but she needed to go home and have a lie down.

Her friend shrugged. 'Well, if you're in a huff and pissed off with me why don't you just say so?'

'I'm not though. I'm just tired and don't feel well.'

'Your choice,' came the reply as she dashed out into the hallway and slammed the door hard behind her.

∞∞∞∞∞

'Hey! You! Where you off to in such a hurry?' A snigger and then a loud guffaw. She turned to see a gang of them, all huddled together in the alleyway behind her. A trail of smoke billowed out from the centre of the crowd, curling up above their heads, hanging over the canopy of lank, greasy hair.

'Fuck off.' Her voice rang around the cobbled floor as she tried to pick up her pace, her legs soft and watery with fear.

'Ooh! Get you, Miss High and Mighty.' Another snort of laughter as she broke into a run.

'Just been giving your pal some of this.'

She stopped and turned to see a young lad, slightly older than she was, step out from the rest of the crowd. He was slowly gyrating his hips and groaning, his head bent slightly backwards, his eyes half closed and his teeth bared with simulated pleasure. A boom of laughter erupted from the rest of the gang. Stomach lurching, she set off again, hot bile rising in her gullet, her head full of visions. Dead children. Lots of them, all beating a path to her door.

'I asked you where you were going.' He ran and jumped ahead of her, the stink of alcohol and tobacco wafting around the air as he grabbed her arm and pushed her against the wall. Her spine stung as it scraped across the rough surface of the bricks, his body too close to hers as he spoke, 'Could have been you I had a go at earlier if you would let me.' He thrust his groin up against her hips. She could feel him harden as he pushed his pelvis closer to hers. Fear swamped her. Her father's temper was bad enough, but this? This was unthinkable. Shaking violently, she gave him one huge push and watched as he reeled backwards, his feet grappling for purchase on the slippery cobbles. There was a collective gasp as he fell backwards, his body landing with an awkward thump on the cold floor.

'You fucking bitch!' His voice followed her all the way down the street as she broke into a gallop, her chest tight with panic. 'You're nothing but a fucking frigid bitch!'

The echoes followed her all the way home, their jeering and swearing trailing her until she hit the underpass and turned the corner on to her road.

Her head throbbed, her limbs were floppy with fear and panic. She couldn't allow herself to even think about Daryl and his gang of disgusting mates. All she could think about was him, the toddler. His tiny face filled her mind. What if he wasn't actually asleep? What if it had happened again, just like it had with Justine White? And then there was the other one, the girl in the park. Her stomach went into a spasm. All she had done was throw a few extra covers over him. That was all it was. He just wouldn't stop crying. That was what she remembered the most, the constant screaming, so loud it felt as if it would crack her skull open. So much pressure and anger; like a cannonball exploding inside her head.

They were waiting for her when she got in, fists at the ready. No particular reason. She just happened to be there and they were drunk and angry. They were always angry. Her mother's torn blouse told her all she needed to know. She stared at them, her eyes dead and unseeing, and let them do it, taking the slaps and punches without trying to defend herself, seeing it as fitting punishment for what she had just done. For everything she had ever done. Nothing could hurt her now.

∞∞∞∞∞

The knock came early next morning as she was getting ready for school. She watched her father stagger his way through the living room, bleary-eyed, his face red and bloated, and heard him fling the front door open, hitting the wall with an almighty bang. She listened to the policeman on the step ask him about his daughter and realised that she was actually flooded with relief. This was it; the thing she knew would happen. The thing that she deserved. It was here now. Her life was over. Everything she had ever known was about to be ripped away from her. And she couldn't have cared less.

LISSY

She is sitting outside the school office when I arrive, streaks of mascara stained on her face; a lattice of black oil running down her cheeks. I stiffen. She knows how I feel about her wearing make-up, especially for school. Not that we need to focus on that right now. We have more pressing matters facing us. I take a deep breath as I approach her and sit down. I have no idea how I will deal with this, what I will say to her to make any of it any better.

'It wasn't me, Mum!' she shrieks as I turn to look at her. 'I swear to God, I didn't do anything.'

She is a pitiful sight, bent double and sobbing into her hands as I lean over, place my arm around her shoulders and pull her into my chest where she lays, her body a crumpled heap on my abdomen. I feel the heat pulsate from her body and let her cry herself out before I speak.

'Sweetheart, what on earth has happened?' I know exactly what has gone on. The person on the phone told me in great detail what it is my daughter is supposed to have done, her purported misdemeanour. They demanded I come straight down and meet with Rosie's head of year to talk about it. So here I am, armed with all the details and absolutely no idea how I am going to work my way through it all. I will defend her. Of course I will. She is my daughter and this is completely out of character. She didn't do it. She simply does not have it in her. However, it would appear that the school believes otherwise.

'Mrs McLeod?' I snap my head around to see a young teacher standing behind me. He is in his mid to late twenties and has black hair slicked into place by a ton of gel. He has the prerequisite designer stubble that all young men now seem to favour and is smiling at me, revealing a row of perfectly white teeth any orthodontist would be proud of. I am tempted to correct him, to tell him that I am a Ms and not a Mrs but decide this is neither the time nor the place. Perhaps later, when we have sorted this thing out, but definitely not now. I don't want to provoke him in any way and jeopardise Rosie's chances of being exonerated from this whole sorry mess; this dreadful predicament that she is currently in.

'If you'd like to come this way, please?' With a sharp, sweeping gesture he swings his arm behind him and stands back in the doorway of the headteacher's office. *The headteacher?* I feel my stomach tighten and grip Rosie's hand as we pull ourselves up and walk inside.

His tone is perfunctory as he speaks, his manner clipped but courteous. 'We felt the need to get you involved, Mrs McLeod, as the money was rather a large sum and this is a very serious issue we have going on here. I'm sure you'll agree?'

He waits for me to say something, to side with him against Rosie, to turn against my daughter, my only child. Two disapproving adults against one youngster. I squeeze her hand and glance at her horrified expression as another glassy tear escapes unchecked and rolls down her cheek. A mesh of urticaria is creeping up her neck; a scarlet web of nervous tension stretched over her throat and across her chest. This is all a big mistake, of course, it is. There is no way Rosie would steal such a large sum of cash. No way at all. There has to be a rational explanation for all of this. My daughter is not a thief.

I stay stock still and watch as he begins to drum his fingers on the old teak desk. It's a sprawling, antiquated piece of furniture, much too big and far too dated for the average sized, modern room we are in. He is beginning to get agitated while he steels himself for my answer. He wants me to agree with him. I can see it in his face. He thinks I am going to turn against my only child. He will have a long wait.

I clear my throat before speaking, 'She didn't do this, Mr ...'

'Cooper,' he interjects, his face devoid of all emotion. I can see what he is doing here. He thinks he can break me. He doesn't realise I was broken many years ago and nothing he could ever do will ever have any effect on me. I am beyond being hurt by the likes of him.

'Right, well, as you can see by the state of her, Mr Cooper, my daughter definitely did not take that money. She is not a thief.'

There is an awkward silence. I watch his face, see how his eyes dart between Rosie and me. I remain silent. I have said my piece. For now, anyway. It's his turn now. Let's see what he has to say next.

'Well, the thing is,' he murmurs, his eyes dark and full of intent, 'the money was found in Rosie's bag. We had to ask the entire year group to empty their belongings on to the floor and the envelopes containing the money were found tucked into your daughter's textbook, which was shoved down the bottom of her schoolbag.'

I blink quickly and wiggle my jaw as I feel a headache set in at the base of my neck. It will creep its way up over my skull and stay there all day if I don't catch it in time. I ask for a glass of water and rummage around at the bottom of my handbag for paracetamol. Pressing the blister pack with my thumb and forefinger I pop two out of the packet and throw them into my mouth, then pick up the tumbler that has been placed on the table in front of me and take a long drink of the cool water. It glides down my throat, a welcome reprieve from having to speak. It is giving me some thinking time. Not that I have any thoughts at the ready. The only thing I am sure of at this minute in time is that my daughter did not steal that money and that I will not be bullied or intimidated by this man.

'OK,' I say with a voice that is a little more delicate that I would like it to be. I want to appear in control, authoritative, formidable even; not some insipid little parent who will immediately kowtow to his accusations. 'I am aware that the envelopes were in your drawer and it was the spending money of some of the pupils for the upcoming visit to York. Can I just ask why they weren't taken straight to the office and put in the safe? Three hundred is a lot of money to keep in a classroom, don't you think?'

I watch his face colour up and his eyes darken until they are the deepest shade of black. Two spots of coal set deep in his face, they glitter menacingly at me. He is furious, a silent, simmering slip of a man who is barely holding it together. I don't care. He doesn't scare me. This is my daughter he is talking about; her reputation, our life. I will not tolerate her being blamed for something she did not do. She deserves better. *We* deserve better.

'The money, if you don't mind me saying, Mrs McLeod …'

'Ms,' I say rapidly, now infuriated by the sound of his voice, his slicked back hair, everything about him. 'I am a Ms, not a Mrs.'

'Indeed,' he hisses, 'I'm glad we've cleared that aspect of our meeting up, *Ms* McLeod, now if we can move on to the more important matter of the stolen money.' He raises his perfectly shaped eyebrow at me and I am not sure whether I would rather stifle my laughter or slap his face. I am inclined to do both but instead manage a slight smile and nod in affirmation.

'As I was saying,' he continues through gritted teeth, 'the money was in *my* drawer in *my* desk and it was locked up.' He stares over at Rosie and then back at me. 'The drawer had been broken into and ransacked in a bid to locate the cash.'

'Which somebody planted in my daughter's bag,' I say abruptly.

I have no idea where that thought came from but don't much care. I do, however, know what sort of reaction it will provoke. I know exactly what type of rage my words will bring from this pathetic looking creature sitting opposite me. For all I try my hardest to live my life in the shadows away from any sort of scrutiny, I will not stand by and watch Rosie be verbally mauled by this man. I simply will not tolerate it.

'Planted?' he says incredulously, his voice going up almost a full octave. 'You're actually accusing somebody else of doing this?'

'Why not?' I shrug dispassionately, trying to come across as unperturbed when I am anything but.

'Why not?' he echoes, the volume of his voice increasing with every syllable that falls out of his mouth. 'I'll tell you why not. Because the money was found in your daughter's bag. Nobody else's. Just Rosie's. Now if that isn't evidence of her guilt, then I don't know what is ...'

I can see his nostrils expanding with rage and watch as his skin grows redder and redder by the second. I suddenly feel euphoric. I am in control of this situation. I can do this. I have rattled his cage and now have the upper hand. I can keep my daughter safe from all the horrors of this incident. I will shield her from this and we will live to fight another day. She will not go through what I was subjected to. I will make sure of it.

'Mr Cooper, since starting at this school my daughter has been bullied. She has reported this to her form tutor and nothing I repeat NOTHING has been done to stop it. It was only a matter of time before something like this happened. There are pupils in this school who are targeting her, making sure she gets into trouble for something she didn't do. And do you know who I blame for this entire event, Mr Cooper?' His jaw tightens and I watch a small pulse take hold in the delve just below his cheekbone, 'I blame you, Mr Cooper. For the past four weeks, you have stood by and watched my daughter suffer at the hands of these pupils and not once have you intervened or helped her.'

I hear a small squeak come from Rosie but ignore her. She will be horrified by my outburst, fearing a backlash from this man at some point in the future. It won't happen. I would like to see him try. Any repercussions from him will bring a swift and hefty response from me and I will make absolutely certain he doesn't forget it in a hurry. I may have spent my life being bullied but I will make absolutely sure it does not happen to Rosie. Over my dead body.

'I beg your pardon?' he says, his lip curling at the edge as he speaks.

I straighten my jacket and tug my sleeves down over my wrists. 'I believe that one of the pupils, or perhaps even more than one, maybe a whole gang of pupils in this school, is trying to set my daughter up. She is relatively new here and has struggled to fit in. Some of the other children here have—'

'Just a moment,' he says, holding his hand up to block what I am about to say. 'Only yesterday we received a report from Rosie's previous school stating that although she was a bright and happy pupil, there were occasions when she was rather surly towards staff,' he coughs for dramatic effect before continuing, 'and on her final day she had been involved in an argument with another pupil that ended with an injury which required the other pupil needing hospital treatment.'

I feel my face begin to burn. Does he think I don't already know about these incidents? Has he not realised that behind every incident, every occurrence, *every fucking dreadful lie,* there is a story? A reason for it all. I am incensed, incandescent with rage. Probably not the best frame of mind with which to conduct what should be a formal meeting with my daughter's teacher, a senior member of staff, but what the hell. I have only one chance to clear my daughter's name and this is it.

'Right, well, if you want the details of those incidents then I am more than happy to enlighten you. Rosie became surly towards staff when the ongoing bullying from a certain pupil wasn't taken seriously, which eventually resulted in Rosie fighting this girl off after she dragged Rosie to the ground. The other girl bumped her head and yes, she needed stitches. Oh, and in case you're interested, Rosie lost a chunk of hair and ended up with a black eye. It was an act of self-defence after months and months of bullying. Is that enough information for you, Mr Cooper?'

There are a few seconds of silence before he speaks again.

'Right, well back to the issue of the money, *Ms* McLeod,' he says, with as much authority as he can muster, 'there needs to be some kind of sanction for Rosie's behaviour.'

'I'm still in the room!' Rosie's voice is shaky and tears continue to roll down her face as she leans forward to remind us of her presence in all of this. 'I'm still here, you know!' she sobs and I watch as Mr Cooper eyes her with complete scorn. If he looks at her like that once more, I fear I might just throw something at him. The old-fashioned paperweight sitting next to me on the desk looks tempting. I squeeze my eyes shut and visualise the large, glass orb hitting his head with force and knocking him sideways onto the floor. When I open my eyes again, he is staring at me. I shiver slightly and look away. His pupils are pitch black spheres and contain more than a hint of menace.

'I'm afraid we have no other option than to exclude Rosie for the next two days. A meeting will be arranged with Mrs Paxton, the headteacher, a meeting which you will both have to attend before Rosie can return to school.'

I remain silent. The decision has been made and fighting it is futile. I grab Rosie's hand and drag her up out of the chair. She follows me wearily, her head almost touching her chest as I stalk towards the door. My head pounds with fury and exhaustion. My legs almost buckle as I turn to face the young teacher, who is now looking rather too smug for my liking. My voice is far louder than it should be as my words explode into the silence of the room.

'You haven't heard the last of this, Mr Cooper. Rest assured I will be back in touch. My daughter did NOT steal that money.' Barely keeping my anger in check, we head out of the room, past the office where a sea of bewildered faces are staring out at us, and into the car park.

CHILD B

*H*er stomach was in knots as she watched it all unfold. All through the night, a steady stream of people traipsed through the house, an army of official looking individuals wearing dark uniforms and even darker expressions. They questioned her for what felt like hours and hours. Where had she been? Why were her clothes torn? Who had she spoken to? Who was with her during the night? On and on it went until she felt light-headed and woozy with it all. Her answers were always the same even though she had been told to stay in the house at all times, she had been out. How long for she couldn't remember, but she had definitely been out of the house for a good part of the evening. She had come back in, checked on him. He was fine. No, she hadn't seen his face and yes, he was under the covers. What else was she supposed to say? What was it *they* wanted *her* to say?

It twisted in her stomach, the worry and fear, the thought of what she had done. Or hadn't done. At one point during the questions she went dizzy. They had told her to place her head between her legs, instructed her to breathe deeply, to close her eyes, to not panic. How could she possibly not panic? Such a stupid thing to say. Her little brother was dead and it was her fault. Somehow, he had slipped away whilst in her care and she hadn't even noticed. What kind of a sister was she?

They would be checking her story, they said. Asking around to see who had seen her. They wanted her friend's address. They would be going round there to talk to her, to get her side of the story. She felt sick at the thought of that. Her friend would blame her, tell them she was gone for hours, that it was all her fault. And in a way, it was. She had neglected him, left him alone to die. She was the worst big sister ever. A complete monster.

They eventually left them alone at 4 a.m. Her mother had been sedated; her father was sitting quietly at the kitchen table, his large, clumsy fingers draped across the wooden surface, his eyes black with anger and hurt. He kept asking her what had gone on, how had it happened? She shook her head miserably. She had no answers. If she had them, she would have gladly given them to him, turned the clock back, made everything all right again. But it wasn't all right and never would be again.

The two of them sat in the dim light of the early morning sunrise, their misery and horror so thick and tangible she could practically taste it. It was implanted in the back of her throat, the sour tang of guilt.

No words were spoken as they watched the watery, orange light filter in through the window and listened to the birdsong in the garden beyond, signifying a new day was upon them. A day without their beautiful little boy; the first for the rest of their lives.

The police came back just as sleep decided it would have her. Through the fog of an exhausted brain, she went with them to the station to be questioned again, her father at her side. She told them once more what had happened, reiterated her story, went through it, step by painful step, going into as much detail as she could until, at last, exhaustion swamped her and the tears finally came. Only then did they let her go home with the caveat that further questions would follow and, should her story change in any way, shape or form, then trouble would ensue. She couldn't imagine that things could get any worse. Whatever trouble they threatened to put her way would pale into insignificance compared with what she and her family were about to face for the rest of their lives.

By the time they got home, she was beyond exhausted, fatigue seeping out of every pore, guilt swallowing her. Her last thought as she placed her head down on her pillow was one that involved death. Not her brother's, but her own. She closed her eyes and hoped to never wake up.

BEVERLEY

The drive home soothes my jagged nerves. Not that I have anything to feel anxious about. Everything is about as good as it can be. Never perfect. Life will never be that. Perfect was rudely snatched away from me many years ago. I have no idea what perfect even *feels* like any more. But I have no real reason to feel nervous or anxious. Everything is going swimmingly. I am simply over thinking things as usual. One of my less attractive traits. It's difficult for me to stop over analysing everything. I always expect the worst from people, from each and every situation I find myself in. Life has taught me to be suspicious.

I message Warren as soon as I get in the house. His plane is due in at 8 p.m. I will be there waiting for him like the dutiful wife that I am. I have missed him and always look forward to the times when he is home; even though he leaves wet footprints all over the bathroom floor and damp towels slung over the side of the bath. Living on your own means you have a routine, a set way of doing things, and an extraordinarily tidy house. Warren being home is always a compromise but we somehow manage to get along rather nicely. We work out a way of rubbing along together, without any of the friction that many couples encounter after living apart for weeks at a time, and then just when we start to get it right, the time arrives for him to leave again. We spend weeks getting used to being an item once more and then we have go back to living our separate lives. Having a husband who works away is a double-edged sword. Love and stability without having to endure toenails clippings all over the floor and whiskers sticking to the side of the sink every morning. And of course, when he is away, my routine also includes my secrets. We all have them, don't we? Warren thinks he knows everything there is to know about me. How wrong he is. What he sees isn't the real me. It never has been. I am an actress playing at being me. But just lately I have developed even more of a clandestine lifestyle. While he is home I will have to make sure I play my cards even closer to my chest. I don't want him getting the wrong idea. He wouldn't understand. His upbringing was starkly different to mine. He had a close, loving family. The worst thing that they had to endure was the death of their gran. She died peacefully in her sleep at the ripe old age of ninety-seven. He couldn't ever begin to comprehend how difficult my life has been, how much we have struggled to leave the past behind us. Nor would I expect him to. So, I will just have to be extra vigilant; be on my mettle. Clear all my text messages and lie low until he goes back abroad. Only then will I be able to relax and continue with my crusade, get the job done.

Once I am inside the house, I carry out a quick check. Don't want any incriminating evidence hanging around. Not that my plans leave a huge paper trail. It's been mainly text messages and emails. Safer, cleaner, easier to keep track. I shuffle a pile of receipts and bills into a folder. Warren rarely looks at any of these things. They are only monthly direct debits and bank statements, anyhow. Nothing that needs hiding away. I just prefer being in an orderly environment, and I like the predictability of having everything tucked away. It gives me some semblance of normality; less chaos to deal with. I like order in my life and am not a fan of surprises.

I cook a meal of salmon and potatoes with a white sauce and leave it to cool. We can eat it later, once he gets home and has unpacked; we can have a late supper before bed. The kitchen is spotless as I head upstairs for a shower. I like to look good for Warren, to show him that I cope well in his absence. He is often under the illusion that I stumble through life, a gibbering wreck of a woman who collapses in a heap at the first sign of a problem, but that is simply not true. Admittedly, there have been times in the past when I have buckled under the strain of it all, but I've changed, grown stronger, become my own person. I now have a goal, something to work towards. An endpoint.

I choose my best outfit to reflect my positive mood. It may only be an airport run but I prefer to feel clean and smart whenever I am out and about. Perhaps it's all part and parcel of my need to be organised, to have everything shipshape. I slip into my navy court shoes and am just about to leave the house when my phone rings. I consider ignoring it but then think perhaps it could be Warren telling me about a delay. He would normally give me more notice than this, but then again, the flight only takes forty minutes from Schiphol Airport so it is certainly a possibility.

I grab it out of my bag and smile as I see the number flash up. A small flush of excitement grips me.

'Hello?'

'How is everything coming along?' the voice asks softly.

'Perfectly well,' I murmur. 'But my husband is home for the next few weeks so—'

'We'll keep contact to a minimum,' the voice cuts in before I have chance to finish.

'Yes please. That would be better.'

We talk for a little while longer before saying our goodbyes and hanging up.

I stride out to the car feeling more in control of my life than I have done for many, many years. Any lingering doubts I had about this undertaking immediately evaporate into the ether as I stare up at the clouds, and speak silently to whoever may be listening that this is definitely the right thing to do. It's the only thing to do. It's just a pity I have left it this long. Still, better late than never.

LISSY

It's been a long day. Rosie has moped around the house all afternoon complaining about her lot in life, about how unfair it all is, about how lonely she is without any friends or family to turn to when times are tough. That's her favourite line when she feels as if life has got it in for her.

Why don't we have any family?

Where are all of your relatives?

Where is my dad?

The last one jars me. No matter how many times I explain to her that he chose to leave us, she always somehow twists it to make it appear as if I drove him away. The last I heard he was backpacking across Outer Mongolia or some other such place that I would never in a million years choose to visit. His loss. The split was acrimonious and what hurts more than anything is his refusal to contact his daughter. His only child. His last remaining contact with me. He claimed he has every right to ignore her. Apparently, anything connected to me is toxic.

As for the other relatives, I have told Rosie time and time again about how Aunt Alice brought me up after my parents and I decided we would all be better apart. Then when Alice died, she left everything to me, which has allowed us to live in comfort, in a nice home; otherwise, we would be living in a council flat. I would be scrambling around for work, taking anything I could find, whether it be waitressing or cleaning toilets. Not living here in a large, four-bedroom house with a huge garden in the middle of the North Yorkshire countryside. If anything, we are blessed; perhaps not in the conventional sense, but financially we are very fortunate indeed. Not that any of it matters to Rosie right now.

And at least at times like this, during these stressful periods, I can spend time with her and am not tied to a nine-to-five job. My home is my career. Painting is a luxury and one that Alice afforded me. Any sales I make are a bonus. In that respect we are very lucky indeed. But whenever the chips are down, Rosie turns on me. I'm the only thing she has, so it's my job to bear the brunt of her dismay and anger and hurt, and on the whole, even though I say so myself, I do it with aplomb. I grew a second skin many, many years ago and it has served me well seeing me through some extremely tough times. Times I would sooner forget. So whatever Rosie throws my way pales into insignificance compared to what I have already experienced. Her insults and moans and relentless digs at me barely scratch the surface.

'You do know I'm not going back there, don't you?' she barks at me as I gather a pile of her belongings that have somehow managed to gather at her feet; magazines, empty cups, a mound of used tissues.

I scoop them up and march past her, ignoring her remark. She is going back. Rosie may not have had the most stable of upbringings but the one thing she has had all her life is an unprecedented amount of love. That's the thing with being wanted and cared for; you don't realise how crucial it is until it isn't there. And mine wasn't there. Not for many years. Alice stepped in when nobody else would and for that I will always be grateful. It can't have been easy for her but she stuck it out, and despite the odds we made it together; me and Alice against the world. Now it's Rosie and me. And sometimes everything runs smoothly and sometimes it doesn't; our lives tick along nicely and then one small thing happens and we are right back to where we started swimming against the tide. Like this school issue.

'We both know that's not true,' I reply dismissively as I scurry into the kitchen and dispose of all the detritus she has accumulated. I don't know how she does it. Rosie seems to have a knack for gathering clutter, whereas I am neat and orderly. In that respect, we are polar opposites.

'You'll have to drag me back there, then,' she murmurs, but already I can feel her resolve weakening. Deep down, Rosie knows that unless she makes a concerted effort, life will pass her by. She is a gregarious soul. She needs to be around people. I am a loner but my daughter has a natural affinity with others. That's why I refuse to be too concerned about her lack of friends. It will all come good soon enough. I am sure of it.

'Can I try to get in touch with him?' she asks, her tone suddenly brighter; perkier.

'Who?' I reply, my mind already on other issues, my latest painting being the main thing.

'My dad,' she replies, and I feel the blood drain from my head.

I try to speak clearly but all I can hear is the echo of my own words as they rattle around my head. 'He isn't in the country, Rosie. You know that.'

'But there must be a way of finding him, surely?' she whines. 'I mean it's all so weird, don't you think? We go to bed one evening and wake up the next morning and he's gone. No note. Nothing.'

I've protected my daughter; did what needed to be done to shield her from the upset and horror. Of course, there was a note, a lengthy, threatening, vitriolic note that turned my stomach to liquid and my skin to ice. I kept it, hid it away, too scared to even dispose of it in case anybody found it. My plan was to shred it and burn it, make sure it leaves no trace, but for some strange reason I have hung on to it, salted it away, along with the rest of my past. Rosie's words have reminded me what I must now do with it. I cannot risk her finding it. I cannot risk her finding out.

I manage to speak through a constricted throat, my head hot with a sudden burst of anxiety, 'Rosie, my darling, he left us. I know he is your dad and everything but we are better off without him. His leaving is an indicator of how unreliable he is. Surely you can see that?'

'What about your parents, then? Why didn't you live with them? And please don't say you just didn't get on. There's more to it than that. There has to be. I want you to start being truthful,

Mum. You're always on at me about being honest and yet you never really tell me about your past. I mean, what about your scars? I've seen the way you hide them away. There's no way you got them by falling over like you've told me in the past. You get grazes when you fall over, not a huge gash across your wrist …'

Her statement knocks me off kilter. So far, I've been able to avoid any deep and meaningful discussions about my upbringing, skimming over it all with trite phrases and empty pieces of information about how we 'didn't see eye to eye,' but now Rosie's questions are gaining traction and I am not prepared. And she is right. Am I really in any position to talk to her about honesty when she barely knows the real me? I shiver at the thought of speaking to her, telling her the whole sorry tale …

'I've already told you about them,' I reply tersely, knowing that I haven't. Not really. All she knows is that relationships between us were strained. Now she wants more from me and I'm not sure I can give her anything substantial to go on. I'm not ready for this and not in the right frame of mind. I should be, I know that, and I also know that none of this is Rosie's fault. The older she gets, the more probing her questions will become. She is a bright girl and deserves answers. But before I can begin to formulate a decent reply, a noise from somewhere behind stops me, cutting through my thoughts. I am constantly attuned to the slightest disturbance, my senses going into overdrive whenever anything different catches my attention. Seeing my chance to escape from Rosie's ever-growing scrutiny, I shuffle off to investigate where the sound is coming from.

In the hallway, I can see that an envelope has been pushed through the letterbox. It sits there, a small, white, rectangular piece of paper, innocuous and yet threatening at the same time with its sharp corners and unusual timing. The postman has already been and we don't know anybody around here. We are strangers in town.

I bend down and turn it over. It contains no stamp and the front is completely blank. I feel a familiar pulse begin to start up in my neck as I tear it apart in one slick movement. My head buzzes as I open the paper that is folded in half and stare at it, at what is typed on the paper, bold and large, jumping out at me. It contains just three words that make my head spin, forcing me to slump awkwardly on the bottom of the stairs whilst reaching up to the handrail to stop myself falling on to the floor in a hysterical heap. The words scream at me, blur my vision, slice at my stomach making me queasy. Words that say nothing but mean everything. They are there, threatening, repulsive, poisonous. Just three little words … YOU FUCKING BITCH.

ERICA

verything is grey. Huge swathes of cloud hang lazily overhead, threatening to spill their innards at any given moment. Their vast bodies cast long, dark shadows on the pavements like some monstrous entity waiting to crash down upon us all. I scurry along, suddenly wishing I had taken the car, keen to get home before the rain starts.

Arthur is just pulling up outside in his BMW as I stride along the street, my heels clicking loudly on the pavement, announcing my arrival to anyone who cares enough to listen. I watch as he wrestles his body out of the car, dragging his briefcase out with an irritated yank. I feel my stomach tighten and hope this isn't an indication of his mood for the remainder of the evening. I'm too tired for bickering and putting up with his snide remarks. All I want is a hot bath and a large glass of Chardonnay. Arthur, no doubt, will want a large scotch followed by numerous gin and tonics. Well, he can have them. Usually I would monitor him, dilute them when he isn't watching, but tonight I am too exhausted to care. I just pray his day has been productive. Arthur is a hedge fund manager and he used to love his work but the last few months have seen a change in him. He wanders around the house in a thunderous mood most evenings. When questioned about it, he simply replies that everything is going 'tits up.' I don't ask why and he doesn't tell. That's just how it is. We have fallen into a routine of putting up with our lot.

I switch on the TV as soon as we get in. The synthetic voices help to fill the difficult silence between us, easing the tension that settles in our home like an unwelcome visitor. Night after night, we amble along, pretending nothing is wrong, avoiding each other as best we can. I'm surprised Arthur hasn't already upped and left me before now. I sometimes think that it's only money that's holding us together; the glue that binds us. So sad, really. I can't even pinpoint when it was that it all started to go wrong. It's been a series of occurrences that have built up and eventually driven us apart. The dregs of our marriage held together for financial reasons. The thought of it fills me with a great sadness. I want it to be better but no longer know how to go about it. We are a jaded couple in desperate need of a makeover.

'I'm not hungry,' I say as we head into the kitchen.

I watch as he wrestles with his jacket and flings it over the back of the chair. Another of his habits that irritates me beyond reason. An expensive, silk lined suit that now reeks of frying smells and old dishcloths. I pick it up and stride out into the hallway where I slot it over the newel post. Arthur is too busy perusing the menu of our local takeaway to even notice. I say takeaway it's actually an upmarket deli that just happens to prepare hot snacks to eat out. My husband wouldn't be seen dead in a fish and chip shop or your average pizza parlour. That's part of our problem. I'm not demure enough for him, not the quiet, little wife who will accompany him to dinner parties and laugh at all his jokes. I am an embarrassment to him; the woman with a chequered past, the sad, old northerner who simply won't let go. He tried to change me, turn me into the wife he had always dreamed of, but it hasn't happened. I'm beyond redemption. Too spoiled and damaged to repair. A useless, broken spouse he can't afford to divorce. So, we stumble along together, fused by a fear of insolvency. Not that we are poor. Far from it. That's the whole issue you see; once you get used to being wealthy, it's difficult to step down from it. And Arthur and I don't do sharing. We're equally selfish. At least that's one thing we have in common. That and the money. Because we do have money and rather a lot of it. I'm not one for bragging but who would have thought that a gritty, working class girl like me would end up having more money than God? Gritty might be too strong a word. Or maybe not. It's a good thing people can't see inside my head because I can almost guarantee they won't like what they find there. I do a pretty good job of covering up, concealing what I'm really thinking. I adapt to all the societal norms and expectations on a daily basis but deep down, I know that I am different. Scarred by the past and terrified of the future.

And that's another secret that I have been keeping from everyone. My illness. Even Arthur doesn't know about that particular aspect of my life. I've only recently been diagnosed and, so far, haven't been given a proper prognosis, but I am fairly in tune with my own body and have a sense that when I get it, it won't be good. So that's why I have made my decision. I'm going to go ahead with what needs to be done, regardless of the outcome. Whether I live or die now seems irrelevant. What is important is that my wishes are carried out, my final dream is fulfilled and I can leave this place a happy woman. If it wasn't for the distance between us I would do it myself, but fate has dictated that I must observe from afar, watch it all unfold, which will be gratifying enough. It will satiate the need that has gnawed away at me for so long, I can't remember a single day when it hasn't been in the forefront of my mind. Perhaps that's what it is that has driven a wedge through my marriage, my distant demeanour and perpetual simmering anger. Soon however, it will all dissipate; the past will no longer eat away at me. My ruptured history will evaporate into the ether along with her memory. This whole thing is just something that needs to be done. That's all there is to it. And as far as I'm concerned, the sooner the better. I have no idea how long I have left. It could be months, it could be years. The outlook may even be a positive one. Regardless of all of that, I intend to carry it through, take it to its final resolution. I suppress a smile as Arthur brushes past me, phone in one hand, menu in the other. Tonight, I will do my best to be convivial towards him, less hostile. Now I know everything is going to plan, I can relax a little. Besides which, I still feel we should try to get along as best we can. It's miserable living like this, having to put up with the caustic remarks and black moods. I don't hate my husband. I just feel like I no longer know him. He is distant, removed from me and despite everything, I would like things to be back to how they were before everything turned sour. I am tired of being permanently angry.

Pouring myself a large glass of wine, I saunter upstairs and run a bath. Since finding out, I actually feel lighter, as if a great weight has been lifted. Funny isn't it, how a possible death sentence can fill me with such joy? I strip off, making a point of avoiding my reflection in the mirror. I am already aware of all my flaws and scars and lumps and bumps. I don't need to see them close up to remind me of their possible toxicity. Not that I am scared of looking. It's more that I am resigned to it and have more important things to be thinking about. I sink down under the soft, creamy bubbles and take a long, deep slug of my wine. My marriage may or may not be falling apart, but at long last, the rest of my life is coming together. Because that's the only thing that's important to me now. Making sure it all runs smoothly and everything goes to plan. With any luck, it will all take place before my body really starts to fail me. I take another sip of wine and close my eyes, feeling confident about it all. It will happen soon. I'll make sure of it.

BEVERLEY

It was luck that brought her to me. After everything I have been through, I think I deserve some good fortune so I don't feel the slightest bit guilty about any of this. Perhaps I should, but I don't. I doubt I have even registered in her thoughts over the years so why should I feel any remorse? She deserves this. And I deserve closure. God, I hate that word. A glib way of saying you are bringing an end to something that, in my case, has no finish line. My torture will never end. So, when I use the word closure, what I actually mean is revenge. I want to get my own back. I want to feel vindicated for what I am about to unleash upon her. I need to feel that she is sorry. I want her to wish she had never been born. Childish I know, but that's how it is. I am probably emotionally stunted and that too is her fault. I blame her for everything that is wrong with me. She has a lot to answer for. I have every right to want her to suffer.

Warren lifts his glass to the waiter to indicate he wants a refill. He has attended too many business functions and thinks this is the way to go on, to get serving staff to be at his beck and call. Ordinarily, he isn't a rude man but there are times when he comes across as abrasive. He spends too much time surrounded by people who wine and dine frequently and he forgets that it is a luxury. He needs to be reminded every now and again that the bar staff are on minimum wage and deserve, at the very least, a modicum of respect.

'Thank you,' I chime at the young man who pours our wine and look to Warren to indicate that he should do the same.

'Yes, sorry, thank you for this. Compliments to the chef.' He coughs gruffly and takes a long slurp of his Merlot. I sip mine, already feeling drunker than I have in a while. I must remember to keep myself in check, to not let him know too much, which isn't easy when the alcohol takes a hold of me. When that happens, all the memories churn around in my brain and spill out of my mouth. This is why I rarely drink. Too many demons, too much hurt. My inhibitions run amok when introduced to wine.

'So, tell me all about what's been going on while I've been away,' he says quietly. I feel my breath catch in my chest and for a fleeting moment, I wonder if he knows. 'You've been on cloud nine ever since getting this job. It obviously suits you.'

I laugh nervously and curl my fingers around the stem of the glass. He's been home a few days now and we've hardly had time to talk to one another. Warren's first few days back in the UK almost always consist of catching up with jobs around the house. I've insisted we get a gardener but he tells me it is his job, something he looks forward to. So, in his absence, the grass grows and grows and the weeds do their best to take over the entire garden, snaking up the side of the fence, their curling tendrils strangling everything and blocking out the light. I think about my activities while he has been working away and wonder what he would think about it all. He doesn't know anything. Of course, he doesn't. How could he? This is my secret, my plan. He is simply making polite conversation, catching up on events that have happened in his absence. I need to relax, not let my composure slip. That would be disastrous. I think back to all those years ago, to my blip, as we euphemistically call it. My memories of that time are vague, like snatches of a dream, disjointed and blurry round the edges. God knows what nonsense came out of my mouth back then. Perhaps Warren knows me better than I think he does. Perhaps he already has my darkest secrets stored away in some hidden recess in the farthest reaches of his brain, and is constantly watching and waiting for a time when they will all come spewing out, which is why he monitors me so closely, questions my every move, makes sure my life is as stress free as it can be. Or maybe I'm just overthinking everything. I take a deep breath and down a long glug of white wine; more than I should on a midweek evening out. More than I should if I am to keep my thoughts in check and keep my mouth shut.

'I love it,' I whisper, my throat closing up against the acidic effects of the alcohol. I cough and stare at Warren to assure him I am functioning entirely as I should be and am not in the throes of another breakdown. I'm not sure how either of us would cope if that happened again.

'That's great,' he says, his voice softening as he places his hand over mine and stares at me. 'I'm so pleased you're happy.' The relief in his voice is tangible.

My happiness, or rather the lack of it, is a constant burden on him. Poor Warren; having to put up with a wife who is prone to bouts of depression. I feel like one of those wealthy Victorian women who used to fall into a swoon at the first sign of trauma, regardless of how easy and casual their lives were. Except of course, my life has been anything but that. I have every reason to collapse in a heap, and wail and gnash my teeth and tear my hair out in great clumps. However, I don't. I did once, and it *was* only the once, which is surprising really when you consider all that I've been through. Put like that, I am far stronger than I think I am. Feeling slightly euphoric, I take another swig of wine. And then another.

I am fortunate that Warren isn't the type of man who is controlling. Not like some of my friends' husbands who question them about their spending, who they have spoken to, and where they have been. As long as everything is running smoothly, he is happy to let things be. This is good. I'm not up to answering a barrage of questions as to why I am so happy in my new job. It is, after all, an everyday secretarial position with no outstanding or defining features, nothing to set it aside from any other office job. Apart from one thing; that is the one thing that attracted me to it in the first instance. I lean back in my chair and savour the moment, the memory of that day when I realised what it meant I could do, should I get the position. Which I did. I sailed through the interview and got a call offering me the position later that afternoon. My face flushes at the memory. It was my chance. It was then that I knew the hand of fate was at play and I could, at long last, let karma do its thing. I could set things in motion, then stand back and watch it all unfold with an exquisite sense of pleasure.

I look over at Warren. He is on his phone. Only home for a few days and already work is taking over. I watch his demeanour change from untroubled to agitated in less than five seconds. He is beginning to lose his temper with whoever is on the other end of the phone. I feel for them. Warren is a hard taskmaster and not to be messed with when riled. I feel the tap on my shoulder while I am staring at him. I turn around to see her standing there. It takes me a while to register her face. We've only spoken a couple of times and her dress code tonight is entirely different, as is her hair. Less formal, sassy even, which takes me by surprise, given her role.

'How lovely to see you here, Beverley!' Her smile is broad and she looks more laid back than the last time I saw her when she was dashing down the corridor, clipboard in hand, late for a meeting, hair flying around in wispy strands as she pelted towards the waiting throng in the room at the far end of the building.

'You too,' I say a little timidly. I have no idea why, but I feel nervous in her presence, which is silly and more than a little juvenile. This is my time; I can spend it however I choose. I stare over at Warren who waves at me lightly and nods at my acquaintance before turning and becoming engrossed in his conversation once more.

'This is my husband, Warren,' I say although the introduction is pointless as he is already turned away from us, gesticulating in the air and becoming a little too animated for my liking. I pity the person on the other end of the phone and picture them beginning to sweat and quake at his escalating temper. He is a different person when he's at work. This is a side of him I rarely see and feel thankful in that respect.

'Anyway,' she smiles, 'I'll let you get on with your meal. Enjoy your evening.' And with that she is gone, striding confidently across the restaurant, weaving through the array of tables that are dotted around with little or no thought to access. Hardly ideal for the staff having to navigate their way through the place with their arms piled high with plates.

I watch as Warren grows more and more disturbed with the poor person on the other end of the receiver. Sweat coats his brow and he purses his lips in anger. I try to catch his eye but he bends away from me, his forehead creased into lines of annoyance. The snippets of conversation I pick up on mean nothing to me. Esoteric phrases about engineering that wash over me and leave me cold with boredom.

It seems to go on for an age until, at last, I hear his voice drift over to me just as I'm beginning to think I should spend the rest of the evening in the ladies' room powdering my nose.

'Who was that, then?' he says nodding over my shoulder at my acquaintance who is seated on the other side of the restaurant.

Warren is suddenly back with me and I am now supposed to snap into action and pick up where we left off. I suddenly feel aggrieved that he has ignored me for the last ten minutes. I try to appear convivial as I speak, even though my mouth is as dry as sand and anger is starting to bubble up inside of me. A hot spring of fury ready to erupt.

'That was Anthea Pa—' I begin, but before I have a chance to finish he is answering another call, his attention once again directed away from me.

Suddenly overcome with a flash of fury, I do something I have never done before. Scraping my chair back, I yank my jacket off the back of my chair and, before Warren even registers the fact that I have moved, I am on my feet and scurrying towards the exit, rage exploding inside me at his behaviour. How dare he be so rude? How bloody dare he?

By the time he reaches me I am outside the restaurant, scurrying along the street, my anger highlighted under the glare of the fluorescent lights.

'What the hell is going on?' he barks at me, which infuriates me even more. He is the one at fault here.

Striding along the path, I scan the street for a taxi. It's empty; a Wednesday evening, and most people are at home saving themselves for their weekend night out. I hear Warren's footsteps trailing behind me, the faint tip-tap of his expensive leather soled shoes; his favourite Loake brogues so shiny you can practically see your face in them. I feel his fingers grab at my arm and before I am able to pull away, he spins me around.

'Beverley?' A line of puzzlement sits between his eyes. His lip is curled slightly as he shouts my name. It bounces around the empty street, a tinny echo cutting through the darkness.

I am completely incensed and do something I have never done before. Clutched by fury, I pull my head back slightly and spit in Warren's face. As soon as I do it I cannot believe my own actions. This isn't me. Or is it? There are times when I barely know myself. I seem to have thoughts and deeds hidden within me that constantly set me on edge; make me wish I was somebody else. Anybody other than me.

I watch his reaction and find I am holding my breath in anticipation. He raises his hand and reaches into his jacket pocket where he drags a handkerchief out and dabs at his face. Maybe now he will see through me, realise what I am capable of, perhaps even get an idea of what I am planning on doing. I hope not. I like to think I am cleverer than that but there are times, like tonight, when I shock myself, let my guard down and almost reveal the true me. I don't want Warren to see her, the real Beverley. She is a sour faced individual; bitter and vengeful and best kept out of view, secreted away from all the decent people.

He takes a step towards me and for one awful moment I think he might hit me, lash out at me with his huge fists. He has never done it before but then, I have never spat in his face before. There's a first time for everything.

Every single noise is accentuated as I wait for the connection that will knock me off my feet, send me reeling on to the tarmac.

Warren is over six feet tall and weighs nearly fifteen stone. He could squash me like a fly if he so chooses. Blood thumps through my ears, roaring and gushing, tearing around my body as I watch him lean into me. I wait. Electricity bolts through me as he tilts his bulky body forward towards mine. I feel his touch on my arm; gentle and reassuring, a whisper on my skin.

'Beverley.' His voice is little more than a sigh in the calm of the evening.

I am rocked to my very core by how sedate he is, how composed and unruffled he is while I am in complete turmoil, my stomach in knots, my head feeling as if it is in a vice that is slowly being tightened by a set of invisible fingers clasped around a cold, metal handle turning and turning, crushing the very life out of me.

'Come on, sweetheart,' he says softly, 'let's go back inside. I need to pay the bill and then we can leave and go home. That's if you want to?'

He thinks I've gone nuts again. Maybe I have. How would I know? Warren's face is soft, rounded into a non-threatening gaze with an easy smile and soft, glassy eyes that are coaxing me into submission. Gone is the frown line, the look of bewilderment. He is staring at me as if I am about to be sectioned. A look of pity. Or fear. The last thing Warren wants is to have to nurse me through another breakdown. Can't say I blame him. It wasn't an easy time for me or him. I need to get myself out of this situation. I do not want my poor husband to start acting as if I am in need of support. If that happens he will start monitoring me too closely, questioning my every move. He will suffocate me with his love and compassion, allowing me no room for manoeuvre, no space to carry out my next move. I cannot let that happen. I absolutely must pull myself together if I am to see this thing through to its conclusion. I've waited too long, spent so many years wanting it and now it has practically fallen in my lap; this *chance* has presented itself, and if I don't pull myself together I run the risk of losing it completely. The last time I had a 'blip,' I was so isolated and pumped full of drugs, I didn't know which way was up. Dark days best left unvisited and not a time in my life I would ever want to repeat.

'Warren, darling, I am *so* sorry. I'm just a bit tired,' I say meekly, hoping I manage to get the balance right. Just enough humility to convey my regret at my outrageous behaviour, but enough strength to set aside any concerns he might have about my sanity. I need to assert myself here, let him know I am not on the cusp of losing my mind. 'Let's just pay the bill and leave, shall we? I've got an early start in the morning.'

He eyes me cautiously, assessing my mental state, seeing if I can hold it together or if I'm about to turn into a blubbering wreck. I link my arm through his, leaning my head on his chest as I speak softly, 'Honestly, darling, I am fine. I cannot apologise enough. Too much wine.' I giggle quickly. 'That's all it is. No more midweek drinking for me.'

'Well, if you're sure?' he says, sounding anything but sure.

I will need to be careful here. Make certain I reassure him. This is the problem with being damaged; people are always looking for cracks to reappear. No matter how stable you think you are, those around you are in a constant state of flux, ready to step in should those cracks start to open again. They are always on the lookout, waiting in the wings to stop those hairline cracks from turning into irreparable gaping holes.

'I'm sure,' I say with a smile. I dip my eyes and stare at the ground.

A clatter in the distance alerts me. A woman is standing outside a takeaway. She leans back against the window, illuminated by the green, flashing sign above her, and lights a cigarette. Taking a long drag, she catches my eye and gives me a cursory glance before grabbing her phone out of the rear pocket of her jeans and staring at it intently. A door slams from the shop next door. A man in his twenties starts to wind in the awning that is hanging over the front of the newsagents. Everyone is shutting up shop, heading home for their midweek routine of a ready meal and early evening TV that will wash over them, mesmerise them while they unwind after a hard day's graft. The woman glares at him as droplets of water from the earlier downpour spray over her as he continues to wind. I watch her mouth something at him, her face screwed up in anger as she wipes herself down, swiping at her wet arms with long, aggressive strokes. He shrugs and continues to rotate the handle regardless. She shouts at him again, telling him he is *a fucking idiot!* before stubbing out her cigarette and storming off inside.

We walk back to the restaurant and I wait outside while Warren settles the bill with a bewildered looking waitress. By the time we manage to flag down a taxi, I am beyond exhausted and ready for my bed.

'You sure you're OK?' Warren slings his big, strong arm over me as we slink down in the back seat, our bodies snuggled together like a pair of canoodling teenagers.

'Absolutely certain,' I reply and lean up to kiss him on the mouth, hoping he can't see through my act.

Inside I am a complete wreck at the thought of how close I came to ruining the whole thing. I mustn't let anything like that happen again. I have no idea what did it, whether it was the sight of Anthea that unnerved me or this thing I am about to embark on. Regardless, I have to keep it together because this time in a few short months, I will have it all sorted, and I am not about to let it all slip away from me because of a few minutes of stupidity, a momentary lapse of concentration. This is too important, too crucial to spoil. I've waited over half my life for it, lived and breathed it. There is no way I will let this opportunity go. It will not slip through my fingers without a fight.

CHILD B

*S*he was completely exonerated. Not that it made her feel any better. If anything, it made her feel worse. She deserved to be punished. He was dead and she was alive and she didn't deserve any sort of happiness as long as her tiny brother was in his grave, cold and alone. He was there because she wasn't. She left him on his own with that monster, a girl who was supposed to be her friend. A girl with a dark secret. How was she to know? How were any of them supposed to have known? She would have done anything to be able to turn the clock back, make everything all right again; bring that little boy back. No matter how hard she tried, she would never be able to get on with her life. Nothing would ever be the same again. This was all her fault.

She was given complete anonymity and assigned a social worker. Big deal. The anonymity meant nothing, and as for the social worker? Well, she was a waste of space. Nobody could help her. Nobody. The judge had decided that revealing their identity would have a detrimental effect on their mental health having to deal with public opinion and possible vigilantism. They were at a tender age, he had said, and had their lives ahead of them. Suicide bids had already been attempted and nothing would be gained from giving the public their names. Waste of time really, since everyone in the local area already knew who they were. Anybody who felt like carrying out their very own vigilante campaign could go right ahead since they all knew exactly where both girls lived. Keeping their names secret seemed like a pointless exercise to her, but the decision had been made and she had no say in it. And anyway, people pitied her, not hated her. It was the other one they hated. Some said they hoped she would die in prison. Unlikely since she was on suicide watch.

The details of the case were harrowing, to say the least. He had been smothered. She had pressed her hands down over his tiny face and stopped him from breathing. How dare she? How fucking dare she do such a thing? And then she had the audacity to try to slit her wrists with a knife she had managed to smuggle out of the kitchen whilst on remand. All of this from her friend; somebody she thought she knew well. Turns out she didn't know her at all. They were complete strangers. And now her so-called friend was being given counselling because of her attempted suicide and 'difficult home life.' The papers had jumped on that particular aspect giving detailed accounts of her parents' history of alcohol abuse and violence, saying she had come from a challenging background claiming violence begets violence.

She sat through the court case, listened to it all. Her father tried to stop her, but she couldn't not go. The police may not have blamed her, but she had caused this. It was all her fault. She barely understood what it was they were all saying, anyway. It was all just words at the end of the day. None of it would bring Greg back. When all the jurors and police and the judge trudged off home, tired and wearied by it all, horrified by her friend's actions, disgusted and outraged at what one human can do to another, desperate for a drink or a sleep or whatever it was they did at the end of such gruelling days, Greg would still be in his grave. None of their wise words would help him or inject breath back into his lifeless, desiccated body.

The court case gave her time to think, to reflect on it all. There was nothing she could do, of course, except watch it all and build up a hatred of such gargantuan proportions, it almost killed her. Eating was impossible and sleep evaded her for what felt like months until, eventually, she was referred to a specialist. A therapist who talked to her. That was all they did talk. And for all her scepticism, she felt that in some small way, it helped her. The problem with him was that, although he was kind and gentle and he got her to eat without feeling guilty for having the privilege to do so when she didn't deserve it, he still didn't truly understand her predicament. How could he? He didn't know her. He couldn't see inside her head. He only knew what she chose to tell him.

As the case progressed and more evidence emerged, it became clear that Greg wasn't the only one. The police were looking into another case; one involving a little girl in a local playground. At the time, everyone had presumed she had fallen, but after further investigations, evidence had emerged that there was possibly foul play involved. Someone, no, not someone, she had pushed that little girl from the top of the slide and left her there to die. Somehow that made it worse, because if they had stopped her then, known about it, done something about it, Greg would still be alive. But he wasn't. What was done was done and could not be undone.

The court case seemed to go on for an age. Teams of psychologists and an army of specialists trooped in, day after day, each claiming to be experts in their field. Some citing Child A as unstable, some claiming she was damaged by her upbringing, having been exposed to violence from a very young age. And if the incident with the slashed wrists didn't convince them of her mental instability, her further attempts at smashing her head against the wall and shoving plastic cutlery down her throat did a fine job. She was cleared of murder, convicted of manslaughter, and sent to a young offenders' institute.

After a while, the papers quietened down and the folk of County Durham soon forgot about her and got on with their lives. But not the families of the dead. They didn't forget. Their lives didn't continue as normal. They no longer knew what normal felt like and probably never would.

The only thing that kept her going through those dark times was her collection. Day after day, night after night, she would sit, hunched over the table, sifting through every newspaper it was possible to get her hands on, seeking out articles about the incident. Articles about her. She would cut them all out, stash them away in scrap books, reading them over and over until her head throbbed and her chest ached from sobbing. It was unhealthy, she knew that, but felt powerless against its draw. She found it cathartic; it helped her to sleep, helped her to restore some semblance of order back into her life. Her parents tried to stop her but it was useless. Nothing they did or said could help her put an end to it. They all had their own way of grieving and this was hers. But then her father's death brought an abrupt end to it all. She needed to drag herself back into the real world, to focus on the future and help her mother cope with the torrent of shit that life had decided to throw at them. Funny thing was, her dad seemed to be the only one who had been coping with it all. He was the one who kept the house running, made sure the bills were paid and that they were all fed and had clean clothes to wear yet he was the one who eventually cracked under the strain. She came home from school one afternoon to find her mother curled up on the sofa, two police officers sitting either side of her, and a family liaison worker gently stroking her hand.

They had tried to coax her father down from the bridge but, apparently, he hadn't responded to any of their cajoling and instead, had leapt on to the cold, hard tarmac beneath, his body crushed beyond recognition. If they thought their lives were difficult before, they found themselves plunged into a nightmare from which they would never wake. Their misery seemed to drag on and on, with no end in sight. Just she and her mother, locked together in their insular world that became a hate-filled place, full of bitterness and resentment and blame. Until she left home that is. University couldn't come quick enough. It was a welcome reprieve from the darkness and angst that permeated their lives on a daily basis. Freed from her mother's suffocating ways she found she was able to forge a life for herself.

Losing her virginity was first on her list. For far too long she had led a cloistered existence, forgetting how to smile or relax. And as for boys? The night they lost Greg was the last time she had even thought of them, but now she was a different person, in a new place. This was a chance to reinvent herself, to be whoever she wanted to be.

High on a mixture of cheap lager and dope, she lost her virginity to a lad whose name she didn't even know. It wasn't important to her. What was important was making sure she did it; got it over and done with so she could get on with the rest of her life without being saddled with guilt. Any thought of sex and boys took her right back to that evening. She needed to break that association. It wasn't exactly the most romantic encounter, but then that wasn't her intention.

They had done it on a balmy summer's evening on a long strip of grass behind the pub, hidden only by the huge bins and piles of black, *plastic sacks that she feared would topple over and smother them. He grunted and she cried, and when it was over they both went their separate ways, each too drunk to remember one another in the cold light of day. She had staggered back to her flat and fallen, face-first, on to the bed where she stayed until morning, the memory of the encounter no more than a blurry image in her mind.*

University was good for her soul. She enjoyed the subject matter and didn't mind the workload that others complained about. It gave her something to go at; it was something to focus her mind on.

She did her best to fit in with the others, hitting the party circuit, drinking hard, smoking the odd joint, but all the time he was there in her mind, her younger brother with his tiny face and dimpled, chubby hands. Her baby.

By the time she met Warren she was in her third year. It was also around that time she took up her interest again; cutting out snippets from newspapers whenever the story cropped up, keeping tabs on her, the one the papers still referred to as Child A even though she was no longer a child. She had been transferred to an open prison and was up for parole, having been a model prisoner for the past six years. It was only manslaughter, after all. That word made her toes curl. She was a murderer, nothing more, nothing less. She took two lives. Two tiny unsuspecting lives ... left two families bereft and heartbroken, and now she had suddenly decided to become a good citizen and they were all supposed to forgive her and simply accept it. As if it made the whole sickening episode acceptable.

The newspaper reports detailing her life told of a hideous upbringing, of parents who were saturated in alcohol, a life where daily beatings were the norm. She did recall once visiting her friend and being greeted by a woman who was most unlike her own mother; she was standing in the doorway, wide-eyed, hair bouncing around her face like tufts of cotton wool, skin grey and baggy. The clothes she wore looked expensive and the house was far bigger and more elaborately decorated than her own, but even at the tender age of thirteen she was able to sense an atmosphere of fear and tension, as if the slightest thing would tip this woman over the edge. She wasn't allowed past the doorway and the one thing she did remember, the thing that stuck in her head and should have set alarm bells ringing, were the marks on her friend's arm as she shuffled past her mother a terrified look in her eyes. Then, as if she were carrying out some sort of childish prank, the woman reached out and grabbed a handful of her daughter's hair and tugged at it, knocking the teenager clean off her feet. She landed in a heap on the front step where she lay for a short while, motionless and stunned, before scrambling back up to the sound of her mother's infantile, caustic laughter, passing the whole event off as a sick joke.

It was no excuse for her friend's actions, though. She wouldn't allow herself to be fooled and sucked in by such tales of pity and woe. So, she continued collecting and storing the clippings and making sure she kept track of her whereabouts as best she could. Because one day she would get even. She would make sure her professed friend paid dearly for what she did. There was no way she could ever forgive and forget. No way at all. No matter how long it took, or how much it cost her, one day she would get her revenge.

LISSY

I try to keep it together to stop Rosie finding the note and seeing me in this state. Shuffling myself forward, I stand up, the floor still swaying slightly, and shove the piece of paper deep into my pocket. Just when I thought our lives were back on track. Just when I thought we could start afresh, a whole heap of shit rains down on us once more.

Everything tilts and sways as I do my best to walk into the kitchen. It's like strolling along a seesaw, the floor leaning precariously under my feet, my head swimming as I teeter along, hands pressed against either side of the wall for balance.

Staggering towards the sink, I fill the kettle and make myself a cup of sweet tea.

I sip at it, the liquid burning my throat as it trickles its way down into my clenched belly. What I actually feel like doing is slumping down on to the floor and crying. I want to bash the tiles and scream to the skies that this isn't right and it isn't fair. I don't. Instead, I finish my tea and nibble on a dry biscuit to stem the vomit that I feel rising in my gut.

Rosie doesn't come through to see me. I listen as she shuffles her way out of the living room, then pounds her way upstairs, still cross at me for not answering her questions. Tomorrow she is returning to school. I need to pull myself together. She mustn't see me like this. Nobody must see me like this, especially Mr Cooper, the gloating head of year who, it would appear, desperately wants to see my daughter fail at her new school before her time there has barely even begun.

I pull the creases out of my trousers and stand up. I've come too far to lose my way now. After what I've been through, this letter doesn't even register on the scale of distress and trauma. I have to remember to keep it in perspective, to keep telling myself that I have weathered storms far darker and colder than this one.

I march into the hallway and double check that the door is locked and bolted, then do the same with all the windows in every room in the house. I rattle them in their frames making sure they are solid and cannot be prised open. That was one of the things that attracted me to this place, the fact that it appeared to be secure and secluded. Sometimes, however, secluded is dangerous. Nobody can hear you scream when you're in an isolated spot. It's all about balance; just enough in the way of neighbours to make you feel less lonely and not so many that you run the risk of … what is it I run the risk of? Being blamed for something that happened so long ago I feel as if it took place in a different life and to a different person? I shiver and pull my cardigan around my shoulders. The temperature seems to have suddenly dipped. Or perhaps my core body heat has iced over after finding that letter and reading those words. I think of the stupid, pedestrian phrase about sticks and stones and all that crap about calling names not hurting. Of course they hurt. How can they not? You would have to be made of solid stone for such things to not hurt you. And although I consider myself pretty resilient, I am still breakable.

I place my hands on the kitchen windowsill and stare out at the hills in the distance. The sight of them calms me, helps to dampen the fire that is licking its way up my body and shrieking through my brain. A grey mist hangs over the top of the highest point of the hills, a craggy shoulder of rock shrouding it in a blanket of swirling cloud. It's a mesmerising sight and one I hope I will never take for granted. When I was growing up in County Durham, the view we had was a little less appealing. Our house had a large garden, for sure, but we overlooked a factory at the front, a huge, grey brick edifice that overshadowed the entire road, blocking out light and making the street a formidable place to visit. Even on the brightest of days, we were cloaked in blocks of granite shade that cowered over us, monster-like and eerily cold. The view I now have of the hills of North Yorkshire is not something I will ever take for granted. Every crumb of comfort thrown my way will always be greedily savoured. I've had that sort of a life.

The thump above me alerts me to Rosie's sudden movement. Her feet beat a steady, solid tempo as she pounds her way downstairs and stands in the kitchen, hands on hips, surveying me carefully.

'Have you picked it up?'

'Hmm?' I drag my eyes away from the scenery and stare into her face. Only as I am watching her, seeing the scowl and her channelled brow, does it begin to slot into place.

'A letter?' she snaps impatiently. 'Apparently there was a letter delivered for me,' she says with her hand outstretched, ready for me to hand it over. She stares at me, our conversation and her probing earlier, still not forgotten. A huge, uncomfortable throb takes hold in my neck. A cold trickle of sweat runs down my spine as her words bounce around the emptiness of our kitchen.

'For you?' I say, trying to control my breathing and sound authoritative and fearless, when all the time I fear the ground will tilt and send me sprawling on to the cold, hard floor tiles.

I need to think quickly. Do I really want to hand it over and watch my daughter crumble in front of me? I don't want to lie to her, although the pattern for that particular game started long ago anyway but would or should any mother in their right mind subject their daughter to such a harrowing read?

'I just got a text saying a note's been hand delivered for me and I really need to give it a read. I've just checked and there's nothing there.' She starts to walk back into the hallway, a determined look on her face.

'Who sent it?' I ask, my curiosity now piqued and my imagination in overdrive. I feel my heart begin to flutter its way up my neck and place my hand on my collarbone to stem the sensation.

Rosie turns and holds out her phone at arm's length, staring at it intently. 'Not sure. Not a number I recognise, but then again,

I've got so many contacts and changed my phone so many times it could be anybody. I was thinking it might be Lara. You remember Lara from my last school?'

I do remember Lara. She was a kind girl. Not the type of person to send a letter dripping with poison and hatred. However, Rosie has no inkling as to what is in it and nor will she. And here I was thinking it was directed at me when all the time it was somebody spouting their filth at my baby girl.

'Well, I haven't seen a note or letter and since it's a number you don't recognise I would suggest you just ignore it. Could be that somebody has sent it to you by mistake.'

I feel relief sweep through me as she shrugs and stares once again at her phone, her eyes narrowed pensively.

'Maybe. Anyway, if you see anything, can you let me know?'

'Absolutely,' I reply a little too enthusiastically, elated that she has gone along with it. I expected a tantrum of sorts; some foot stamping and lip pouting, not this resigned acceptance.

Shoving my hand into my pocket, I lightly finger the edge of the envelope, tracing my nail along the length of the paper. Later, when Rosie is safely out of sight, I will dispose of it; tear it into tiny strips and stuff it down into the bottom of the bin where it belongs with all the other rubbish. I could keep it, show it to Mr Cooper tomorrow, when Rosie returns to school, as evidence that she is indeed being targeted but I'm not sure what that would achieve. I have no proof that it came from anybody at the school and, Cooper being the pedant that he is, would use that argument to destroy any complaints I bring against his claim that trouble seems to follow Rosie around. He's wrong on that score. It's me that it tails so closely. Best to get rid of this letter and hope we don't receive another one. I bite at a loose flap of skin on my lip and wince as it comes loose and the familiar metallic taste of blood trickles over my tongue and oozes down my throat. Perhaps I should never have moved here. I should possibly have chosen somewhere further afield; somewhere down south; Southampton, Brighton, London any bustling city we could disappear into. I don't want to start thinking like that but when the heavy shroud of fear begins its descent, it's hard to see beyond it and think rationally. When Davey was here, at least there was somebody else to help around the house, to put the bins out when it got dark, to help with the cooking and cleaning, to share the general workload, but now he's gone it's all down to me. I refuse to think about where the note came from. Therein lies the road to madness; a cold and lonely route from which there is no return. I just need to be more vigilant, that's all it is. I will not move on again. I've spent my entire adult life running away from my past, from an act that most certainly does not define me. This time I am here to stay.

BEVERLEY

The next few weeks pass by in a blur. I managed to convince Warren that I am of sound mind and he returned to work a happier man. Work is busier than I ever thought it would be, with so much to do on a daily basis and a whole raft of new skills to learn. I had no idea how rusty I had become. The social life within the entire building is hectic. Every week there is a function or a party to attend; a fiftieth birthday bash, an engagement, a retirement. The reasons for celebrating are endless. So far, I have only attended one; Shirley who sits opposite me decided to hang up her hat and spend her days pottering around her garden and looking after her grandchildren in her twilight years. It was a High Tea at a local stately home and we were finished by 6.30 p.m. I returned home satiated and mildly giddy after chatting to a lady who went to the same university as me and vaguely knew one of my ex-boyfriends. It filled me with a sense of euphoria, remembering the past, thinking about the wild, young thing I once was. Anybody seeing me now would struggle to marry the two; the mild-mannered, middle-class lady who lives such a safe life it borders on practically dead, against the young student who smoked, drank, and slept with anyone who breathed. I smile and roll my eyes. I have worked extremely hard to reach this point in my life, to shake off the shackles of my past and refine my bitterness. It took a lot of effort and continual self-appraisal. I have overcome many barriers and lived through so much heartache it would have felled a lesser woman. Yet here I am, trudging through life, just getting on with it.

I push the trolley around the supermarket, my back beginning to ache after sitting for so long typing up the minutes of a meeting that lasted almost three hours. I often wonder what they find to talk about at these events; how they have the stamina to sit through it all.

My eyes scan the shelves as I run my gaze along the huge stack of items that I will never, ever purchase. My list is short. Warren isn't due back for another week, and when he is away I am inclined to live on nothing more than cornflakes and jam on toast. However, I do the right thing and fill the trolley with fresh fruit and vegetables, thinking I can make a casserole and freeze it. That's when I spot him; a man on the opposite side of the aisle who is staring at me, his eyes sweeping over me like an animal sizing up its prey. I am unsure whether I should let him know I have caught him looking over by taking a slightly aggressive stance and placing my hands on my hips while glowering at him, or whether I should do the sensible thing and shuffle away with my head dipped, too afraid of what he might say if I confront him. It turns out I don't have time to do either. I watch; a mix of horror and curiosity creeping up my spine as he smiles and starts to walk towards me. I am rooted to the spot, my mind in full whirl as to who it could be; one of Warren's colleagues? An old neighbour who knows my mother and will take great pleasure in telling me what a terrible life she has had? A complete stranger who is mentally unhinged? He thrusts his hand out for me to shake and that's when I begin to wish I had walked away taken heed of the inner voice that has served me well over the years.

'Daryl. Remember me?' he says, so full of confidence and gusto I almost want to cry. Of course, it's him. I can see it now he is standing so close to me. He still has the same charming smile and twinkling eyes but that is all that remains of the boy I once knew. His hair is almost gone save for a few straggly wisps he has dragged over his forehead in a vain attempt to hide his baldness, and a large stomach protrudes out over the top of his jeans. His T-Shirt is stretched to capacity revealing an unsightly navel and a generous amount of hair-covered gut. He is every inch the middle-aged man who has let himself go.

'Yes, of course. Sorry, my eyesight isn't what it used to be,' I lie as I sweep my eyes over his bulky frame once more. 'How are you?' I mumble, wishing I could somehow escape from all of this; from his probing gaze, the stifling reek of his body odour, which is now wafting around the air between us, the inevitable stream of questions that will no doubt follow if I hang around here and allow him to make polite conversation. I step to one side in a bid to move away but he reaches out and places his hand on my arm, a touch so soft it almost takes my breath away.

'It's been a long time,' he says quietly. 'A very long time.' His face suddenly darkens. A shadow flits behind his eyes. 'I saw her, you know?'

I should have known this was coming, been prepared for it, but as always it catches me by surprise, knocking the air out of my lungs, draining the blood from my head. I swallow hard and grasp the handle of the trolley, my hands slick with sweat.

'Sorry, Daryl,' I gasp, my breath hot and rapid, 'but I need to get on. I have an appointment to go to after this and I'm already late.'

He steps to one side and smiles at me, his head nodding up and down as if he understands my plight. I want to slap him. How can he possibly begin to comprehend what I have been through? The devastation that has been my life.

'Hang on a minute!' he shouts after me as I break into a swift march. 'We should get together one of these days. I work around these parts sometimes. We can meet for coffee.'

I have to stop myself from turning around and yelling at him that I would sooner sever one of my own limbs than sit with him and reminisce over a cappuccino. I feel the heat of his hulking body as he sidles up next to me, forcing me to grind to a halt.

'Here. This is my business card,' he says with a huge grin as he slips it into my palm. He still has a way of making his presence known even after all these years. I stare down at the small piece of card in my hand.

Argent Cars No journey is too much trouble.

There is a telephone number on it and an emblem of a vehicle some sort of people carrier. I look up to see him still smiling at me, 'I have my own taxi business now. Airport runs, business pick-ups, that sort of stuff. Not just an ordinary cab or anything like that. We're exclusive to certain successful businesses.'

I have no idea how to respond. I nod and try to muster up a smile without it appearing like a manic, nervous smirk. Daryl is part of my past, a past I monitor carefully and discuss with a select few. Not here and not with him. Besides which, why on earth would he want to socialise with me after our last encounter? He was rude and obnoxious; excessively so. My mind almost goes into shutdown at the thought of it. It's a memory I have tried hard to block out for many, many years. I don't want him here, forcing it to resurface. I want him gone.

'That's great, Daryl,' I reply. My throat is dry and my head feels as if it is quivering, a visible movement that I am powerless to control. I want to walk away again but he has somehow managed to step in front of me and is blocking my path, my only means of escape.

He reaches back into his pocket and brings out a phone which he brandishes at me. 'What's your number? I'll put you in my contacts and we can stay in touch. It'll be good to talk about the old days. We had some real good laughs back then, didn't we?'

I don't know what to say. He is standing in front of me, his fingers hovering over the screen on his phone, ready for me to speak. An iron hand claws at my windpipe, travels round my head, and knocks at the base of my skull. I have to get away, to remove myself from this situation as quickly as I can. In a moment of madness, I find myself telling him my mobile number, relaying it automatically, my voice flat and robotic as I say the numbers out loud. As soon as I have finished, I push past him, white lights blurring my vision.

'Great!' he shouts after me, 'I'll be in touch.'

By the time I make it to the exit, I am almost blind with panic and horror. I stumble along to my car and fling myself inside, my arms and legs a jumble of ungainly limbs as I try to arrange the bags and belt myself in. I sit for a short while, drumming my fingers on the steering wheel, breathing loudly as I try to calm down, telling myself it is just the shock of seeing him after so long that has caused this reaction. An unexpected face from the past it's only natural I should feel distressed. The last time I saw Daryl was the evening Greg died. *That night.* Guilt oozes from every pore as I shove the key in the ignition and start the engine. I don't want to think about it, those lost hours, that terrible atrocity, all those lies. I turn my vehicle out of the car park and head for home, trying to expel all thoughts of Daryl from my mind. He is the last person I should be thinking about. This was a minor occurrence, bumping into him, no more that, a tiny distraction. He is not a part of my life any more and nor will he ever be.

∞∞∞∞∞

The lights turn to green and I swing the car round into the village, feeling more in control. My breathing has slowed down and the shock has dissipated. He is just a face, that's all he is. Just a minor person from my past from that day. I can't allow him to wheedle his way into my life and up-skittle everything I've worked so hard for.

I pull up on the drive and let out a small whistle of relief. I have a week before Warren finishes work. Seven whole days of doing whatever I want before he comes home and instils in me a sense that I am still under close scrutiny. After the previous incident, he is being extra careful around me, treating me as if I am a fragile object, a porcelain doll that may shatter at any time if the circumstances take a downward shift. I will be tiptoed around, upon his return, until he feels that I am not about to have some sort of mental failure.

I glance at my phone before getting out of the car. I am relieved to see that nobody has called. No lists of unknown numbers. No Daryl.

The sight of her huddled there in the doorway is a shock to me. It shouldn't be, but it is. She did this once before, came to me in desperation when she had nowhere else to go. I am surprised she actually remembered where I live. Just goes to show what she is capable of achieving once she sets her mind to it. I climb out of the car, drop the bags at her feet and sigh heavily.

'Come on, Theresa, up you get. Come inside and you can have a bath and get something to eat.'

This isn't what she is after. I am well aware of what it is she really wants but I refuse to give it to her. Any cash I press into her palm will go straight up her nose or into a vein. The best I can do is clean her up and feed her.

She stares up at me and shuffles to her feet. Her skin is grey and although she is fourteen years younger than me, anybody seeing us together could be forgiven for thinking she is my older sister.

'Give me a hand with these bags and we'll get inside and put the kettle on.'

She complies like a small child and helps me haul the shopping inside, her tiny body shivering violently despite it being late spring and relatively warm outside.

'Right,' I say chirpily, 'let's see what we've got here to eat.'

I watch her slump into the chair, and stare long and hard at her face, at her saggy eyes and mottled skin, and think of my parents, our mother especially, and the heartache our actions have caused.

'Today is a day for forgotten faces.' I smile as I grab a couple of plates out of the cupboard, thinking about Daryl and his huge gut and rancid smell, hoping he doesn't contact me.

'Huh?' Theresa stares at me, no recognition behind her dark, dull eyes.

'Oh, nothing,' I say, 'just forget it. I'm only thinking out loud. Just wondering who is next. That's all it is. Just me speaking my mind.'

Even as I say it, I can see that Theresa is elsewhere, her gaze darting around, flitting around the kitchen, her eyes fixed on anything she can steal to feed her addiction, her mind definitely not fixed on me. I finish making us a snack, wondering if she knows that her current state is apparently my doing. According to our mother, this pathetic creature before me ended up in this condition because of me. Even having a child growing in her belly after it all happened wasn't enough to keep our family together. I saw to that. I was the one who split us apart a long time ago and she has continued to punish me ever since. She done her level best to remind me of my terrible misdemeanour. Like I am ever likely to forget.

ERICA

A rthur is staring at me as I tap away at the screen on my phone.

'Work?' he asks as he points the remote at the TV screen and turns the volume up. He does seem to enjoy it, letting me know I'm intruding on his listening, spoiling his programme. I could quite easily turn the sound off but then I also like to antagonise him sometimes, to let him know I am still here. It's not that I enjoy the conflict, far from it but it is nice to be acknowledged, to have somebody realise you are still in the room. We have been sitting here for an hour, both locked in our own little worlds, the words we should be saying to each other trapped and out of reach. Eventually, the silence became so unbearable I decided to glance at my messages.

Arthur is being facetious. He knows I don't bring work home. My job is not something I ever get involved in outside of office hours. I work part-time for a pharmaceutical company and leave everything behind the minute I walk out of the door. I stopped enjoying my job a long time ago, and have often considered leaving but then wonder how I would fill my time, those endless hours spent rattling around the house while Arthur is working.

'Just a friend,' I say and turn my phone on to silent as a stream of messages slide on to the screen.

I hear him sigh and watch in my peripheral vision as he flicks the television off and turns to look at me, his expression unreadable. There is a moment's quiet where a small frisson of fear pounds through me. His eyes trail over the room before casting them back on to me and speaking softly, 'I think it's about time we talked, don't you?' His voice is indistinct. I have no idea what is coming next but don't like the tension that has suddenly settled in the room. I am at a loss as to what to say or do. I place my phone on the arm of the sofa and cross my legs. An uncomfortable pressure builds in my chest; tendrils of apprehension winding and bending around my body, tightening and choking me. Is this it? The moment we have both been avoiding for so long? The moment when our lives become detached from one another and we are sent skittering off into new and very different directions? Dear God, I hope not. I want something better for us. We both deserve more. I clear my throat and nod, pushing my hair behind my ears hoping he can't see the tremble in my fingers or the throb that has taken hold in my neck.

'Where to start?' I half laugh and find myself suddenly fighting back tears. Months and months this has gone on for. The pair of us, scraping through each day, ignoring our problems, pretending it will all just go away. And now here we are, sitting opposite one another in silence, and it looks like we have reached this point. The point of no return. I feel quite sick at the thought of what he is going to say. There are days when I feel so angry at the world in general that I hate everyone, including him. Then other days I find myself saturated in nostalgia, overwhelmed with a deep longing for the love and connection we used to have, wishing it would return, hoping we can salvage something from it all, from the wreck that is currently our marriage.

'Well, how about we come clean about everything?' he says with a smile and I suddenly feel a collision in my head; stars bursting behind my eyes, blotches and dark shadows marring my vision. My knees begin to bang together and I have to hang on to them to keep them rigid. I press my open palms on to my calves to stop the tremble from showing.

'OK, I'm not quite sure what you want me to say, Arthur?' He smiles at me and I don't know whether he is being genuine or if he has an ulterior motive with his words. We have been distant for so long now, I am unable to read his emotions, to work out what is coming next. This man, the husband I once knew so well, the man I married, the father of my only child, feels like a stranger to me. This is not how I want it to be. It is not how it should be. I used to know every inch of him; the smell of his skin, every strand of hair, every single part of his body. Heat rises as I remember those times, the times I now know I would like back. Arthur isn't a bad person. Neither am I. Life seems to have pushed us apart. My childhood has forced me into a dark place that I don't care for. I want to be rescued from that dank, miserable place but fear everything is too far gone for that.

'I think we both have some secrets we need to share, don't we?'

I swallow hard and try to think of something to say, hoping he will do the decent thing and speak first, tell me what he is hiding. I blink and cough again. Another woman is my guess. It isn't something I have given a great deal of thought to until this point, but then as I start to dwell on it, to give it some serious contemplation, it makes me feel incredibly sad. I am surprised to find that I don't like the idea of Arthur with somebody else; somebody who isn't me. Out of nowhere, tears spring from my eyes and in an instant, Arthur is up out of his chair and kneeling beside me, his hands stroking my hair and cupping my face with a tenderness I had forgotten he possessed, a tenderness that takes me by surprise, catching me unawares and making my heart pound.

'Erica, I opened your letter from the hospital. Why didn't you tell me?'

My senses are muffled. I feel disorientated, as if I have been submerged underwater, an ocean of confusion distorting everything I thought I knew. More tears flow at his words, a river of pent-up anxiety and disquiet leaking out of me. He has seen my future. I think of that crisp, white piece of paper, the prophecy of my life detailing what is going to happen to me. Arthur opened it first and now knows what I have always known. A sob escapes. This isn't how it was supposed to be. I had it all planned in my head, how I would deal with it; all the treatment, the arrangements back home up north. I thought I had it sorted, was managing to keep it all in order, not let it bog me down, but now here it is swamping me with emotion and fear. I try to speak but the words won't come. They stick in my throat, dry and heavy. A lump of pent-up anguish locked inside me, trying to break free.

'I was going to,' I hiccup, 'when the time was right.' I stop and stare at him, my face tight with emotion.

'But the time was never right, was it?' He sighs and leans back on his haunches, his hand locked in mine. 'It hasn't been right for a long time now.' He stares up at the ceiling and shakes his head despondently. I shake mine too and sniff loudly. Arthur leans back and grabs a tissue from the table then passes it to me. 'We've made a bit of a mess of it all, haven't we?'

I nod in agreement and blow my nose. It sounds like an off-key trumpet and I let out a small laugh, my face aching from the effort. He smiles at me and narrows his eyes,

'You can't do this on your own. I know I haven't been the best lately. I've been under a fair amount of strain and been a bit of an arsehole. But we'll get through this together,' he says, squeezing my hand and out of nowhere, I feel as if a huge weight has been lifted. Suddenly his tone changes, his expression darkens, his voice becomes dry and sombre, and I feel myself go cold as he speaks, 'but I also need to talk to you about something else. I know now might not be the best time, but since we're coming clean, then I think I need to tell you. I should have told you a while back, really.'

I steel myself, ready to hear her name being spoken out loud, ready for him to tell me that prior to him finding out about my diagnosis, his bags were packed and he was moving in with her. Funny, isn't it, how scenarios you have prepared in your head rarely turn out the way you have pictured them? I always assumed we would just fizzle out, Arthur and I, eke out the dregs of our marriage until there was nothing left but retirement and an endless greyness that blanketed our days together. I didn't visualise a woman. Another female was never on my radar. The world becomes suspended, held in a vacuum while I wait for him to speak. When he does, his words shatter my illusion; erase everything I thought I knew about our life together.

'I've lost my job, Erica. I'm unemployed, out of work, call it what you will. I've been fired.'

I try to not gasp, to cover the shock I feel at his revelation. No mistress, no affair. He is not packing his bags and moving out. He is simply out of a job. That's all it is. I widen my eyes and try to speak but all that comes out is another wet sob. And the strange thing is, I am not crying because I am ill, neither am I crying because my husband, the wealthy businessman who has always supported us financially, is now no longer an affluent, prosperous individual. I am crying because of the honesty we have suddenly discovered we still have. It is such a relief to let it all out, to watch as our secrets flutter out into the ether, wild and untethered. I close my eyes and breathe deeply; nearly all our secrets anyway. I still have one tucked away, stashed in the back of my mind, bolted into place by the padlocks of my past. Thoughts flicker in my mind. Should I free them? Unburden myself of all of this? I consider Freya, still at university, and what she would think of me should Arthur choose to tell her, and then my mother, still living in my childhood home, so close to where it all took place. Am I really prepared to saddle them with all of this? My plans for an act of unrefined retribution now suddenly seem pointless and silly, carried out in a moment of anger and sadness when Arthur and I hadn't spoken for days, when I felt like the whole world was against me.

I turn my gaze to Arthur who is waiting for me to respond. I know what sort of reaction he is expecting from me. We are used to being more than comfortably well off. We live in a large house in Holland Park. We have no mortgage and a brand-new BMW. A lifestyle most people can only dream of. He thinks I can't live without it; that I am unable to function without money. At one time, he may have been correct. But things have changed between us tonight. We have modified our stance, changed our priorities. Money used to be our god. And yet did any of it make us any happier? Was it really our funds holding us together or was money one of the things that drove us apart? I am almost certain I already know the answer to this as I dry my eyes and wrap my arms around Arthur's neck, wetting his collar with yet more tears that refuse to stop. It feels alien, touching him, seeking comfort from a man who, for the past few months, has been so distant from me.

'When do you leave?' I ask quietly, and watch as he throws his head back and lets out a huge belly laugh. The kind of laugh that is usually reserved for cartoon characters. A booming guffaw that fills the room, rattling the window frames and shaking the foundations of the entire house. I feel myself freeze. I have no idea what it is I've said that has caused such a furore and begin to wonder if there is another hammer blow coming; another deep, dark secret that I've not yet cottoned on to.

'Oh, Erica, this is such a relief, being able to finally talk to you about it. Sorry, sweetheart, it's not anything you've said or done. It's me. It's just me,' he says as he wipes his eyes and shakes his head sadly.

I grit my teeth, unsure how I should reply to this coded message. What next? What else can there be? I wait, hoping he isn't wanting me to dig or prompt him. I'm too exhausted for such games.

He pulls at his collar and lets out a deep sigh. 'I lost my job over a month ago.'

'A month?' I half screech, 'So where—'

'Have I been going to every morning for the past four weeks or so?' Arthur interrupts, eyebrows raised at me. 'Silly, isn't it? You see people do this in films, pull off this kind of stupid prank because they're too embarrassed or too proud or too ashamed to admit to their family that they have lost their job. They get up every morning and go through the same ritual having breakfast, setting off at the same time, driving the same route, even though they are out of work and have nowhere to go to. Then they spend the day in coffee shops or wandering the streets until it's time to go home again, at which point they step in the door and pretend that they've spent the last eight hours at the office.'

I am speechless. Completely and utterly dumbfounded. This isn't like him. The Arthur I know is a proud and dignified man. Quite a snob, actually. There was a time he would have laughed at anyone who did something like this, called them an idiot, a buffoon, told them to get off their arses and find another job. And now here he is, a middle-aged man, an intelligent man, wandering the streets of London while everyone believes he is at work holding down an important job in the city. I'm not sure which is worse, this sad state of affairs, or my rapidly deteriorating health. In less than six weeks our lives have taken a downward turn and now everything hangs in the balance, our home, our finances, my health.

'I realise it isn't the answer,' I say softly, 'but I'm going to open a bottle of wine and we are going to have a drink.'

Arthur nods dully, his eyes heavy with worry. 'One upside of this is that I can come with you to your hospital appointments. Now that I've got plenty of time on my hands …'

I half laugh and stand up, my legs suddenly weak and unsteady, and head into the kitchen.

Reaching into the top cupboard for some glasses, I think about the messages on my phone and make a decision there and then. It is now patently clear to me what I need to do. Life has thrown me a curveball and I have to run with it, adapt and do what I need to do to weather this storm that Arthur and I are currently battling our way through.

I fill our glasses, and as steadily as I can, make my way back into the living room where Arthur is sitting waiting for me. He looks lost, like a small child, vulnerable and in need of help. I hand him his glass and place mine down on the marble coffee table that sits in the centre of the room.

'I just need to send a message to Deb about cancelling my aerobics class,' I lie and watch, ridden with guilt, as he nods and takes a gulp of wine, his Adam's apple wobbling up and down as he drinks.

Perched on the arm of the chair I read the messages that came through earlier: *It's all underway. Now for the next step.*

With trembling fingers, I key in my reply: *Afraid things have changed here. Major family issues. I no longer want to go ahead.*

The reply comes back almost immediately: *What? Why the sudden change of mind? I thought we had a deal …*

I shiver and turn the phone off, throwing it over the back of the sofa where it lands with a dull thud on the rug behind us.

'All done,' I say sheepishly before leaning back and savouring the sensation as the ice-cold wine slowly slithers down my gullet, coating my throat with a slightly vinegary tang. She will soon get sick of not receiving a reply. And she will also say nothing. I think of the consequences of her talking and blank it out. It is no longer my problem. I will simply deny everything. Every message we have sent to one another has been deleted, our tracks carefully smudged out, leaving no trace. I was stupid to think I could do this, to get away with such a ridiculous act. It all happened in a moment of madness, a time of weakness when Pamela had been preying on my mind after I had travelled back up north to visit my mother.

Mum and I had been to my sister's grave for the anniversary of her death and were on our way into town when I bumped into her. One horrible coincidence after another, that's all it was. We exchanged numbers, feeling we had some common ground. Both middle-aged women with murdered siblings. We started to speak on the phone, exchanging pleasantries, chatting about our lives, our jobs, talking about the past, opening up about our guilt. And from that point on, the idea was born; a slow growing seedling, sprouting and flowering until it got to a point where there was no going back. We made plans. We had made a cast iron decision. Or at least that was how it felt. We spoke almost daily, feeding off one another's grief and anger, giving each other more reasons to be furious, to feel perfectly justified with what we were about to do. We knew where she lived. What more did we need? And then fate played its part and an opportunity landed in our laps.

It fell from the sky above like a gift from the gods. And all the while I managed to convince myself that it was the right thing to do. Freya was away at university in Sunderland, my marriage was crumbling and then I found a lump. Finding that hard, pea-sized lump that day should have brought me to my senses. But it didn't. If anything, it gave me greater impetus, filled me full of bitterness. After a morning of being poked and squashed and jabbed with large needles that felt as if they would rip my entire breast apart when inserted, I'd had enough. Life, I felt, had dealt me a cruel blow and somebody, somewhere would pay. Fuelled by pain and worry and acrimony I agreed to go ahead. Stupid move, very silly. I can see that now. It's all in the past. I now need to focus on the future my future, if indeed I have one.

Arthur squeezes my hand as I take a sip of wine and another tear finds its way out and rolls down my face.

LISSY

Typical, isn't it? Just when you start to think your tiny existence isn't so bad after all, something comes along and gives you a kick in the guts just to put you in your place; to remind you of who you actually are and where you stand in the pecking order of life.

Rosie went back to school. Our meeting with Anthea Paxton, the headteacher, was quite positive, and Rosie was starting to settle down, to mingle and make a few friends. The matter of the letter and the missing money seemed to be a thing of the past. I burnt the letter and repaid the money back to the school despite myself; I figured it was best put behind us. The sooner the entire matter was forgotten about, the sooner we could get on with our lives and settle into our new home. My painting was also coming along a treat. I sold two canvases and had a request for another, an entirely new experience for me. Life was ticking along nicely. Until this morning, that is, when I received what can only be described as a double whammy.

I was flitting about doing not much at all really, when the phone rang. Reticent as always, I picked it up and felt my stomach sink to my boots when I was greeted by the voice of Mr Cooper, in his arrogant, smug tone telling me I was to go and collect Rosie immediately. A meeting had already been arranged with him prior to picking her up, to discuss the matter of her exclusion for bullying. I almost choked on the air I was breathing as I listened to him telling me about how she had been on her final warning and they now needed to take further action since the incidents had escalated.

Dropping the phone and pulling on my coat, I was in a complete meltdown, a tangle of limbs as I snatched up my keys and opened the front door, sweat blinding me and my heart trying to claw its way out of my chest. I almost stepped on something as I half threw myself over the threshold and out into the fresh mid-morning air. After the dead pigeon a few weeks back, I initially thought it had been another accident, a freakish coincidence, but as I stared down at the pile of flea infested fur and rotting flesh on my doorstep, I began to realise it was more than that. Much, much more than happenstance or a completely unrelated run of bad luck. This was somebody targeting us. Somebody who felt it was their God-given right to unleash their hatred upon us by planting a dead animal directly outside my door, ready to greet me as soon as I step outside. Picking the fox up with the very tips of my fingers I quickly dragged it and shoved it to one side; its soft, floppy body curling into an amber fleshy heap on my front lawn. I knew that it would attract all manner of vermin, but I was in a rush. I would have to sort it out properly when I got back. At that point in time, Rosie was my priority. I needed to get down to the school as quickly as I could to sort out this latest issue.

And so here I sit, my hands pressed tightly together in my lap, waiting for that odious creep of a man to show his face, to tell me in great detail what the problem is this time around. He enjoys it. Of that I am certain. It seems to give him a warped sense of superiority, having us sitting in front of him, seeing our shell-shocked faces as he reels off a list of Rosie's purported misdemeanours.

I feel the eyes of the office staff on me as I shift about in my seat, the vinyl sticking to my legs in the growing heat of the reception area. I try to rotate my body round to meet their gaze, to let them know that I refuse to be browbeaten by this man, by their system, their allegations against my child, but my view is blocked by an array of paper notices that are littered over the glass partition. I sigh with disappointment and turn my head back to see him standing there, surveying me with his fixed stare. I let out a small shiver. He reminds me of a corpse, his eyes black and unseeing.

'If you would like to come this way, please,' he says in that clipped, perfunctory timbre he adopts whenever we meet. 'Mrs Paxton and I can fill you in on all the details and then we will send for Rosie and she can give us her side of the story.'

I feel my stomach shrivel and fight to stop tears filling my eyes. This is all too much. Rosie bullying other pupils? It's ridiculous. Completely and utterly absurd. I find myself unable to think straight as I follow Cooper into the office and listen to him slam the door behind me before he tells me to take a seat.

Anthea Paxton has a warm and compassionate face and kind eyes, and I pray she will be gentle with me, tell me it's all been a huge mistake and that they are terribly sorry for dragging me down here. But she doesn't. She sits, her back straight, her hands placed on the desk and proceeds to inform me, with military-like precision, about the atrocities my daughter has committed. Unlike Mr Cooper, she doesn't appear to take any pleasure in it, however, she is a woman who holds a position of authority and I can tell by her behaviour that she intends to conduct this interview in a formal manner, to see it through to its conclusion. She will leave no stone unturned.

'Good morning, Ms McLeod,' she says softly, and already I feel under scrutiny. Cooper has obviously informed her of my insistence on being addressed as Ms and not Mrs. The thought of him discussing me when I'm not there makes my skin crawl. 'I'm sorry we have to meet like this. I wish it were under better circumstances but unfortunately this is a serious matter. At Knottswood Academy, we take any incidents of bullying very seriously and do our utmost to sort them out immediately.'

I nod vigorously, my hair flying out of the ponytail I put it in earlier. I reach up and smooth it back down. I want to speak, to tell her that, once again, they have made a huge mistake, but the words won't come. My head buzzes as she lifts a pile of books out from under the table and lays them out for me to look at. There are half a dozen exercise books spread out on the table and as soon as she opens them I feel my abdomen go into spasm. The words jump out at me, a scribble of disjointed phrases in black, marker pen. The words *fucking cow* and *will kill you, you bastard* imprint themselves on my brain. I can see them all, there on the page. And I recognise the handwriting. There is no denying it. The room spins as I lean forward and scan the books. One after another after another after another. Rosie's thick scrawl covering each and every page. *Die you skinny bitch ... will stab you ... scratch your fucking eyes out ... wait for you after school and murder you ...* On and on it goes. A torrent of vitriol and poison filling the pages. I try to speak, but it's impossible. A wave of heat clutches me, my skin burning as I peel my cardigan off and sit motionless, my legs like blocks of wood, my mind racing as I try to make sense of it all. I have no words. All logic leaves me. I sit, a frozen figure, too distressed and confused to do or say anything. I need to think, to snap out of it and do something, but am unable to move or speak.

'As you can see,' Mrs Paxton says quietly, her voice breaking the dreadful silence that has settled in the room, 'this isn't something we can ignore.'

I nod my head numbly and listen as she continues, 'These books belong to a student in Rosie's class. What makes the entire incident even more distressing is the fact that this young person is one of our more vulnerable pupils who has additional needs. She is now refusing to come to school and is, by all accounts, absolutely terrified after discovering these comments in her book yesterday afternoon. We received a call from her parents this morning and they are absolutely furious, and understandably so.'

Despite my vow to remain calm and be untouched by any of this, to make sure I am cool and detached enough to defend my daughter against their accusations, I feel tears begin to build and am unable, or unwilling, to stop them as they begin to roll their way down my face; a deluge of despair. I make no attempt to wipe them away. What is the point? I can see those words and feel their insidious intent from here. I recognised Rosie's handwriting immediately. I have no idea how to get out of this situation, how to defend her when all of this is completely indefensible. I feel totally and utterly lost, and for one horrible moment I am transported back to my childhood, to a time when there was nobody to help me or to protect me against the blows that life put my way. Taking me by surprise, Cooper touches my arm softly and hands me a tissue, his face the picture of concern. With misty eyes, I blow my nose and wipe my face, everything in the room now blurred and out of focus.

Seconds turn into minutes until at last I find my voice and blurt out a stream of apologies both for my mini-breakdown and for the defacement of the books. Those dreadful, unforgivable words that have punctured the heart of another child, destroyed her faith in human nature and made her frightened and anxious. Given her a memory she would sooner forget. And God knows I know all about those. I have a glut of them stored away, ready to jump out at me when I least expect it. Just when I think I have them beaten they make an appearance, vivid and painful, armed and ready to taunt me. So clear and lucid, as if it were only yesterday.

'And this isn't the only thing, Ms McLeod,' she says, her head bowed as she produces a handful of typed letters and hands them over for me to read.

They are more of the same. Notes filled with hatred and swear words that I have never ever heard Rosie say. *You are a fucking slut ... get a life you whore ... everybody hates you ... wish you were dead...*

'How do you know these are from Rosie?' I manage to croak quietly. 'Anybody could have typed these up and—'

'They were traced back to her login,' Cooper interjects quickly. 'In fact they're still there in her documents folder. It was all pretty easy to work out. After the incident with the books we knew exactly where to look ...'

I nod and lower my head despondently. I cannot meet his eyes, to stare at him and see the look of triumph in his face. He must be elated.

'I'm afraid this is a very serious matter,' Mrs Paxton continues, 'and although I am sure it won't happen, the parents of this other pupil are threatening to go to the local authority, and are even talking about informing the police, if we don't sort this out as soon as possible and make sure Rosie is dealt with appropriately.'

My scalp prickles and I am so hot I fear I might faint. *The police?* I breathe hard and grip on to the edge of the chair. The room slants at a peculiar angle. I hang on to the wooden legs as I make a concerted effort to remain upright. This is ridiculous. They are upset, these parents. And rightly so. I would be too. But bringing the police into all of this? An overstretched force who are already struggling to find enough manpower to sort out real crimes? The idea is ludicrous I know it is. But the thought still fills me with terror. I can't let this happen. I cannot entertain the idea of an officer sitting here interviewing Rosie, or worse still, one turning up on my doorstep … it is too horrific to consider.

'So, we have taken the step of excluding Rosie until further notice. Until we can meet with the other parents and come to a decision as to what our long-term strategy is going to be. I'm sure you understand that behaviour of this ilk simply cannot be tolerated. There is no place for it here at Knottswood Academy …'

I stare at her, and then very slowly lift my face up to look at Mr Cooper, who suddenly appears to be embarrassed by the whole situation. I am trying to formulate a coherent response, to let these people know that I am a good parent, not some roughneck dunderhead who has recently stumbled into their lives with my disturbed daughter, when the knock disturbs me. We all turn and watch as she glides into the room, a sheath of papers balanced on her arm, her face composed into a look of complete calm as she nods at Mrs Paxton before depositing the papers on her desk and strolling back out again. Time stands still. I feel the blood drain from my face and the swaying room begins to rock about violently. The ticking of the clock on the wall crashes around my head. The air suddenly becomes too thin. I do my best to practise my breathing techniques, use every calming method I have ever been taught, to bring my terror under control but fear that none of them will serve me well this time. Not today, here, under these circumstances. Today has just turned against me, showing me yet again that life will always have the upper hand. No matter how hard I try to escape from it all, no matter how hard I work and how straight a path I walk, day after day after day, my past will always catch up with me.

Standing up, my head thick and muggy, I offer my hand to shake to both members of staff and listen to my own voice as it projects across the room, a distorted version of its usual self, an echoing reminder of how close I am to passing out. 'I apologise unreservedly for all the trouble my daughter has caused you. If you would like to go and fetch Rosie I'll take her home, and I'll talk to her about this incident.'

I watch from another world, a dim and distant planet of fear and uncertainty, as Mr Cooper waltzes out of the room and comes back a few moments later with Rosie behind him, her eyes wracked with horror and trepidation. There is a sudden silence and before anybody has a chance to say anything or to try to stop me, I hold Rosie's arm and lug her out of the room, our feet the only sound to be heard as we scurry along the corridor and disappear away from the sea of staring faces.

CHILD A

*B*eing released was almost as chilling as being incarcerated. The big, wide world was a truly terrifying place filled with people who wanted to destroy her, to wreak their revenge for crimes perpetrated on children they hadn't even met, to maim her or hurt her in some way so they could sleep easy in their beds at night.

Contact with her parents had been minimal while serving her sentence. During that time, she had built up a relationship with Aunt Alice. And of course, there was her probation officer who did the best he could to assist her transition into the real world. But Alice was the one she latched on to. She was her saviour. Alice had moved back to England from America following a split from her partner of ten years, and was horrified to step back into the turmoil and pandemonium that was their family life. She distanced herself from her abusive and alcoholic sister, telling her in no uncertain terms what she thought of their life choices, and took her niece under her wing. With no children of her own, she saw it as her duty to take care of her niece, to give her as much love and guidance as she could. If Alice didn't help this damaged child, then who would? The poor girl would be flung into a loveless world with no protection from those out there who wished her harm. And there were lots of them; people everywhere trying to track her down, making it their mission to see to it that she would suffer. Even giving the girl Alice's surname didn't stop them. People were intent on getting their own back. They found ways of seeking her out. The inception of the Internet compounded the problem, allowing the world and his wife access to public records without the inconvenience of having to shift out of their armchairs. But Alice did a good job of protecting her niece. She used her money wisely by sending her to a wide range of private classes to arm her with skills she could use in her future; creative writing classes, dance classes, painting sessions, even flower arranging, which the girl hated, claiming it was full of retirees who treated her like an errant grandchild. Turned out her niece was quite the artist, producing paintings that, according to the teacher, were reminiscent of Edward Hopper. From that point on, her direction in life was mapped out for her. Alice bought her the equipment she needed and they never looked back.

But then Alice's untimely death from a heart attack plunged the girl back into the unknown. Still only in her early twenties, she found herself alone and without direction in a world of bitterness and retribution. Only after her aunt's death did she discover just how hated she was. The letters that Alice had kept hidden from her for so long, continued to arrive with nobody to dispose of them; notes telling her exactly what everyone thought of her, and how much they wanted her dead. And so, being the only beneficiary of Alice's will, she found herself with the means to move, to hide from the masses who wished her harm. Like a shapeshifter, she travelled about, changing her appearance, chopping her hair, altering its colour, doing what she could to keep them at bay. And it worked. She relaxed her attitude, became less defensive, more approachable, left the house without fear. Got herself a life.

Then she met him, the first and only person she felt she could trust since Alice. He was a PE teacher, full of life, a man who was always on the lookout for the next challenge. She had to make the decision soon after meeting him. Should she tell him about her past? Encumber him with such a heavy burden? Or should she break free from her guilt and heartache and look to their future together? The longer she took to decide, the harder it became to actually do the right thing and inform him of what had happened to her, and so, before she knew it, six months had passed and the person she was, was far behind her, a ghost of a former life she felt sure belonged to somebody else.

Her pregnancy was a bolt out of the blue, something that took them both by surprise. It wasn't planned but they soon adapted, their lives fast becoming a steady routine of work and preparation for their life with a baby, a child they could pour their love into. The letters and hate mail had stopped and she found herself in a state of complete relaxation, something she hadn't felt in a long, long time. Not since Alice took her in and looked after her, kept her from harm.

The child came along and everything was perfect. For the first time in her life she felt blissfully happy. They were a family. A real tight-knit unit with love and laughter in abundance and a future to look forward to. The baby grew into a toddler. She had emerald eyes, a chubby face and she ran everywhere, her small, fat fists pumping the air forcefully, her smile lighting up every room in the house. Nothing could dent their happiness or take any of this away from her. And then it happened. She let her guard down, became friendly with one of the other mums at the nursery. At first it was good. They took the kids to the park, went for coffee, ventured into town with two toddlers in tow, searching the shops for clothes together, chatting about local schools and their aspirations for their child's future. But then something changed, an imperceptible shift the way her friend watched her, the questions she started to ask, the sudden, endless stream of probing about her upbringing.

∞∞∞∞∞

He had already opened it and was sitting at the kitchen table when she got in after taking the little one to the library to see a children's author. Her friend had declined her invitation. She should have seen the signs then, but was desperate for any sort of company after being alone for so long, and had subconsciously ignored all the alarm bells that were ringing in her head. A tingle of apprehension travelled up her spine as she saw the piece of paper in his hand, noticed the look on his face ...

He didn't leave straight away but the damage was already done. The questions and accusations were endless, his anger exploding into the room day after day. Why hadn't she told him? What had possessed her to do such a thing? What sort of a monster was she, for God's sake? She talked to him, tried to soothe him, get him to see her side of the story and tell him the truth not the distorted version that the press bandied about, not the version that everyone was so sure was accurate and defined her as a person. She hoped she had talked him round, got him to see how bad things had been for her, how difficult her childhood had been and how circumstances had simply spiralled out of control. But then one morning, a few weeks after his discovery, she got up to find him gone. A note was propped up on the kitchen table, spelling out his sentiments, telling her exactly what he thought of her and her child, claiming the girl probably wasn't even his anyway and if she was, he no longer wanted anything to do with either of them. The kid was tainted by association, he said. Her mother was a liar, a deceitful piece of shit, a murderer.

And so, it was back to how it had always been, just her against the world. Back to keeping her defences up, back to constantly checking over her shoulder. No more visits to the park with her toddler, no more days out in town.

The friend must have done her absolute best to let everyone know who she was, as more letters started to arrive, spelling out exactly what they thought of her and all the ways in which they hoped she would die.

Moving around again became a way of life. Every little glance, every innocuous comment, every letter that dropped on her doormat left her frightened for their safety.

She lost all contact with her parents and visualised them living in some seedy hostel, a pair of alcoholics with ravaged faces and blackened souls. They meant nothing to her. Nobody did any more. Only her daughter had the capacity to stay in her heart, to keep her going through all the bad times. And there were plenty of bad times. But that girl gave her a reason to get out of bed every morning and face the world with all its threats and dangers. Yet still, the fear drove her. Each and every time people passed her in the supermarket she would feel herself shrivel up, feel her world tilt on its axis under their watchful gazes.

The moves continued. House after house. Town after town. Until she felt she could no longer do it, keep running away. Her job and the use of online shopping meant she could actually live her life without having to leave the house. She could stay in one place and watch her daughter grow up into a fine young woman. They could do this together. Be a team. This house would be their last. They were there for keeps.

ERICA

B reast conserving surgery they call it, apparently. I feel like one of the fortunate ones. Mine hasn't spread and is in its early stages. Not like the many other women I have spoken to in the hospital waiting rooms and the various online chat forums I have visited, many of whom are facing a much grimmer future than I am. I'm trying to stay positive, to keep my chin up as they say. Some days are easier than others. Arthur is still looking for work and we are doing our damnedest to remain positive and get our marriage back on track. It's not been easy. I won't pretend that, after our soul-baring discussion, everything fell easily into place and we became a loving couple once again. Life isn't like that, is it? Life is full of bumps and pitfalls and cliff edges that you have to hang on to with your fingernails, despite feeling as if you are about to plunge into a gaping abyss. But we are doing our best and that is all we can do.

A weekend away from it all helped. Two days spent wandering round museums and shops in York. Two days trying to rebuild a marriage that, up until two weeks ago, seemed beyond redemption. We tried. We are still trying. And it isn't easy but it's certainly a damn sight better than it has been for some time.

The messages from up north have continued; questioning, desperate, threatening. I have done my level best to ignore them, keeping contact to a minimum. Every now and again I reply, outlining my reasons for stepping out of the whole silly palaver. A lot of people have a massive mid-life crisis: buy a ridiculously expensive sports car, run off with a younger partner, sell their home and sail around the world. Agreeing to go through with that ludicrous plan was mine. For so many years I hated that woman; loathed her with every fibre of my being. Pamela was my little sister, our gorgeous six-year-old girl who went to play in the park one fine, spring day and never came home. It was the deception that got us, my parents and me. For so many months we had believed it was an accident, a tragic, unavoidable set of circumstances; a small girl playing on a slide, a slip of the foot, a fall from above. We cried and grieved and campaigned for greater safety in local play areas, did what we could to try to alleviate the gnawing emptiness that clawed at our lives on a daily basis. And then it happened, the same teenager, babysitting a small boy. Another mysterious death …

For so long I wanted to get even for Pamela's death. The sentence didn't seem long enough. Our suffering would never end. Me, my parents, even my daughter and my husband suffered because of her. She almost wrecked my marriage, but only because I let her. I let her actions get under my skin for so many years. I simmered with anger, fury burning away at the very centre of me, scorching and ruining anything and everyone who I came into contact with. Her actions were very nearly the undoing of me. Until recently that is. I have no idea why it took me so long to get over it. Perhaps it was the lies, the fact that she almost got away with it. Or perhaps it is just me. Maybe I have a darkness tucked away deep within me that will only settle when I feel justice has been done. I hope not. I hope that was the old me, the bitter and twisted version of me who needed a sharp wake-up call to tell her to start living, to begin appreciating life instead of focusing on death. The new me now has important matters that need my full attention. That woman and her phone calls are no longer a part of my life. I have a marriage to save, a disease to fight.

I shuffle along my seat to make room for a man who looks every inch the country gent. He is wearing a green, checked tweed jacket and is carrying a highly polished walking stick with a brass top. He has yellow, canvas trousers on and has a copy of *The Times* tucked under his arm. Opposite me is a young woman wearing earphones and chewing on a matchstick which rolls about between her teeth. I catch her eye and am met with a scowl and a flick of her lavender coloured hair as she narrows her eyes at me and juts her chin forward. Feeling my face flush, I turn away and stare out of the window at the rush of landscape whooshing past us; a smear of greens, browns and blues as we cut through the countryside at 100 mph. It felt far easier to make the journey by train. Driving out of London is an ordeal and, not knowing how my body will respond to the operation and treatment, I didn't want to risk not being able to visit my mum for a while so am travelling north to see her. I plan on seeing Freya too. I spoke to her on the phone and told her about my diagnosis. We cried together. She wailed and sobbed, said she wanted to come home. I told her to stay put and that I would visit her. So here I am, on my way back up north, back to see my mother in my childhood home in Durham and my daughter in Sunderland.

I feel the vibration of my phone and am tempted to ignore it but worry it may be Arthur. We have made a point, recently, of communicating with each other about everything, doing our best to be transparent with every aspect of our lives. Guilt stabs at me. Not completely transparent.

I lift my phone out of my pocket and stare at it. A hot flush creeps up my face. I quickly glance around to see if anybody is watching me. Country gent is engrossed in his crossword and matchstick-chewing girl has her eyes closed and is humming along to her music. I stare down at the message once more and swallow hard. This woman knows no shame. Despite my many refusals and protestations of late, she is determined to go ahead with her silly plan, to plumb to the very depths of hideousness. And from what I gather from this latest text, she is going to take me with her.

BEVERLEY

It took me three days to get rid of her. Three long days of staring at her lank, unwashed hair, which hung in front of her eyes despite my best attempts to get her to take a bath; three days of her dreadful stink clogging up my olfactory system. Three days of her whining about how shit her life is and how much better it would have been if our father was still alive. She never even met him. Our mother was seven months pregnant with Theresa when Dad jumped from that bridge. All these years and she still hankers after a father she never even knew. If it hadn't have been him, it would have been something else. Or someone else. His suicide, Greg's death, they are all the excuses she needs to justify her actions, to explain the path she has chosen to take, resulting in the sad and miserable existence that is now her life. And all of it comes back to me. Every single time. She has even managed to convince our mother that it's all my fault. To be fair, that wasn't the most difficult of tasks. Mum already held me responsible anyway. All she needed was that extra little push to shove the blame for everything that happened my way, make sure it sits firmly at my feet. A huge glaring reminder of all my inadequacies for the whole world to see, the sins of my past emblazoned on my soul for all eternity.

I gave Theresa some food and shoved fifty pounds in her hand as I practically pushed her out of the door and sent her on her way. I told the taxi driver to drop her at the women's hostel in the centre of Durham. It was only after she left that I realised my watch was missing, as well as an old bracelet and some spare cash I had lying around in the bedroom. A small price to pay for getting rid of her. Over the years I have tried and tried to help her, to coax her, cajole her, get her to counselling, get her to see a doctor. Nothing has worked. I now feel powerless to do anything. I have lost another sibling to the ravages of life. It's just me, on my own against the rest of the world.

Sighing, I slump down on to the sofa. Even my one-time ally has deserted me. So much for friends. She has pulled out and now expects me to just sit back and take it, be let down and accept it all with good grace. Well, she is in for a shock because that is most certainly not going to happen. I have had a long time to think about this, to plan it, to avenge Greg's death; so if this woman this coward thinks I am going to let her get away with it, then she can think again. We had an agreement. Come hell or high water I am going to see this thing through. Otherwise Greg's life will be forgotten. And what about her poor little Pamela? What about her memory? Where does she fit into all of this? Surely, she wants some sort of revenge? I know I certainly do.

I take out my phone and send her another message, another one she will undoubtedly ignore, just like the many others I have sent that I've not received replies to. No matter. It won't deter me. I am nothing if not tenacious. I wait and watch as my words disappear and float off into the ether, snatched up by an army of invisible demons as they carry it off to its recipient. Warren is only home for a few days this time then he is heading off to Switzerland to oversee a project there, so time will soon be on my side. I will have nobody around to keep tabs on me, to monitor my movements. Free as a bird.

I smile and stare up at the ceiling, thinking how good it feels, how empowering it is to take the world by its shoulders and give it a damn good shake, to stare in its face and scream that this time I will not be walked on, trampled underfoot, and ground into the dirt. This time, everything will run to plan and people will congratulate me instead of pointing the finger and blaming me. I may not have been the perpetrator of the crime, but by God, over

J.A. Baker

the years, I have served my time, done my penance and now I am ready to move on, to get my own back. So, if Erica Ridley thinks she is out of this thing, then she can bloody well think again. We are in it for the long run, both of us together, and we will see it through to its bitter end.

LISSY

'What the hell is going on with you?!' I scream at her as we drive out of the sprawling car park and head home. Flecks of spittle land on the steering wheel and run down the side of my mouth. I feel as if my body is about to split apart, small pieces of me spreading far and wide. I am absolutely livid.

Rosie's sobs turn into a frenzied howl as we swing on to the main road, narrowly avoiding another car. The driver honks his horn and makes a rude sign at me, his face grimaced in anger. I am too furious at my daughter to respond. The rest of world can go to hell. I need to get her home and find out what is going on inside her head, work out what her motives are. I think of the disturbance back there in the head teacher's office, *her* entrance into the room while I was sitting there, and feel my head begin to spin. The world blurs before my eyes and the steering wheel slips from my grasp. I grab it back, my palms clammy, my heart clawing its way up my neck. I try to take a deep and steadying breath without being sick, but acid and bile have begun their ascent up my throat. I need to do something, and quickly. Craning my head, I spot a side road to my left and swing the car in, grinding to a screeching halt in seconds. I need to calm down if I am to drive the six miles back home. I feel dizzy and shaky and perspiration runs down my back. Opening the door, I lean out to take a few deep gasps of air, but before I can stop myself I throw up in the gutter, a splash of warm vomit exiting my body. I gulp loudly and wait for the stomach cramps to stop.

'Oi!' I hear a voice close by, 'I hope you're going to clear that little mess up.'

Bleary-eyed, I look up to see an elderly man leaning on his front gate. I am in a street of post-war terraced houses that I guess are probably occupied by retirees on a limited income. They have small, neat gardens and tiny, bay windows. Further along, an elderly lady with an ample backside is out washing her windows. She is wearing a large apron and curlers that peek out from under a hairnet.

I heave some more on to the side of the road, then look up, panting and shivering, and give him a small wave to indicate that I have heard him.

'We get so fed up of this, don't we, Maureen? People using this street like it's a bloody toilet.'

The woman stares over at me and nods before going back to her window cleaning, her upper arms wobbling as she sweeps her hand across the top panes of glass, dragging a yellow cloth back and forth until the window gleams.

I feel his eyes bore into me as he shouts over again, 'Just 'cos we're close to the centre of town doesn't mean any Tom, Dick, or Harry can cut through here and mess the place up. Make sure you clean that lot up!' He nods vigorously and I see his bushy eyebrows flicker up and down, then watch as he disappears into the house, slamming the door behind him.

Reaching into the centre console, I grab a half-full bottle of water and weakly pour it on to the trail of thick, yellow liquid that is snaking its way down the road and dripping into the drain, then close the car door.

'I'm sorry, Mum, for putting you through all of this, I really, really am but I *swear* to you I didn't do it!' Her howls fill the car, bouncing around the vinyl seats and dashboard and ricocheting off the windscreen.

'Rosie, just shut up, will you? Just stay silent. Say nothing, OK? Not another word until we get home.'

She stares at me and I watch as tears stream down her face. My hands shake and my legs are liquid as I manoeuvre the car back out on to the main road. If I can just concentrate, get us home safely, then I can sort this thing out. Whatever this *thing* actually is. Right now, I am having difficulty thinking straight.

I try to stem the rising fear I feel as I put all my efforts into getting us back in one piece. Have I not been paying her enough attention lately? Is that what this is all about? Or is it the constant moving about that has brought this on? A deep and unwelcome thought stirs somewhere deep down inside me. I try to blank it out. It's not possible. It's just a stupid, random flickering memory from the back of my brain that has snuck its way in and is trying to weaken me, to scare me into thinking that it will never be over. That this *thing* will be with me, with us, forever. I shake my head. She is not like me, nor is she *anything* like my parents. Haven't scientists shown over the years that nurture can overcome nature? Rosie has had a loving background. OK, so her father left us in the lurch but the world is now stuffed full of single parent families. I think of my childhood rages, the blackouts, then bite my lip hard and put my foot down on the accelerator. I refuse to entertain such thoughts, thoughts that my daughter could in some way be disturbed or damaged. Rosie is an inherently good person. She is not me. Even *I* am no longer like the old me. There is a reason for all of this. There has to be.

My mind wanders back to *her*. That woman, there in Rosie's school. *Her!* Did she recognise me? Did she even see me or notice my presence in the room? Another wave of sickness hits me. I blink and swallow, my hands gripping the steering wheel for dear life. I'm not sure I can do this. I know I swore we would never move again but this is all getting to be too much to bear. But then, if we move once more and Rosie switches schools, am I just stoking the fires of her resentment and discontent? Giving her more things to be miserable about and another reason to misbehave in this way?

By the time we pull up on the drive, I feel certain my skull is about crack open. My nose is streaming and my vision is so blurred I cannot believe we made it home safely. Stars burst behind my eyes and shadows creep in on my peripheral vision. Rosie has done as I asked and remained silent all the way back, which is just as well as I don't think I was in any fit state to answer her. Surely if she were the damaged pupil the school thinks she is then she wouldn't have complied, would she? She would have kicked up a huge stink and fought me all the way back, screaming and yelling at me that she is innocent, that this is all my doing for moving her about so much. I cling on to that thought as we step out of the car, our feet crunching on the gravel. Then I see it and remember. The dead fox. Another wave of nausea hits me and a film of horror and dread coats the roof of my mouth. I stare at Rosie who is, in turn, staring at the mangled, furry heap on the front lawn. Her eyes are wide and her mouth is gaping open. A smear of blood covers the lawn where I dropped it earlier, and as we watch, a flock of magpies land on its back and begin to peck at its innards, one of them clawing greedily at the fox's eyeball; a pack of hungry creatures pulling and tugging at its sinewy, bloodied flesh. I need to get her in the house away from it all; from this hideous sight before us, but before I can do anything she lets out an almighty shriek that could shatter glass. I watch as she doubles over and sobs, her breath coming out in rattling, laboured gasps. She stops and stares at me before letting out another ear-piercing scream. We have to get inside. I need to get her away from all of this and calm her down before anybody hears us. I rush over and wrap my arms around her body, half limping and half dragging her to the doorway, where we stand jumbled together while I grope with my keys, a mass of wet, jangling metal that slides about in my sweaty hands. I somehow manage to find the right one and keep it still long enough to slide it into the door. We stumble inside, Rosie falling on to the bottom step while I throw my bag into the corner with a thump, not caring if anything breaks. I am just about to shut the door when I see him. He is running up the driveway, his face full of concern. He stops and lets out a gasp when he sees it there, the heap of red fur, deeply incongruous against the sprawl of lush, green grass. I quickly turn around and bark at Rosie to go up to her room. She does it without question, scrambling up to her feet in seconds, a terrified look in her eyes as she darts upstairs, taking them two at a time. I feel a sudden stab of guilt and pity as I watch her go. As soon as I get rid of Rupert I will go and see her and we will talk about all of this. Time for some honesty, time for us both to start opening up.

'Everything OK?' he asks and I want to laugh out loud at his words.

My daughter has just been excluded from school for the second time in under a month, we have received a hate-filled note, I have just found out that somebody I hoped I would never see again for the rest of my life is the secretary at Rosie's school, and to top it all off, I have a dead fox on my front garden. *No*, I want to scream at him, *things are definitely not OK*. But I don't. Instead I do what I always do, what I have done for all of my adult life, I smile at him and tell him we are absolutely fine. I can see by the bewildered look on his face that he doesn't believe me. Of course, he doesn't. Why would he? My hair is wild and tangled into knots, my face is a sticky smear of tears and snot, my daughter, only minutes ago, was shrieking and howling at the top of her voice, and I very probably reek of vomit. I am a mess, both physically and emotionally, but do my best to assure him that we are both OK and that yes, we will give him a knock if we need any help. It's only as I shut the door that it crosses my mind. I try to shake the thought away but it refuses to budge. Him, Rupert. Could he be the one who put the fox there? And is he the person who posted the note a few weeks back? And what about that blasted pigeon? I swallow and tell myself this is no more than mild hysteria talking, that I need to get a grip and start thinking rationally. Why would a neighbour target me? Unless … I banish the thought away. And then what about *her* at the school. Just a coincidence? Is that what this all is? Simply an awful twist of fate? Maybe. Or maybe not …. I don't believe so but I have to tell myself I'm imagining it. If only for Rosie's sake.

I place my hand against my forehead. My face is hot, my skin like parchment. I am dehydrated and need a drink in order to think straight. I stagger through to the kitchen and stick my head under the tap, gulping water down in great, sloppy mouthfuls. It runs over my face, down my chin, cooling my burning flesh and soothing my aching throat.

Standing up, I wipe my mouth and wait for a few minutes. I need to compose myself. I am a complete mess, my head tight with anxiety, my limbs like liquid. I sweep my gaze over the garden then remember that I have forgotten to lock the front door. I also need to dispose of the carcass on my lawn. So much to do. Such a terrible day this has turned out to be, and one I don't want to repeat.

As I make my way through, I have the most awful sensation in the pit of my stomach. I can see it as I slowly edge my way round into the hallway. There is another letter on the mat. I am frozen for a few seconds, my limbs locked with terror. My brain is screaming at me to move, to do something. Somehow, I am able to free myself of the paralysis and, wrenching the door open, I lunge forward and run down the driveway, my eyes scanning every possible hiding place, every way out of here. There are a handful of cars in the distance but nothing or nobody else. I stop and try to control my breathing, the buzzing in my head like an attack of killer bees. Am I going mad? Is this what it feels like to lose all control? Is it all coming back after all these years? I think back to the rages I suffered as a child, to the blackouts I had, and slump to the ground, suddenly exhausted by it all. Is this ever going to end? Or is my life forever going to be spent running away, bolting in?

I try to stand up but my legs buckle. I stay on the ground; my entire body weary. I just need a few seconds to think, to gather my strength. I look around the garden once more and then stare over the hedge at the terracotta roof that is Rupert's house. It has to be him. There isn't anybody else it can be. I haven't even seen any of the other neighbours and he was the one who initiated contact. I am too tired to do anything about it at the minute but tomorrow I will go around there and confront him, tell him to leave us alone or I will call the police. I stare around again, my pulse slowly returning to normal. I let my eyes travel around the perimeter of the front lawn and garden, taking in the sprays of wild flowers and small splashes of colour. Usually I would admire it, take time to appreciate such a lovely sight, but today I am too tired, too harassed and overwrought to value the beauty of it all.

I twist around, straining my neck, suddenly thinking that something is different, something has changed. Then I realise what it is. The fox has gone. I should care but don't. It's one less thing for me to do. I am all out of energy and not in the least bit bothered. I have bigger problems to sort out when I go back inside; a whole host of issues waiting for me. I climb to my feet. I am not worried about where it has disappeared to or who has taken it. As long as it's not on my lawn any more, I honestly don't give a shit.

When I turn around and see Rosie there, I feel the ground begin to pull me down again. She has opened the letter and is holding it out to me, her hands trembling, her eyes glassy with more tears.

'I'm coming in now, Rosie,' I say in a voice that doesn't feel like mine. The sound of it echoes around my head, thick and rasping as I manage to stagger to the doorway, wondering how I am going to get through this. It's only at times like this I begin to understand just how much Aunt Alice protected me, kept me away from the rough and tumble of living. She gave me a sense of direction and purpose and taught me how to deal with the day to day worries of life whilst keeping me from harm. And now I am alone with nobody to care for me or show me what to do. It's all down to me. Nobody to tell me what to do or to help me. I am completely on my own.

'Mum, what is this?' Rosie cries as I fall through the door and almost land in her arms.

She thrusts the letter out at me, her hands quaking, her fingers white with the strain of gripping it. The sound of crisp paper being straightened out booms in my ears as I snatch it from her and let my eyes wander over what is written there. My heart gushes and pounds as I stare at the letter. More sickness, a terrible headache. I fight it, my breathing erratic, my eyes sore and heavy. The words scream at me, loud and brutal, tearing into my soul like a bullet from a gun.

Thought you could leave it all behind you? Think again. I know your every move you murderous, old monster. I am watching you. I am watching your every fucking move, you old bitch …

Fuelled by anger and outrage, I snatch the note out of Rosie's hand and storm back out, crunching my way down the drive, leaving her behind me, yelling at me that she has no idea what is going on, crying out that she is frightened and scared and wants to go back to our old house.

I am at his door in a matter of seconds, my temper at boiling point. There is nobody else around here. It's him. It has to be. I ball my hand into a fist and batter it against the wooden door, hammering with all my strength, a relentless pounding that fills the air around me, drowning out the birdsong. I don't stop until the door swings open and he is standing there, his face frozen with confusion and alarm. He doesn't fool me. I know what his game is. I've been stupid lately, too soft. I've let my guard slip, been friendly with him and this is the net result. My first thought is to show him the letter but I think better of it. I need to keep it for evidence of his continued harassment. And if he thinks he is going to get away with this, he can think again. I am done with the bullies, with all the threats and aggravation and stalking. I have had enough. I have spent my life on the run, moving from place to place to avoid people like him. But not for much longer. This is where it all ends.

'What the fuck do you think you're playing at?' I wail at him, brandishing the paper in his face.

He takes a step back and lets out a low whistle. 'Whoa there, tiger! I'm not sure what's going on here but I think you need to calm down a bit.' His smile is warm and it stops me in my tracks.

But not for long. An iron fist in a velvet glove is what it is. His wily charms won't work. Not with me, not this time.

'Don't pretend you don't know,' I hiss at him and feel my blood pressure rise even further as he steps to one side and motions for me to go through. Go in there with him? Not a chance in hell.

'I don't know what it is you think I've done but I am not prepared to stand here on the doorstep and have you scream at me like a fishwife. I am, however, more than prepared to do it inside in the privacy of my house over a cup of tea. Your choice.' He glances at my clothes, my snarl of hair and softens his voice, 'Look, I can see you're really upset. If it's because I moved the fox, then yes, I admit I did move it. I'm pretty sure you would have wanted me to, wouldn't you? But as for this?' he stares down at the letter that is hanging limply in my hand, 'I'm afraid I have no idea what it is. I can see that it's obviously causing you a great deal of distress so can I just suggest you just throw it in the bin?'

I stare at him, my anger slowly dissipating as his words gradually sink in. I try to think clearly, to work out what to say next. Of course, he is going to deny it. He would, wouldn't he? He is not about to admit his culpability in all of this.

'Look,' I say, the fury of fog beginning to clear from my brain, 'I know what you are up to, and no, I am not prepared to go in there and sit with you while you pretend you don't know anything about what is going on. We both know that you know, OK? What I am telling you is this, don't fuck with me and my daughter or I will come down on you so hard, you won't know what hit you.'

I turn and start to walk away then stop when I hear his laughter, a bellowing growl that takes my breath away. What sort of man is he? This Rupert guy who seems impervious to my screaming accusations? I have pointed the finger of blame at him, shouted and sworn at him, and threatened him and all he does is offer me tea and laugh. Spinning round on my heel I am incensed to find him still standing on the step, head thrown back as laughter spits out of him like machine gun fire.

'What the hell is wrong with you, anyway?' I holler, my voice no more than a whisper above the sound of his guffaws. I watch as he wipes his eyes and runs his long fingers through his mane of glossy, thick hair.

'Sorry,' he says, shaking his head and rubbing his face, 'it's just that you're what five feet four and weigh probably about eight or nine stone. Nine at a push. Am I right?'

I say nothing, all too aware of where this is heading, what it is he is about to say.

'And I'm over six feet tall and weigh thirteen stone. Now I don't want to blow my own trumpet or anything like that, but I'm also a bit of a fitness freak and probably lift more than your body weight every day at the gym. I'm also a kick boxer and am partial to a bit of jujitsu. Lots of time for fitness workouts when you work away from home. Not much else to do, I'm afraid. So, when you make idle threats like that, make sure you can see them through.'

His voice suddenly sounds very serious and has an edge to it; a hint of menace. I feel my face flush and start to scurry away, stones and dust kicking up in small clouds beneath my feet.

'Look, I don't want to scare you,' he shouts after me, 'but you can't blame me, can you? You turn up here, yelping at me like a hysterical fishwife, accusing me of all sorts of mad stuff. I've every right to defend myself, haven't I?' The edge has gone now, replaced by the usual gentle tone he adopts.

I consider stopping but feel too washed out, marginally delirious even, by the day's events. Instead I continue walking back home, feeling hollow, as if my insides have been scooped out. I am at a loss as to what to do next. It's as if the world is conspiring against me and forcing me to spend my entire life running. And I am too tired for it all. I don't want to do it any more; living my life looking over my shoulder. I promised myself we would stay here, and we will. I owe it to Rosie, the stability. There will be no more running away trying to escape my past. It seems that wherever I go, it will always find me.

I trudge back home, bolt the door, and ignoring Rosie's weeping and wailing, protests of innocence and her questions about the note. I climb the stairs to my bedroom, fall on to the bed and close my eyes, only too happy for the darkness to engulf me and keep me safe in its clutches.

BEVERLEY

She saw me. I just know it. It was obvious by the way her face crumpled and her body practically folded in on itself. And the timing was perfect too. I had just sent a message to Erica telling her all about it, about how she was in the office next door, her daughter in trouble yet again. I didn't actually have to go in. I had no need, but simply couldn't resist it. All these years I have waited. As if I am going to allow a situation like that slip out of my grasp. And I had the perfect excuse. I had forgotten to take the documents through that Anthea had asked me for earlier, so it seemed like the ideal opportunity to present myself to her; to subliminally say to her, *Remember me? Here I am, back in your life once more ...*

Her expression was priceless. That alone was worth waiting for. And that daughter of hers ... well now the world knows exactly what sort of family they are; how you can't rub out the past no matter how hard you try. It will always be there snapping at your ankles. Sooner or later everybody's sins catch up with them, don't they? And now hers have. There is no way she will be able to scurry away and hide again. I will make sure of it. Soon enough everyone will know what kind of family they are, what sort of daughter she has reared. They will see that evil is in the genes, running through their veins. There is no escape route when your mother is a murderer. It will follow you for the rest of your life.

A frisson of excitement surges through me as I think of what lies ahead, the plans I have mapped out. Such a sensational feeling and one I have waited for, for so long now I never actually thought it would ever happen. A part of me no longer cares about Erica and her sudden cowardice and lack of allegiance to our cause, but then there is another part of me that is furious with her. We talked about this for so long, formed what I thought was a deep and lasting friendship and then out of the blue, she turns against me, leaving me in the lurch. And I don't like being let down. It's not that I can't do this on my own. Of course I can. I'm not an idiot. It's more to do with the fact that she has chosen to ignore me, to lead me on and then swat me away like a fly. I am suddenly a nuisance to her, an annoyance, an intrusion in her life that she can do without. Well, I'm afraid that doesn't sit easy with me. We have come too far to break our pact. She is in on this whether she wants to be or not. I'm doing this for Greg, for Pamela, for all the forgotten children out there who deserve to live on, who deserve better than the paltry sentences our justice system doles out on a regular basis. A three year old and a six year old whose lives were snatched away from them. Somebody has to pay for such crimes. I will make sure of it.

Excitement clutches at my stomach as I log on to my computer and wait for Shirley to leave for lunch. I watch as she scurries about, picking up her bag then putting it down again, rummaging around for her cardigan even though it's warm outside. As lovely as she is, Shirley is a real old fusspot, dithering about, taking an age to do the smallest of tasks. Her retirement will be welcomed in the school. She has been here for forty years but the time has come for her to let somebody else do her job; somebody younger, somebody far more competent. I'll have the office to myself when she finally goes for her sandwich, leaving me free to print off *her* particulars; full name, address, contact details. Even her daughter's dietary requirements and medical details are at my disposal; the name and address of her doctor and any conditions we may need to know about. Delicious stuff I have waited years to get hold of, and now here it is, at my fingertips. All I need is for Shirley to stop dawdling and start being more time efficient. These are the sort of things that rankle with me. Truth be told, I'll be glad to see the back of her when she retires.

'Is this what you're looking for?' I ask, trying to keep the irritation out of my tone as I spot her purse down the side of the desk.

'Ah yes! Of course,' she says in that childish tone of hers that makes my skin crawl. 'I have no idea how it got there. Never mind, it's here now. Are you sure you'll manage on your own? I've got a doctor's appointment straight after lunch but I'll be back as soon as I can.'

I wave her away, giving her a hundred assurances that everything will be fine in her absence. She rubs my hand softly and just stops short of giving me a hug.

'Go on,' I say to her quietly, 'off you go or you won't even have time to do anything.'

She nods in agreement and finally scurries away. I breathe a sigh of relief and lean back in my chair. Jesus. How can something so simple be turned into such a gargantuan task? I wait until she is out of sight then quickly switch seats and take over Shirley's computer. I stare at the screen, scroll down to Rosie's details and smile. There it all is, just waiting for me. I take a couple of different screenshots and then print them off before stuffing them in my bag. My computer isn't connected to a printer yet so I've waited for what feels like forever to be able to do this, to get a hard copy of her details. So far, I've had to hold it all in my head. Shirley practically lives in this office. No matter how early I get in or how late I leave, she's been here, watching my every move, making sure I complete each and every task properly and to her liking. A noise behind me sends my senses into red alert. I need to be careful here. Can't have anyone thinking I'm doing anything wrong. I turn around to see Laura, one of the dinner staff, rummaging through the cupboard behind me.

'Sick bags!' she shouts as she pushes a mountain of stationery aside and dips her head deeper into the darkness. 'Little Robbie's just spewed up everywhere. Right over his dinner and all over the table.'

'Sounds like it's all a bit late for sick bags,' I say as I move her aside and grab a box full of them, pushing them into her hands. 'I think you're more likely to need a mop and bucket.'

She shakes her head despairingly and mouths, *'Kids, eh?'* at me before dashing off to the canteen, her long, blonde ponytail swishing about behind like a huge, white pendulum.

The afternoon passes quickly and I am relieved to be out of the place. My back is aching and my eyes are sore from staring at the computer screen for too long. All I want to do is get home and read through the printout again.

Tired as I am, I can't resist having a drive past the house after school. *Her house.* This Peartree Lodge where she lives. Sounds idyllic; smack bang in the middle of the North Yorkshire countryside. How is that fair? She should be in a tiny flat somewhere, scrubbing floors to try and make ends meet, working as a waitress in a greasy cafe as a second job, not in a big house in a glorious location. Initially I googled it, her home, this Peartree Lodge, and then I couldn't resist a visit. It's an amazing place, set up on a grassy mound in a tiny hamlet, surrounded by the hills and fields and a long streak of blue sky and fluffy, pearl white clouds where the swallows and doves and blackbirds fly. She doesn't deserve that. She definitely doesn't deserve that kind of life.

I say goodbye to Shirley, leave the office and sling my bag into the car, suddenly furious at it all. Driving much faster that I usually do, I swerve out of the car park and head over there. Just a quick look. That's all I want. Just to get an idea of how she lives. I won't hang around long. I'm not that stupid. Just long enough to get a glimpse into her life. The one she doesn't deserve to have. Then I will be on my way. Back home to my plans.

ERICA

She is looking old. She *is* old. And yet for a lady in her eighties, she has such a young soul. I take my mother's hand and stroke it lightly. Her skin is crisp and dry. Her nails are long and slightly yellowed with age and her hands are dotted with liver spots, and yet I still think she is an utterly beautiful lady. Never cross or sulky. Never does she ever claim to be hard done by. Always with a ready smile and words of wisdom. I wish I could be more like her. I have spent the last few years of my life almost crippled with anxiety and hate. So much loathing and bitterness. And for what? It hasn't made me a better person or brought Pamela back. And it certainly won't cure my cancer or save my marriage. Only effort and time and love can do that and who knows, in the end, even all of that may still not be enough. None of us really know what the future holds. All we can do is work at it, give it our best shot and hope that lady luck is smiling down on us.

I don't tell my mother of my diagnosis. She has had enough heartache to deal with over the years. To give her something else to worry about, another thing to dent her small but peaceful life, would be unutterably cruel. So, we talk about Freya instead. We talk about her studies and aspirations to become a journalist. We chat about my mother's weekly visit to the library, and the coffee morning she attends every other Thursday at the nearby community centre. We even speak about her love of crosswords and how she is convinced that such activities can stave off dementia. Perhaps she is right. Who knows? One thing I am sure of, however, is that I will never, ever let myself become bogged down the way I have done in the past. Life goes on. Pamela is gone and no amount of vengeance or retribution will bring her back. It is what it is and I was a fool for not seeing it before now. My life was a vicious circle of blame and revulsion, one feeding off the other until I couldn't see a way out. No more. From now on I will look to the future. Do what I can to support Arthur, and be the best patient I can be, by looking after myself and staying healthy both physically and mentally. One is as important as the other.

'I'll make us another cup of tea, shall I?' I say and carry our used cups through to the kitchen. It's strange how this house seemed so huge when I was a child, yet if I spend too long here as an adult, it feels as if the walls are closing in on me; the dated, striped wallpaper, the heavy, jacquard curtains they all seem so small. Everything about this house has shrunk with the passing of time.

I wait for the kettle to boil and drag my hands across the worktops. Clean as a whistle. Age hasn't allowed my mother to become one of those people who doesn't see the dirt and the dust. Everywhere is immaculate. I have offered to get her a cleaner but she won't hear of it, claiming she would get bored if the cleaning was done by somebody else. I personally think it is more to do with the guilt of watching somebody else do all the chores and take care of her house, but regardless, she insists on doing it herself and from what I can tell, she is doing a sterling job despite her advancing years.

The kettle boils and I refill our cups then head back into the living room where she sits, regal and graceful, her face suddenly the picture of concern.

'I saw her a few weeks back,' my mother says, narrowing her eyes in concentration as she speaks. 'I think it was a few weeks anyway. Perhaps longer,' she says contemplatively.

I place her cup down on the table in front of us, making sure the coasters are in place. 'Who did you see, Mum?' I ask as she picks her cup up and blows over the rim, a wisp of steam curling up around her slightly puckered mouth.

'The other mother.'

I freeze at her words. That's how they often referred to each other, how folk in the neighbourhood spoke about them. The other mother. It became a well-known phrase around these parts. There was Vera and then there was Anne my mum. And when one was spoken about, the other lady was referred to as 'the other mother.'

'You mean Vera?' I ask, a little too brightly, my voice taking on a new and much higher tone.

'Yes, of course. Greg's mum.'

That's the other thing. After it happened, they didn't speak of their living children. They, along with everyone in the neighbourhood, used their murdered children's names as a bond that seemed to tie them together, a way of cementing their strange and unwanted union. I have never heard my mother being called 'Erica's mum.' Not once. Not when I am back here in my childhood town. Strange, really. I may well be the living child but I am definitely the forgotten one. Perhaps it was the little things like this that fuelled my anger and hatred and filled me with a need for revenge. Or maybe I am just a bitter person at heart. I sincerely hope not. I like to think I am better than that, but life has taught me that we often have no idea what we are capable of until we are truly put under duress.

'How is she?' I ask, simply because I have no idea what else to say. Her statement required a response and at this moment in time, this is the best I can do.

'Oh, as well as can be expected, really. Under the circumstances …'

We leave it at that. There is no need to mention her husband's suicide all those years ago and her daughter's drug habit. Some things are better not said.

Right on cue my phone vibrates and beeps, saving us both from the awful, uncomfortable sensation that has settled between us.

I reach into my pocket and drag it out, expecting it to be Freya asking what time I will arrive. I told her to text me mid-afternoon before I caught the train into Sunderland.

Beverley's name jumps out at me. I ready myself and open the message. Her words are laced with such revulsion and animosity, they take my breath away. I did the right thing, refusing to go ahead with this thing. I re-read the message, each word sending a wave of fear through me. I am so relieved to be out of it. And yet, I'm not out of it, am I? She is determined to keep me embroiled in it. I read the message again, unable to comprehend what I am seeing, unable to link these words to the middle-class, middle-aged lady I spoke to all those months ago.

Sat in the car outside her house. Fucking bitch is set up for life living here. So upset and furious. Feel like taking a brick and caving both their heads in …

Sickness grips me, a bolt of dread searing through my brain, rendering me speechless. Not like this. It wasn't meant to be like this. It was meant to be a case of letting the press know where she was, getting her to move on, making sure her daughter knew what her mother had done. All we spoke about was outing her. Not this. Not violence. That would make us as bad as her. Surely Beverley can see that? The pair of us hurting her never came into the equation. It was never, *ever* part of the plan.

I smile at my mother and excuse myself, telling her I have to go in the hallway to get a better signal so I can send a reply to Freya, who is on her way to meet me at the station. I hate all this deceit, but will do what I have to do to protect her. She is a frail, old lady and doesn't deserve to become embroiled in any of this nonsense. Because that's what it is; complete and utter nonsense. A stupid idea that has grown and grown and been blown out of all proportion. After tracking her movements for many years, Beverley realised with a great deal of joy that Lissy had moved to North Yorkshire, not far from where she lived. Then she struck pure gold when she also found out that the school Lissy's daughter attended had a vacancy for an admin assistant. She applied and got the job. It was handed to us on a plate. We could actually see her when she visited the school, see how she had aged, perhaps throw a little trouble her way by way of spreading a few rumours around about her daughter, making her so miserable she would beg her mother to let them move again. Then they would be somebody else's problem. That's all it was supposed to be. Just a way of getting all this anger out of our systems. For me anyway. Looking back, I should have known that Beverley wanted more than that. Her messages and conversations always had an edge to them, a hidden meaning that I didn't always pick up on. Or didn't want to. I was so wrapped up in my own rage and loathing that I was blind to it all.

I almost go back into the living room to speak to my mother about a memory that has jumped in my head but stop myself. It was a conversation we had many years back. Something about Beverley; something that happened long before I met up with her and we became acquainted. I screw my eyes up to concentrate, wishing I'd taken more notice of my mother's words. But at the time Beverley meant little to me. I wouldn't have had any reason to listen closely, to pay attention to the details. She was practically a stranger to me, someone who suffered a tragedy similar to ours but not a person I associated, or mixed, with. We were very different people back then. We still are. I screw my eyes up and try to think. It was something about an incident involving a child. *Did she take a child?* My head feels tight. I recall my mother telling me about Beverley being taken into hospital, her husband being frantic with worry but can't for the life of me recall what the actual incident was. There's been so much gone on since then, it's all tucked away in the back of my thoughts.

I take a deep breath and tap away at my phone, panic now searing across my skin like a wave of electricity. She has to stop this. I have to stop her. She isn't well. So far, I've ignored her pleading, sharp messages and turned a blind eye to her threats. But now she has upped her game, taken it in a whole new direction. Maybe that's what has caused her to do this, my refusal to communicate with her. Is this what she is trying to do? To draw me back in to her awful little plan using possible violence as a tactic? Is she having another breakdown? Is that what happened to her last time?

I tap away at my phone, thinking I will possibly regret this.

Go home. Leave them be. You are not solving anything by doing this. Give it up. Please, I'm begging you, don't do this.

I hit send and hope she comes to her senses. If anything happened to Lissy and her daughter, Beverley and I would be blamed, having messages like this on our phones. I quickly hit delete and slip it back in my pocket. Because they are targets, the pair of them. I don't doubt that there are plenty of people out there ready to avenge the death of my sister, a child they never even knew. People who would take it upon themselves to carry out their own sentencing, take the law into their own hands. You see it all the time on the television and in the newspapers; gangs of them torching the house of a man they believed was a paedophile, bandying adult photographs online of the Bulger murderers in the hope somebody somewhere recognises them. They are everywhere, these vigilantes, fully believing that what they are doing is for the good of the people. And I was nearly one of them. I still can't quite believe I let that happen, that I even considered it. I don't think Arthur or my mother would have ever forgiven me. I don't think I could ever have forgiven myself. And then, of course, there is Freya to take into consideration. Quite ironic really that she wants to become a journalist, to spend her days writing about other people's lives and problems when her own family almost fell apart without her even knowing.

'Everything OK, darling?' My mother's voice always manages to instil a sense of calm in me. The timbre of her delicate, hushed tones washes over me, transports me back to a time when I felt safe in her arms. Our family was fortunate in that respect. We coped far better with our loss than Beverley's family did. It wasn't easy for us, far from it but we always had a lot of love to keep us going, whereas Beverley's family seemed to run on bitterness and blame. And as far as I can tell, they still do.

'Fine, Mum. I'm just checking the train times, making sure they're not running late.'

I run my fingers through my hair and shake my head. More lies to a person who doesn't deserve them. I tell myself I'm doing it to protect her, to keep her from all of this. I only hope Beverley is doing the same thing with her mother. If nothing else, both ladies deserve a modicum of peace in their twilight years. God knows they've suffered enough.

My phone beeps and I give it once last glance before heading back to the living room. As I expected, it's Beverley and her reply is simple enough. Just one word that tells me all I need to know about just how deep rooted her hatred is. I stare at the screen and feel my stomach clench. It simply says, *NEVER.*

LISSY

The light is fading as I sit bolt upright in bed. I have a dressing gown draped over me and the house is silent. For a few seconds, I can't think where I am and I feel besieged with nerves. I lie still, waiting for the pulse in my head to disappear and for my thoughts to assemble themselves, to slowly slot into place like pieces of a jigsaw coming together to form a complete picture. I spin around, my eyes darting about the room, catching shadows, glancing in corners, checking I am safe. I swing my legs over the edge of the bed and stand up. The room seems to move. I lean back and hang on to the bed sheets to steady myself. How long have I slept for? An hour? Two? I suddenly remember Rosie and the school bus, thinking she will be in soon. Straightening myself up, I tear out of the door, my head tight with confusion. And then I remember. Horror and disappointment roots me to the floor. I think of Mr Cooper and his supercilious smirk, and Anthea Paxton and her gentle but firm words. And *her,* in there with us. Together in the same room after all these years. Then Rupert's face lodges in my head. His laughter, the mockery. *And that letter.* Fuelled by fear, I race downstairs, almost falling over my own feet, and barge into the living room. Rosie is sitting on the sofa, feet curled up under her legs, a book on her lap, *Dirty Dancing* is playing on the television in the background. She is the very epitome of calm. The picture of innocence.

'You were out for the count, so I covered you up,' she says, not looking up from the page she is reading. I stare at the book and tilt my head slightly to get a better look at the title. Rosie is a book fiend. Literature is her greatest love. I still cannot believe what she has done. My head pounds with disbelief. Somebody with such a passion for the written word would never deface a book in that way, would they? Subject another person to such horror? Surely not.

'*The Tempest*,' she says, and lifts the book up for me to see.

I nod in recognition and shiver. It feels cold in here. How can I be cold when summer is on its way? Outside a flock of great tits are feeding en masse, a tight bundle of them huddled round the bird feeder, their small beaks digging into the food I put out yesterday. A blackbird swoops down and I watch as they all fly away, their tiny wings beating furiously as they flutter and hide in the nearby shrubbery.

'Have you read this one, Mum?' Her voice is soft, almost a whisper.

I shake my head and push my hair behind my ears. It is tangled and in need of a wash. My mouth is coated in a greasy film and the slightly sour smell of sweat is all around me, on me, permeating the still air and filling my nostrils. I need a shower and a drink of water to rinse away the residual coating of bile that is clinging to the back of my throat.

'This is one of my favourite quotes from this play,' she says, her voice suddenly growing in crescendo, a sharpness to it I don't care for. I turn to stare at her, my eyes probing her features for clues.

'In this scene, Ariel is speaking to Prospero, and you know what he says, Mum?' A degree of caution creeps over me as I watch her face, see a look in her eyes that puts me on edge. 'He says, "Hell is empty and all the devils are here."'

I nod, unsure what it is she wants me to say. Her eyes are dark. She narrows them as she looks up from the book and turns to stare at me.

'Do you like that quote, Mum? I think it's perfect. One of the best quotations ever. What do you think of it?'

I gawp at her open mouthed, my chest suddenly tight with apprehension. She unfurls herself from the sofa and sits up straight, her body tight with barely disguised aggression.

'I think I need a shower, Rosie, and then we can talk about everything that's happened because I think we're both really upset, but right now—'

'Talk?' she barks at me, her shrill voice freezing my blood. 'Talk about what? Where should we start, Mum, eh? You tell me!'

A quietness descends, an ominous hush, our eyes locked together in a moment of unexplained darkness. And then I realise. It crashes into my mind, hot and inescapable, a gushing tide of guilt submerging me, dragging me under, crushing me, taking the breath right out of me. I sink to the floor, collapsing in an undignified heap, my legs splayed out around me. I see it there, the horror of its presence is a sickening reminder of who I am. The letter. Davey's letter, the one he wrote to us the morning he left all those years ago, the one he propped up against the condiments on the kitchen table before he stepped out of our lives, never to return. It sits next to Rosie alongside the one we received earlier, as sharp and clear as the day he wrote it, its neat edges and cutting words slicing into my heart, tearing our family into tiny, little pieces.

I try to speak but nothing comes out. I swallow, take a few small, deep gasps and stand up, my legs wobbling under me as I take a few tentative steps towards her. She stops me dead, holding out her outstretched palm to keep me away, to keep me, her own mother, at arms-length.

'Stay there. Don't come anywhere near me!' Her voice is unrecognisable, loaded with such hatred and unadulterated rage it takes my breath away. 'I swear to God, Mum, if you come any closer I will scream that you are trying to murder me.'

'Where di—' I stammer.

'Where did I find it? After I covered you up, after I had calmed myself down after seeing *that note*,' she says icily, staring down at the paper sitting next to Davey's letter. 'After seeing that *fucking note*, I went through your bookcase looking for something to read. The one you always claim contains only boring books. Nothing there I would like. Isn't that what you've always told me in the past? Anyway, tucked away at the back was an envelope. But I don't need to tell you that, do I? Because that's where you hid it, isn't it? Stuffed right at the back, away from me.'

I lower my eyes and blink away a lifetime of unshed tears.

'Anyway, at that point you were asleep and I was pissed off so I thought, why not? I'll give it a read …'

Sweat trickles down my spine. My eyes mist over and small needles stab at my flesh. This cannot be happening. It just can't. I have to do something, anything to get her back on my side. A ticking sound in my head grows louder and louder making me feel sick. I need to focus, to concentrate all my efforts on getting our little family back on track. I cannot let this happen. I should have told her everything before now. I am painfully aware of that, but the time was never right. When exactly is it the right time to tell your teenage daughter that at the same age she is now, you were sent to prison for killing two small children? The time is *never* right for such a disclosure.

Slowly, I reach out my hand to her, taking small steps so as to not alarm her. Never taking my eyes from her face, I very gently shuffle forwards, careful to keep my expression as neutral as I can. Her face crumples and she lets out a shriek as I reach her and pull her into my arms where she collapses in a snotty, wet heap. Pain beats its way through me as she leans back then throws herself at me, pummelling her fists against my chest. Then reaching up, she starts to slap at my face, her soft, small hands stinging my cheeks. I don't try to stop her. I deserve this. She should have been told. Keeping it from her was unforgivable. I thought I was protecting her but all I've done is punish her, make her feel as if she has been living with a complete stranger for all of her life.

'I hate you! I HATE YOU!' The slaps continue to come, sharp and raw against my bare flesh.

We go on like that for another two or three minutes, until eventually Rosie wears herself out and she slumps in my arms, her body a dead-weight against mine. She stays there for another minute or so, heaving and sobbing like a baby. I remain silent, not wanting to lose the moment. It could go either way. Just one word out of place, one sharp breath and I could lose her again. Everything could shatter into a million tiny fragments, impossible to piece back together. I can't let that happen. This is Rosie, my only child. We are a team. The two of us together. Never apart. Never …

'I'm so sorry, my darling,' I whisper, my chin resting on the top of her head. 'I was wrong for not telling you, but there's so many things you need to know. So many things.'

I daren't breathe, terrified of her response. She is in fight or flight mode. I wait, my body so tense that a pain shoots up my back and wraps its way around my neck, snaking up the base of my skull. A sharp ache cracking against the bone. I pull Rosie closer to me in case she tries to escape, just a small hug to my body to keep her near me.

'You often asked about my family and why I never saw any of them.' I wait to see if she responds, and when she doesn't say or do anything, I continue, 'My parents were both alcoholics, Rosie. They were very abusive. We lived in quite a big house compared to some of my friends but ours was a miserable existence. Although my dad had quite a good job as a manager at a local factory, when he was at home there was a completely different side to him that not everyone knew about. My mo—'

'NO!' Rosie pulls away from me and is screaming at me once again, 'NO, Mum! Please don't try and pull that shit about it being down to your parents and how it's all their fault!'

'Rosie, I'm not. I'm really, really not. I'm just setting the scene, telling you how it all started. Please, just hear me out?' I hear the desperation begin to creep into my voice. I'm losing her. She is drawing away from me. I have to stop her, bring her back to me. She is my life. Everything is pointless without Rosie. Time stands still as I wait for her to do something anything. As long as she stays seated next to me, I can do this. All I want is for her to listen, to hear me out, to take notice of the sorry tale I am about to tell her. But she doesn't. I start to speak again and in a heartbeat, she is up and out of the chair, eyes blazing.

'NO! I don't want to hear anything you have to say! You're a liar. Nothing but a cheap, pathetic, fucking LIAR.'

The entire house shakes as she slams the door and storms upstairs, screaming a shower of obscenities at me from the top, about how dare I accuse her of misbehaving when all the time I had the darkest secret of all stashed away in my past and how she always thought I was a shit mother. I try to let it all wash over me, to let it slip over my skin, telling myself this is to be expected and it's just a fleeting emotion, something that will change with the passing of time. And then another still voice taps away at me, screaming that this is the beginning of the end; a gaping fissure that is beyond repair. A bubble of air catches in my chest. I can't let that happen. Not ever. Without Rosie, I am nothing. A husk of a person. I may as well be dead.

As delicately as I can, I follow her upstairs. I have to say this and she has to listen. Passing the hallway, I check to make sure the front door is locked and bolted. I slip both sets of keys into my pocket and tiptoe up to her bedroom. The door is closed, possibly barricaded with her chest of drawers to stop me getting in. I'll find a way. I have to. If I don't, then I can kiss everything goodbye; Rosie, my paintings, the rest of my life. It will all have been for nothing.

I take a deep breath, tap my hand against the panel of the door, and wait.

BEVERLEY

Disgust courses through me, saturating my brain, chilling my flesh. I have never felt this way before, known a loathing so deep that it takes root in me and refuses to leave. When she was an image in my head it was different. I hated the memory of her, the thought of what she did, how her actions destroyed my life; but now she is here, flesh and bone, just a stone's throw away from me, our lives separated by only bricks and mortar, behind which she sits with her daughter, relishing in their nice little life I have realised that I want to kill her. Nothing would give me greater satisfaction than watching her squirm with fear as I take a knife to her throat while her daughter stands by and watches.

I sit with the engine running at the bottom of her immense driveway, my stomach churning with anger. How can it be fair that she is in there, living a life of luxury while other people suffer because of her actions? How is any of that acceptable? White hot hatred eats away at me as I picture them both sitting inside, luxuriating on their expensive furniture, chatting, laughing. Not giving a toss. And just look at this place! I stare at the grandeur of it all, the wide and sweeping views of the North Yorkshire hills she has, the sprawl of her garden. Her house is flanked on either side by houses of the same ilk, all exuding wealth and a sense of genteel tranquillity. She has it all, living here. I ponder over how she came by this sort of money. I know for a fact her parents are still alive and have pissed any money they had up the wall. The woman who brought her up after she was released from prison, perhaps? She didn't seem overly wealthy but then you never can tell, can you? Or is this what the British justice system does to people once they are released after committing terrible crimes? Set them up for life so they don't become a drain on society and are less likely to re-offend? The thought of it sickens me to the pit of my stomach. My mother still lives in the same tiny, terraced house in County Durham where it all took place. She exists on a pittance of a pension, still has the same dreary, threadbare carpet and yellowing wallpaper, and all the while *she* is here, lording it up in her bloody mansion, living like *fucking royalty*.

I sit and seethe for what feels like an age, my veins bulging with fury. I have to use all my self-restraint to stop myself from marching up that wide, gravel driveway, knocking on her door and dragging her out by her hair telling her that if she doesn't give it all up, and get the fuck out of here, then her face will be printed across every national newspaper by tomorrow morning. But then that would make it all too easy for her. I want her to suffer a bit more, to try to work out why everything in her life is suddenly falling to pieces, why her daughter has turned out to be such a bitch. Just like her mother.

A noise alerts me, drags me out of my thoughts. My eyes flicker over to the house to the right of hers. A man is at his car; an expensive looking, black Audi, long and sleek and polished to within an inch of its life. He opens the boot and heaves a large, black sack up off the ground then places it inside before slamming the lid closed. I watch him turn around, his hand up to his forehead to shield his eyes from the glare of the sinking sun, and on instinct, I duck down behind the dashboard, my heart suddenly thrashing around my chest. I have no idea why. I'm not doing anything wrong here. I'm not breaking any laws or hurting anybody. There are some dreadful people out there committing all kinds of atrocities but I am most definitely not one of them. The things I have done pale in comparison with those awful criminals. I am a decent citizen whereas *she* is a complete monster, sitting in there, in her huge house, wearing a mask of decency when all the while she is entertaining evil thoughts.

I peek my head up a fraction and watch as he gets in his car and reverses off the drive. I consider pulling away, but it's too late. This man already has me in his sights. He stops at the end of the gravel path, his rear tyres slowly edging over the pavement and on to the road where I am parked. I sit up, my face hot at being caught out. His Audi is directly in front of me. He reverses some more, slowly edging closer until our bumpers are almost touching. My cheeks burn with shame as I look ahead to see his eyes, a narrow strip of darkness in his rear-view mirror. He is watching me intently, his close scrutiny of me clearly obvious by the concerned and lingering expression in his gaze. For a split second, I wonder if I should pretend to be lost; get out of my car and stroll up to his window to ask for directions to one of the outlying villages. But I get the feeling this man is no idiot and would see through my tissue of lies. So, I sit, my fingers clutched tightly around the steering wheel, my heart banging around my ribs, and hope he gets fed up and leaves. I fumble with the keys in the ignition, ready to drive off when he doesn't move. What if I do that and he follows me? Reports me for loitering or some other such nonsense? I take a deep breath and tell myself not to be so stupid. I am not doing anything wrong. I just need to calm down and start thinking logically. And then, just as I am going through all these possible scenarios, his car growls into action and he drives away, the wheels kicking up a storm of dust.

I almost laugh out loud. Alone once more. I reach into my bag and grab my phone, my palms still slippery with nerves, and compose a message to Erica. As I type, telling her the sort of things I would love to do to that bitch and her daughter, I am almost dizzy with euphoria at not being caught. She replies almost immediately some garbage or other about me going home and leaving them both alone. I send one back saying that will never happen. A shiver of exhilaration ripples through me as I picture Erica's sour little face now she's decided to be all pious about the whole thing. Sod her and her prim and proper little ways. I made myself a promise and I'm sticking to it.

I throw my phone on to the passenger seat where it slides about on the leather, and turn the key in the ignition. Actually, this place is perfect. Almost deserted, apart from one nosy neighbour. Still, I can always check to make sure his car isn't here next time I come back, park my vehicle further up the road, around the bend. There are loads of options open to me. I just need to man up a bit and think laterally so I don't get caught.

I swing out on to the main road and turn the stereo up loud, listening to *Snow Patrol* on the radio, thinking it's everything I ever dreamed it would be, this retribution caper. Everything and so much more.

ERICA

I try to forget all about Beverley and her message as I head north on the train to meet Freya. I am determined not to let her ruin the precious time I have with my daughter. Freya has herself a summer job in Sunderland and, unlike the other students who are heading off home at the end of this semester, she is staying there to work. The local newspaper has offered her a position in the office carrying out menial tasks and she jumped at the chance. It gives her an opportunity to see what the environment is like and gain some experience in the world of journalism. It was too good a chance to turn down. I feel a pang of worry when I think of her in the student accommodation on her own. Arthur and I tried to convince her that she should come home, but she was so excited about this opportunity that there was no swaying her. Until I told her of my diagnosis, that is. Then she was ready to jump on the next bus and head home, jack it all in to be with me. We had to do an about-turn and tell her to stay, that she was right about it being too good a chance to miss, and she should give it her best shot. And so here I am, my head almost bursting with excitement at the thought of seeing her again.

My phone vibrates and I snatch it up greedily, ready to savour every one of my daughter's gorgeous words. She is meeting me at the station, and I sent her a message to say we were slightly delayed at Newcastle so I would be a few minutes late. She has spent the last ten minutes sending me every emoticon she can find that contains love hearts and people blowing kisses at each other. I smile and shake my head, then feel myself freeze as the message opens. Not Freya but Beverley, this time. Again. She has sent me a photograph of something, a piece of paper. It's too small to see. I bite at the sides of my mouth anxiously and open the picture, a loose flap of skin coming away between my teeth as I swipe my fingers over the screen to enlarge it. It's an address. I can guess who it belongs to before I even read what she written underneath it.

Peartree Lodge
Oaklove Hill
North Yorkshire
DL6 9DP
Mobile number 07491 188192

I close the message and lean back on my seat. Why won't she leave me alone? How did I not see it before; how odd she is? Completely unhinged. If only the memory of her hospitalisation had come to me earlier I may well have had second thoughts about speaking to her and getting involved in all of this. I don't doubt for one minute that she has been damaged by the murder of her brother and the awful circumstances of his death, but then so have I. My family and I lost my sister. My poor dad went to his grave a heartbroken man, a shadow of the person he was. We all have our emotional baggage to lug around day after day. I only hope she doesn't do anything too rash, but I fear she has begun a downward spiral of vengeance and is too far gone now to back down.

I close my eyes and hug the phone to my chest, feeling the dull rattle of the train as we chug into motion and leave the station. Perhaps I should contact Lissy, tell her she is being watched and to be on her guard. I quickly dismiss the idea. That would very possibly make me look like the crazy one. She would be well within her rights to report me to the police for harassment.

I am still mulling this over, thinking how close I was to losing it all and how blessed I am to have, somehow, been given it all back again, when the train pulls into Sunderland and I spot Freya on the platform waiting for me. She is wearing a pair of low slung jeans, that hang just above her narrow hips, and a white T-Shirt. A green knitted bag is slung over her shoulder and she is carrying an armful of books. She looks like a typical student, slightly frayed at the edges whilst managing to maintain an air of studied calm. My heart beats solidly and I have to stop a crazy, wild smile from spreading across my face when I see her through the window.

The crowd of people on the train shuffle along the aisle at a snail's pace, everyone murmuring and chuntering on about how dreadful it all is, and that with the prices of trains nowadays you would think the least they could do is be on time. Eventually, the doors slide open and we all spill out on to the platform, a sea of passengers spreading over the area like scurrying ants, some searching the throng of waiting faces while others march towards the exit, eager to get home.

I feel a warm hand slip into mine and turn to my daughter beside me, her face the picture of concern. 'Mum, you look shattered!'

She reaches up and plants a soft kiss on my cheek, then takes my bag from me, pulling at my arm as I resist.

'No, Mother, I'll take this,' she says with a grin. I try to stop her, to tell her I'm not an invalid, but she puts her hand up to stop me and I find myself going along with whatever she says. I am putty in her hands.

The taxi takes us through a busy street of Victorian town houses, some still residential while others have been changed into offices for solicitors and accountants. They tower over either side of us, casting long, grey shadows in the dying light. It's a short ride, no more than five minutes, and I protest that I could easily have walked it, while Freya tells me to hush before leaning forward, tapping the back of the driver's seat and saying, 'Here is fine, thank you.'

The flat looks empty, most of the other students already packed up and gone to their respective homes scattered across the country.

'There's only Dora left. And me, of course.' She laughs as she drags my bag across the hallway and into her room. 'She's leaving in a few days so I'll have the place to myself.'

I think of her here on her own and carefully eye the lock on the door. It looks sturdy enough. She'll be fine, I know she will. I must keep telling myself that or I won't get a wink of sleep for the rest of the summer.

'I thought we might go out for a meal tonight. You know, you and me in a posh restaurant?'

She laughs and kicks a pair of battered old trainers out of her way before flopping down on to a chair. 'Round here? Are you kidding me?'

'It looks fine to me,' I say chirpily, 'we can get a cab into the city centre. You can show me the highlights of Sunderland. Give me the grand tour.'

She juts out her lip and nods, a mischievous twinkle in her eye as she speaks, 'We can go clubbing, eh? Get you signed into the local strip joint, see if they can give you lessons.'

I laugh and she gets up and throws her arms around me. 'Mum you're being really brave about it all. If it was me I swear to God I would be shitting myself, but here you are looking bloody amazing, and I know I don't tell you it often enough, but I think you're an absolute star; the best mother in the world.'

'Yes, well, you would say that, wouldn't you?' I chuckle softly. 'Seeing as I'm paying tonight.'

∞∞∞∞∞

The evening is a riot. We eat, drink, tour the town, enjoy the relative calm of the pubs now the university has all but emptied itself of students. We send a series of grinning selfies to Arthur, who replies with a row of kisses and hearts, then we return to Freya's flat satiated, mildly drunk, and giddy with happiness.

I flop down on the bed still half dressed, and fall asleep almost immediately.

When I wake the next morning, Freya is still snoring softly in the chair next to me. I stroke her hair before getting up and showering. I'm making us both a cup of tea when she saunters in, bleary-eyed, hair sticking up comically at opposite angles. Her mouth gapes as a yawn escapes. She brings her arms up and stretches like a cartoon cat, her lithe limbs looping around her body.

'Morning, lovely. Cup of tea?'

She nods enthusiastically and flops into a kitchen chair. 'What time's your train?'

I stare up at the clock and let out a low whistle. 'In an hour. Best get a wriggle on, hadn't I?'

The kettle boils and we drink in silence for a short while. It's highly likely that the next time Freya sees me I will be in a hospital bed. But we don't need to talk about that. Instead, we discuss her new job, next year's course and how her application for her student loan is going. Mundane stuff, but then, sometimes boring is what's required to keep the bad stuff at bay.

My taxi turns up with only ten minutes to spare before my train is due to leave. I hope traffic is light and, for once, pray for a delay at the station. Freya hugs me tightly and I have to prise myself away with promises to call her as soon as I arrive back home.

The train is sitting on the platform as I dash through the station, sliding past the crowds, saying *excuse me, excuse me,* over and over until I am finally in the carriage and safely ensconced in my seat. I am flooded with relief at having booked a train that requires no changes. After last night's shenanigans, I don't think I would have the energy for it; dashing from platform to platform, pushing through people, dragging my bag along behind me. I'm too tired for it all. I rest my head on the back of the seat and let myself be carried along with the soft, lulling regularity of the engine. We set off and power through the greyness and shadows of the towns and cities, passing the towering red brick walls and industrial skylines and head off into the countryside once more.

I pull out my book and read for a while, then check my phone, a small shiver of dread running through me as I stare at the screen. One new message from Arthur telling me to have a safe journey and saying he'll be waiting for me when I get to the station. And that's it. I close my eyes and let the relief wash over me. No manic messages from Beverley, no idle threats. Nothing. I feel a huge release of tension seep out of me and close my eyes to stop the tears I feel welling up from spilling forth.

When I wake up, we're pulling into King's Cross and I can't quite believe I've slept for that long. Groggy and disorientated, I stagger up and am close to tears again when I spot Arthur on the platform. I grab my bags and shuffle along, suddenly eager to be home.

Arthur kisses me lightly on each cheek as I teeter over to him, tiredness folding in on me. We head off for the car in near silence, the gulf between us not yet fully mended.

I practically fall through the door after we pull up outside the house, the familiarity of it all such a welcome sight it makes me feel quite giddy. My phone vibrates and I reluctantly pull it out, afraid of what I might find written there. It's Freya checking to see if I'm home yet and sending me lots of kisses. I scroll through my previous texts and consider deleting the messages that Beverley sent me. Incriminating evidence is what they are, if she ever does anything stupid. I stare at them and am just about to hit the delete button when Arthur strides up behind me and tucks his arm around my waist, taking me by surprise. I swing round to see a bouquet of flowers in his other hand. Tinged with guilt I stuff my phone into my pocket, hoping he didn't see anything. I will do something about all of this. Get rid of her messages, detach myself from it all. Tomorrow. I will do it all tomorrow. Right now, I have a marriage to mend.

LISSY

I slept on the sofa, afraid that Rosie might sneak down during the night and try to leave me. I hung on to all our sets of keys just in case but, as far as I'm aware, she stayed in her room all evening. I gave up trying to get in there. She refused to communicate with me and I got fed up of talking to a piece of wood. Sometimes I could hear her sobbing in there and it tore me apart, but no matter how hard I tried she stonewalled me. There seemed little point in the end. I kind of hope that today will be better, that time has allowed her to cool down, and she will let me talk to her without any shouting or crying, but I'm not holding out a great deal of hope. She is in shock. This is all to be expected.

I make us some breakfast, desperate to keep things as normal as possible. The paradox of my actions isn't lost on me. We are about as far from normal as it is possible to be, at this moment in time, but if I don't do this, I fear the void where our life used to be will grow so large it will swallow us both. We need normality. We need each other. Rosie is my anchor in the choppy seas of fear and uncertainty that are ahead of us.

I set the table, making sure everything is in place; the best cutlery, a jug of juice, a toast rack; things we rarely ever use, I lay them all out with military precision. I want to make a good impression, show my daughter I am not the monster she thinks I am. Laying the table is the easy part. The difficult bit will be coaxing her down from her bedroom. A horrible idea forces it way into my brain. I swat it away but like an annoying fly it keeps coming back to me, a persistent, insidious thought that taps away at the back of my skull, resolute in its need to terrify me.

I dart upstairs, my heart suddenly growing inside my chest, thumping against my ribcage as I turn the handle on Rosie's bedroom door. It opens. No barricade, no heavy furniture propped up against it to keep me out. I step inside and am immediately struck by how tidy it is. No clothes strewn over the floor, no magazines lying around or half-filled glasses of hot chocolate or cherryade occupying every surface. And the bed is made. Terror grips me. I stare at the window. It is ajar. Tears well up and dizziness overwhelms me. I stagger over to the bed where I flop, my head dipped, my shoulders hunched. I stem the wave of sickness I feel rising and take a deep gulp of air.

'What are you doing?'

The sound of her voice behind me almost knocks me off balance. I spin round, a surge of relief blooms in me and I stand up, my heart battering with gratitude.

'I-I thought …'

'That I'd gone? Climbed out the window, on to the kitchen roof, and scarpered? Don't think I didn't consider it, Mum. It was only the fear of falling and cracking my head open or breaking both legs that stopped me.'

Her hair is wrapped in a towel and she is wearing a pair of grey joggers and a T-Shirt that has seen better days. I have never seen her look more beautiful. I want to run to her, wrap her in my arms and keep her there for as long as I can. Protect her from it all, all the horror and fear and malevolence that is out there. She stalks into the room and shakes her hair out from the turban-style wrap on her head. It springs free and falls in small, wet curls down her back.

'Your room is—'

'Tidy for once?' she says, her mouth a tight, firm line as she speaks. 'Yeah well, I couldn't sleep and the drop was too high so there was nothing else to do, was there?'

I nod and sit in silence, watching her as she darts around the room, throwing cupboard doors open, dragging clothes out, and yanking a shirt over her head.

'Rosie, look,' I say softly, not entirely sure where to start, but she stops me, her eyes blazing, her voice a near shriek.

'Don't, Mum, OK? Just don't. Whatever it is you're going to say, I don't want to hear it. Everything about you is a huge, fat lie! All those years I asked about my dad, all those questions about your parents and you lied to me. Time and time again. Lie after lie after lie.'

She is furious now, stomping around the room, her face scarlet with anger. I stand up as carefully as I can. The window is still open but I don't want to make any sudden movements. There's no telling how she might react if I get too close to her. I visualise her stepping back, her senses out of kilter, her body plummeting to the cold, hard ground below. My head buzzes as I speak.

'I know I did, sweetheart. And I am so, so sorry but I did it to protect you. To keep you from all of this because I knew it would be horrible if you ever found out. This is exactly what I wanted to avoid.' My pulse is racing, my head swimming with dread. I edge close to the window, Rosie too distracted to notice. Her head is dipped and I watch as a lone tear courses down her cheek and drips on to the rug where she stands. Desperation twists my gut. I have done this. I have made this terrible thing happen, and now I have to mend it; to make everything all right again, back to how it was before. Before wasn't ideal, far from it, but it was better than this.

'You're not the person I thought you were.'

Her words cut through me. Perhaps she is right. There are days when I question who I am; when I think back to that time and wonder if that was me, that desperately unhappy, dejected child, or whether it all happened to somebody else. My memories of my childhood before it all occurred are so deeply troubling and unsettling they often scare me. I try to not dwell on them and make a concerted effort to keep them in the darkest reaches of my mind. Easier that way. It allows me a modicum of clarity for the events that followed. Those grisly crimes. The ones that haunted me for so many years, stopped me from sleeping, eating and kept me from living. Because if I allowed the beatings and the neglect to clutter my mind, like so many other people who were only too keen to blame me, I could have gone down the route of believing it all; those terrible accusations levelled against me. But I didn't. I made a determined effort to focus my mind, sift through the debris in my memory banks, make space for logic and reason. And it worked. Bit by bit, the events came back to me, lightening the weight that had dragged me down for so many years, allowing me access to memories I had forgotten existed. Because although I had a blighted childhood, was feral, angry, explosive even, the one thing I became certain of after all the soul-searching and therapy and psychiatric assessments that I have endured over the years, the one thing that is now crystal clear in my mind is the fact that I did not kill those children.

Even as I say the words inside my head, they sound alien; a discrete thought that doesn't belong to me, something that has quietly crept inside my brain and is growing and taking hold of me, making me question everything I ever knew about my past. And yet it does belong to me. I know it does. This isn't something I have dreamed up, like a criminal who, over the intervening years, has managed to convince themselves that they are innocent; twisted their memories, tinkered with the timelines and images in their head, applied their own judgment to it all, I am certain of it all. The girl on the slide, little Pamela, she fell. I know she did. I can see it, her limbs flailing as her tiny body reeled backwards. I can remember my fear, the icy sensation in my stomach as I stood, unable to move or cry or do anything at all to help her. I had been out all morning, doing my best to keep out of my parents' hair as they rolled around the house, bleary-eyed and bad-tempered after a particularly heavy drinking session the previous evening. I had met her at the park. There was nobody else around, just the two of us together in the fresh morning breeze. She had been down that slide at least half a dozen times, squealing with excitement each and every time. Her long, blonde hair flying behind her as she slid down the brightly coloured length of metal, hurtling through the air as she propelled herself forwards, before clambering back up again. I cheered her on, loving the connection I had made with a younger child. I had longed for brothers and sisters if only because it meant I wasn't alone in the house with my parents. I feared them so much it pains me even now to think about it. I watched as she climbed the steps again, her face creased with excitement. Then something happened. A turn of her foot, a sudden surge of adrenalin resulting in one fatal slip, one momentary lack of concentration; I have no idea what caused it, but she fell backwards. The world slowed down for those few seconds. I watched horror-stricken as she fell; I listened to her scream, heard the crack, saw the river of blood that oozed from the back of her head a dark, oily, scarlet slick trailing over the slab of grey concrete.

I stare at Rosie. She is now watching me intently.

'What?' she barks, even though I haven't said anything. 'Why are you sitting there looking all miserable and depressed? It's true. I have no idea who you are any more. You're a stranger to me.'

I pat the bed, certain she won't come over. She takes me by surprise by settling herself on the edge of the mattress, her back rigid with anger.

My voice filters through the warm, muggy air of the room. It's still early but outside the sun is a shimmering, amber promise of the day to come. Perspiration gathers under my armpits and around my hairline. My fingers tremble as I wipe it away and rest my hand on my jeans.

'Please hear me out. In my entire life, nobody has listened to me, heard what really happened. You'll be the first.'

She makes a grumbling noise and I gently traipse my hand over hers. She pulls it away but stays seated, making no attempt to move. I am grateful for such a small mercy; I feel as if I could cry. And so, I talk. I tell her about the day at the park, about my parents, about the rages I suffered, about how damaged I was. I tell her about Beverley, the popular girl at school, how desperate I was to be friends with her, how I hung around her and about how she took me in and we formed a friendship that was asymmetrical; the balance of power always tilted in her favour. But I hung on in there, eager to be part of her gang, a forlorn creature who had nobody. And then I tell her about the day; that day. I relate the tale of the babysitting, how she went out leaving me alone with him. I tell Rosie everything, the whole sorry story, and when I am finished I close my eyes, too afraid of her response, too afraid to see the hatred and disbelief in her eyes. Too afraid to hear the words that she doesn't believe me, that like all the others before, she too thinks I am a liar; a worthless human being. A murderer.

The impenetrable silence seems to go on forever. We sit, side by side, locked together in a shroud of misery, mother and daughter drowning in this cesspit of despair because of who I am.

When she turns to face me, I can barely bring myself to look at her. She is completely innocent in all of this. None of it is her fault and yet here she is, trapped by my past, terrified of the future. Everything we are going through is all because of me.

'Why did they all think you did it?' she whispers.

'Because of my upbringing? Because there were witnesses who said they had seen me suffer huge meltdowns at school? It was a chain of events that, once set in motion, seemed to gather strength, people believing what they wanted to believe, making things fit. We all want to find answers, don't we, Rosie? Nobody likes loose ends. They need tying up, putting away somewhere. It makes everyone feel better having someone to blame. And I was that someone.'

'Did you tell them you didn't do it?' Her brow is furrowed and for one awful minute I fear she might turn against me, start shrieking that I'm making it all up, trying to get out of it with more of my lies, but she doesn't. She sits and waits, her eyes searching mine for answers that are so hard to give.

'I tried, but you have to remember I was a blighted child; deeply damaged, underweight and covered in unexplained scars and bruises. They were determined to portray me as another Mary Bell. People were angry and upset. There were two dead children and they needed somebody to blame. I was the obvious target. I was there, on both occasions. What are the chances of that happening? The prosecution team jumped on those statistics. At least a million to one, they said. And they were right. But at some point, those statistics have to be proven wrong, don't they? Look at the chances statisticians give of being involved in an aeroplane crash or winning the lottery. Yet it does happen to people, doesn't it? Just because it's improbable doesn't mean it's impossible.'

My breathing is shallow and for one horrible moment I fear I might pass out. I don't feel any lighter after speaking out after so many years. I don't feel as if a great burden has been lifted. I just feel sick. My innards shift and churn and my skin is caked with sweat.

'I didn't do it either.' She begins to cry, softly at first, followed by great, heaving sobs as I pull her closer and wrap my arm around her to protect her from all of this. That's all I want to do now; keep her from all harm. Stop the world from throwing any more hurt our way.

'Somebody has it in for me at that school, Mum. All I've done since starting there is work hard and smile at people. I've tried to work out who it is that's doing these things to me but I can't think.'

Her howls penetrate the soft, sultry air, dig into my soul and rip my heart out. I know she didn't do it. I should never have doubted her. Me of all people. Don't I know how it feels to be wrongly accused of something? I let her cry herself out and stroke her hair, keeping my own tears for when I'm alone. They don't come easily to me. Too many memories of things I would sooner forget.

∞∞∞∞∞

Later, when I have showered and cleaned myself of the grime of the past few days, and we're in the kitchen after eating, Rosie tells me something that stops me in my tracks.

'What sort of car was it?' I ask, panic growing inside me.

She shrugs and pouts slightly, her bottom lip jutting out to indicate her uncertainty. 'I don't know. A red one. Too far to see. It was parked up on the road, opposite our driveway.'

'Could you see who was inside?' I ask breathlessly, already acutely aware that anyone from that distance would be too small to see, just a featureless outline.

She shakes her head, and I feel fear tighten inside me, a wide band of unease that wraps itself around my body, tracking its way through my organs and leaching into my veins. I suddenly feel exhausted by it all. I am tired of running, trying to escape from a past that didn't happen. I am utterly powerless against the tide of hatred that follows me wherever I go. No matter what I say or do, people will always think me guilty. This is a life sentence.

'If you see it again, or anything different, anything at all, you must tell me straightaway. You do understand, that don't you?'

She nods, her eyes suddenly wide with anxiety. 'Is this why we moved about all the time? Because people don't believe you and think you haven't been punished enough?'

My breath comes out as a ragged gasp. I am beginning to feel desperate and will do what I have to do to protect Rosie. 'Yes. I'm afraid it is. People want revenge. They don't want the details or facts, sweetheart. Just revenge.'

'Can't we go to the police?'

I shiver at her words. 'As a last resort we can, but I'd rather not.'

She seems to understand this and doesn't take it any further, knowing the complications involved in such a move.

'Why didn't you change your name? Wouldn't that have helped? Given you anonymity?'

I pick at the edge of my shirt. It is starting to unravel, cotton spilling out and trailing down over the hem. The irony of this isn't lost on me.

'Our names were never given out to the public,' I murmur. 'The judge thought it necessary to protect us; well me anyway, so we were only ever referred to as Child A and Child B. And then, when I went to live with Aunt Alice and she gave me her surname, I thought that would be enough. Obviously not.'

Tears prick at the back of my eyes. I swallow and hold them in. Too late for crying now. Way too late. What I need is some kind of inner strength to draw on. God, I hope I have some in reserve. I am worn out by all of this. So tired I could sleep for a lifetime.

'Maybe we should have moved to another part of the country? London or Birmingham or somewhere like that where they would never find us?' Rosie's eyes have a glimmer of hope in them. She doesn't understand the hatred people have for me, that they will do anything to find me, go to any lengths to track me down.

'I thought about it, sweetheart, but when I was with Alice I felt safe, and she had already set up home in the north-east when I moved in with her. I was beholden to her and couldn't ask her to traipse halfway across the country so I could hide. And then she died and I met your father and I thought I was settled. But after he left I felt vulnerable, frightened. I had you to think of. I knew this area quite well, so thought we would be OK, but I found myself constantly looking over my shoulder, convinced people knew who I was.'

'You could have done it then,' she interjects, 'instead of staying around here, moving from one town to another, you could have upped sticks and moved further afield.'

I shrug listlessly. She is right. But would the feeling of being watched have ever left me? I doubt it. At least here, I knew my way around. It isn't so easy moving hundreds of miles away with a small child when you're at such a low ebb

'I hear what you're saying,' I whisper, 'and with hindsight maybe I should have. But I was focused on you and just getting through each and every day. Making such a big move was beyond me. I knew the remote villages round here were the best places to avoid people …'

'Didn't work, though, did it?' Her tone is sharp again. She is starting to develop an edge to her voice, her attitude and body language suddenly harsh and defensive.

'No, it didn't,' I say faintly, 'and I can't apologise enough for that. I am so, so sorry for what I've put you through. All the moving about, the changing schools ... the lying.'

She sighs and we sit there for what feels like an age, two helpless souls drowning in a vast ocean of hopelessness and despair.

'Mum,' she says at last, 'do you think somebody at school knows about all of this? Is that why those awful things keep happening to me?'

Her words barge into me, knocking me off balance, taking all the oxygen out of my lungs. It suddenly feels as if all the air has been squashed out of me. How did I not see it? Make the connection? Jesus ... there are none so blind as those who cannot see. It's her, Beverley. Even saying her name in my head makes me feel sick.

'Rosie,' I say as I stand up, careful to keep my voice steady, 'I'm sure nothing else is going to happen around here, but if you see anything different or odd, let me know straightaway, OK?'

She nods, apprehension written all over her expression, and wraps her arms tightly around her body.

With legs that still feel as if they are about to crumple under me, I head upstairs, checking every window and door is locked as I pass.

BEVERLEY

Work isn't the same without her here. Everything is bland. Just a long and drawn out monotonous stream of dreary tasks. My days are colourless; drab and bleak. They stretch out ahead of me, a dismal streak of nothingness. I did too good a job, that's the problem. I have seen to it that that girl won't return for at least another two weeks. The entire issue was taken to the governors at the behest of the other girl's parents, and they made absolutely certain that her penalty was as severe as school policy allowed. So now I find myself with nothing to focus on, nobody around to punish, nobody to go at. She was such a soft target too. She made it all so easy for me, leaving her computer logged on so anybody could access it. Silly girl. So naive and trusting. And her handwriting was so simple to emulate; no fancy curls or intricate swirling descenders. It was a piece of cake. And after the debacle with the money, well, I kind of knew they would come down hard on her, so I should have expected it, really. This is a good school with a reputation to preserve. They don't take kindly to thieving and bullying. So here I am with nothing to go at, nobody to direct my anger at. She is suddenly conspicuous by her absence.

The hours drag by in a stultifying haze until it is time to leave. This place has suddenly lost its allure, all the sparkle gone out of it. I used to love coming here. It was more than just a job. It was my project, but now I have two long weeks ahead with nothing but a whole host of menial admin tasks waiting for me when I get here every morning. I need to do something to keep me focused, to keep the momentum going. If I back off now, Lissy and her daughter will forget about it, and I don't want that to happen. I most definitely do not want them relaxing, thinking it's all over. Because it will never be over. Not for me, not for my mother. Ours is an ongoing punishment, a lifetime of anguish. And if our lives are such, why shouldn't theirs be the same?

I close the office door and head out, thinking I should really visit my mother, perhaps even take her to the graveyard. Every time I go to see her she asks me about going there, tending to Greg's grave and taking fresh flowers, but I always seem to find an excuse to not visit. I don't know why I find it so difficult to make the journey. It's not far; it isn't the travelling that bothers me. Truth be told, I have no idea what it is about going there that perturbs me. Perhaps it's the thought of being so close to death all those bodies, all that heartache. A sprawling expanse of rotting flesh and old bones beneath my feet. It makes me shudder just thinking about it.

I shake my head. Not today. I cannot face it today. I always have to prime myself before I visit my mother, mentally prepare for her frosty disposition and snide remarks. A lifetime of shouldering the blame for Greg's death is a heavy burden to bear and I find it draining to be reminded of it time and time again. I would also have to inform her that Theresa visited me and stayed over and anything involving my sister is an ordeal. Mum would find excuses for her, tell me she lost her way in life after being surrounded by distress and misery while she was growing up, try to give me another reason to feel guilty. Just a few hours away from the house when I should have been watching Greg, that's all it was. Probably not even that. Then afterwards my life was turned on its head. And it's all because of *her* Lissy bloody Smyth or McLeod or whatever the hell it is she calls herself these days. It's not as if she was even a real friend; she was just someone who followed me around, hung on to my every word, until eventually I relented and took her under my wing. And all because I felt sorry for her. She was the lost kid at school, a true loner, until I took her in. And for a while, we did grow pretty close. We hung around together, went shopping in town, exchanged used bottles of nail varnish and scrappy pieces of make-up that we pilfered from our mums' limited supply … I blink back tears. Just goes to show what happens when you let people into your life. A lesson I will never forget.

I check my hair in the rear-view mirror and slip the key into the ignition. I know I made a promise to myself that I wouldn't visit her house again. Not after last time. Too risky. But the temptation is so great. It eats away at me as I swing my car on to the road. Just a quick drive past. It can't hurt, can it? I'm not breaking any laws, not doing anybody any harm. All I'm doing is satiating my need to do something, *anything* to settle the nagging sensation that is sitting in the bottom of my belly; the one that keeps telling me I haven't quite done enough to scare them, to make sure they don't sleep well at night. Just a little bit more. That's all I want. Just enough for her to snap and confront me. Then I can make my move. When that happens, I can really get things moving. The thought of it sends a bolt of excitement through me, a welcome sensation after such a tedious day. I visualise her, the look of shock on her face when I inform her what I'm going to do, how I have passed her address on to every newspaper I can think of. Then I envisage the next part and shiver; the part only I know about. The part I have waited for all of my adult life.

The draw proves to be too great as I take the road that leads past her house. It's a long drive through curling country lanes that are full of potholes and hemmed in by overgrown hedgerows that blinker my view, but it is so worth it. Everything I do now concerning Lissy is worth it. It's all turning out far better than I ever anticipated. It'll actually be a pity when she's gone. I'll have nothing to throw my energy into, no more planning and lying awake at night mulling over my next move. It will be just me and Warren. Back to how it was before I found her, before she moved so close by. The thought of that fills me with dread. The past few weeks have seen a new me. I have never felt so animated, so alive. I have a renewed sense of purpose and it feels fantastic. The thrill of it all sends a shiver up my spine as I pull up on the road opposite her house and get comfortable. Neighbours or no neighbours, I intend to sit here as long as I damn well please. And if anybody asks what I am doing here, I will toughen up and tell them to go to hell. This is a free country and I have a strategy which I intend to see through to its conclusion. So what if my initial idea has changed and Erica thinks I've taken it all too far? It was never set in stone to begin with. A plan. That's what we had. A fucking brilliant plan and she is now trying to ruin it, to shove her big, fat voice of reason in there and spoil everything. Well, I won't allow it. I absolutely will not allow it.

I feel a burning pain begin to fizz about in my head, flames pulsing and burning my skull. Heat travels through me, growing and expanding, throbbing through my body, energising me. My fists crash down on to the seat. I thrash my legs about and roar into the quiet of the car, my voice filling the calm of the surrounding countryside.

Once I am finished, my fury and frustration vanished, my energy spent, I lean back and smile. I sweep a trembling hand through my hair and smooth the creases out of my clothes ready for the next part the best part. The bit I have longed for, dreamt about, spent my entire adult life waiting for. The thought of it elates me and sends me soaring to another plane. I lean my head back on the seat and let my body be carried away by the thrill of it as it rips through me in a huge orgasmic wave.

LISSY

We spend the day milling about the house, doing not much of anything at all. I am sapped of energy and Rosie is so jumpy and nervous she practically crackles. Anthea Paxton called me and I spoke to her alone in my bedroom. I didn't want to unnerve Rosie and put her even more on edge, so I hid away, did my talking in private and feeling pretty shitty about it all. I've done enough lying and been deceitful enough to last a thousand lifetimes and I just keep adding to it all, scurrying away, discussing my daughter's future without her even knowing. I told myself it was for the best that I was doing it to shield her from yet more worry and distress, sheltering her from it all.

The school haven't taken it lightly, and decided to exclude Rosie for ten days, after they'd called an emergency meeting with the chair of governors and the parents of the other pupil. I doubt boys fighting in the playground, inflicting wounds on each other, possibly even drawing blood, receive anything as harsh as this. But I don't doubt it was to pacify the parents and shut them up, to stop them from spilling the beans to the local newspapers, who love nothing better than to criticise teachers and school policies especially when it comes to the issue of bullying. I didn't disagree or try to make any waves. We need to keep our heads down, Rosie and I, not make ourselves the centre of attention or project ourselves into any unnecessary limelight. I thought it was pointless trying to persuade Mrs Paxton of Rosie's innocence. She would think me completely mad if I were to claim that a member of her staff has perpetrated the deeds of which Rosie has been accused; a member of her staff who has a vendetta against me because of a crime I was accused of committing when I was a child. She would have every right to think me insane and call social services to protect Rosie from her dangerous and crazy mother. I haven't told Rosie that I have spoken to the school. I will, later, when things are less fraught. Instead, I wander around the house, double-checking doors, tugging at windows, pulling at curtains to shut out the outside world, a place full of terror and peril. I'm being overcautious, paranoid even. I know this but I can't seem to stop it. Since making the connection with Beverley being behind the events at Rosie's school I am constantly on edge, my imagination dreaming up all kinds of horrible scenarios. That's the problem with having been exposed to the seedier side of life in prison, I know what people are capable of and how they will stoop to any new low to get what they want.

We eat our evening meal on our knees in front of the television. Our world has suddenly shrunk. The dining room feels too big, too formal. All we want in this time of need is comfort food, and a plate of mashed potato, chicken and gravy seems fitting. I pick at my food, constantly watching for shadows, unexpected movements flickering in my peripheral vision. I am exhausted with it, unable to relax, expecting a bang on the door at any time, listening out for any noise that might indicate somebody is hanging around the house.

I finish my wine and refill my glass, desperate to blur everything, to soften the sharp edges of my overactive mind. I take a long slug and finish the glass then stop. There's a fine line between being relaxed and being so drunk my reflexes no longer function as they should.

I am just beginning to loosen up slightly, to feel marginally safer in my own home, when Rosie calls me. I am in the kitchen washing the pots when her shouts from upstairs alert me, sending me into panic mode. Despite talking myself round, telling myself we are safe here, I still feel apprehensive, my skin suddenly clammy with fear. I have spent the best part of my life on red alert, my senses attuned to the slightest whiff of danger, so it doesn't take much to push me over the edge.

I thunder up the stairs, my body buzzing, perspiration coating my flesh at the sound of her shouts. She is in her bedroom, standing at the window with her back to me when I get there. My first reaction is to drag her away, rip the curtains closed and shriek at her that she must never, ever stand there again, that there are people out there who want to hurt us, do terrible things to us because they think they know my past. They don't. Nobody knows me. I've only just started to reacquaint myself with the person I am. They can't possibly know me when for years I barely knew myself.

'There!' she shouts and I feel as if an invisible hand is pushing me to the floor.

Rosie turns to look at me and then back to the window, her eyes wide with a glimmer of what looks like mild excitement. 'The car I was telling you about. It's parked down there again!'

I can hardly breathe. My chest wheezes and my legs are like lead as I force myself to stagger over to where she is standing. I have no idea what it is I expect to see there, but feel certain that whatever is out there will come to no good. I step forward, every breath an effort, every noise in the room accentuated. A pain whistles round my head as I lean in to where Rosie is standing. I narrow my eyes and stare outside.

There in the distance, at the side of the road opposite our house, is a red car parked up in a lay-by. My blood thickens. The world tilts. I grab hold of the windowsill to stop the room from spinning.

'Do you want me to go down and see who's in there?'

'NO!' My voice is a scream, a frantic, hopeless screech that sends Rosie reeling backwards, her green eyes wide with horror.

I pull her close to me as gently as I can, eager for her to listen. 'Sorry, Rosie. I didn't mean to scare you, but what you're suggesting could be dangerous. We have no idea who is down there.'

She nods and I find myself thanking whichever greater deity is listening for giving me a level-headed daughter who, when the chips are down, knows exactly how to react. So far, she has been superb. Upset yes, angry most definitely, but her comprehension, her ability to unpick the complexities of what has gone before, far supersedes her age. Many would have fled, raged around the house breaking things. But not my Rosie. She is my rock, my reason for getting out of bed every morning and painting on a smile. She is everything to me.

'Who do you think it is, Mum?' she asks, her eyes searching mine for answers I cannot give.

I shrug and pull her away from the window. 'Could be any number of people, sweetheart,' I murmur into her hair as we sit on the bed. I rest my chin on the top of her head, drinking in everything about her; the smell of her apple shampoo, the softness of her pale skin, the delicate feel of her body as she cuddles into me.

'You really should write to somebody, you know, tell them you didn't do it. It isn't fair, all of this. People shouldn't be blamed for things they didn't do.'

Once again, tears threaten to fall. I blink them away. If only she knew of the many cases of wrongful imprisonment, the people who are locked up for crimes they didn't commit, and the ones who walk free for crimes they did. But I can't tell her. What good would it do to colour her judgement of a world she barely knows? I want her to be free of such constraints. I want my daughter to view the world from a neutral stance, to make her own decisions and not get bogged down with all the possibilities of how atrocious a place it can be. It can be a decent place too. I am desperate for her to see that. I so want her to see the good in people.

'Perhaps,' I say softly as I stroke her hair, 'maybe when all of this is over, I might consider it,' I add, knowing fine well I will do nothing of the sort.

We sit for a while in comfortable silence, each of us locked in our own thoughts. The hushed calm of the room is disrupted by a sound beneath us. I sit up, my skin prickling with dread, and listen. Another noise thumps its way up to us. There is somebody at the door. Rosie pulls away from me and we sit and stare at each other for a few seconds before I snap into action.

'Stay here!' I hiss at her before bolting down the stairs. I stand in front of the door, terror soaring through me.

The knock comes again, loud, determined. Whoever is on the other side of that door has something they need to tell me. Or do to me. I step forward and open it a crack, the chain rattling in its casing as I peek through to see Rupert there, standing on my front step, a puzzled expression on his face. My sense of trepidation and mild alarm steps up a gear.

I give him a courteous nod and wait for him to speak. He clears his throat and rubs at his face looking marginally anxious.

'Please don't shout at me. I just wanted to ask if you know who is in the car at the end of the road?'

I feel my face heat up and shake my head at him, my throat suddenly too tight to respond.

'Ah, OK. I was kind of hoping you might know them. I certainly don't,' he says, turning around to glance down at the vehicle before looking back at me. 'And I've asked the other neighbours and they don't know who it is, either.'

A needle of dread races its way down my spine. I suddenly feel hot and cold at the same time. I feel his eyes bore into me and have no idea why I do it whether I am clutching at some kind of hapless idea that he is here to help me or if I am simply desperate for a friend in these torrid times but I slide the chain off the door and step back to let him enter. He hesitates, unsure of what my response is going to be, then strides over the threshold and walks in.

We're sitting in the living room when Rosie comes down. I offer to make tea for him but he refuses and stands up to go to the window.

'She was there yesterday,' he says, his back to us as he speaks, 'I was pulling off the drive when I saw her. She was just sitting there staring up here. Bit weird, don't you think?'

I hope he can't see my shirt pulsating as my heart thrashes around my chest.

'And since she was staring up at your house, I just wondered… well with the dead fox thing and everything…well, that was what alerted me. I was putting it in the boot of my car to take it to the local waste disposal site when I saw her …'

His words hang there, filling the void between us, the great chasm of doubt we now have after my performance yesterday. I should thank him, tell him how grateful I am for getting rid of it, but am unable to speak.

'It's somebody who wants to get back at Mum,' Rosie blurts out and I go cold.

What is she thinking of? We barely know this man, this Rupert who, on a whim, I let into my living room. What was I thinking of? What is Rosie thinking of, saying such stuff to him?

'It's OK, Rosie,' I say as I glare at her. She makes a face as if to say, '*What? What have I done?*'

Fortunately, he doesn't seem to hear her, or if he does, he is wise enough to not show it.

'I'm sure Rupert doesn't want to hear of our problems and woes.' My eyes are wide as I signal at her to stop, but she doesn't.

'A lot of people think Mum did something that she didn't, that's what it is. That woman in the car down there is probably one of those people. Things have been happening to me as well …'

'Stop it, Rosie!' My voice is loud enough to make Rupert turn back to us.

He is the picture of serenity and calm. I can't work out whether he is doing it to lessen an embarrassing situation, or whether he is actually part of this thing. Does he know anything about it? Is it simply a coincidence that he turns up and then all these horrible things start happening to us? Or is he here to do me harm; to do *us* harm and is currently in my living room sizing us up, working out what his next move is going to be? My head aches and it feels as if a red-hot poker is being inserted into my stomach and slowly rotated; my internal organs turning round and round on a burning spit.

'I'm sorry, Rupert,' I mutter croakily, 'but we're having a bit of a problem at the minute, so thank you for letting us know of this person. We'll certainly keep an eye out, won't we, Rosie?'

She nods, a defeated expression in her eyes, and turns her back to me.

'Right,' he says as he begins to edge towards the door. 'Well, I'd better be off. Just thought I'd check; see you were all right and make sure this person hasn't been bothering you.'

I nod and thank him.

'You could take the registration number and pass it on to the police, couldn't you?' Rosie quickly glances at me then looks away, arms crossed, head tilted up, a flicker of defiance in her posture.

'Rosie!' I bark and apologise to Rupert as I chivvy him out.

'No,' he says quietly, 'it's no problem and she is probably right.' He stops and I want to yell at Rosie that she must stop this right now, but they are both suddenly on a roll, their faces fizzing with excitement. 'Tell you what I'll do, if it's still there in a day or two, I'll pass my concerns on to the police, tell them the registration plate and they can maybe find out who it is and why they're parked up there. Just seems weird, don't you think? Nothing but fields for miles and miles and someone just sits there staring up here?'

Rosie nods animatedly.

'I mean, I could understand it if it was a workman eating his lunch, having a break, but it's not, is it? It's a middle-aged woman just sitting there …' He stops, suddenly aware of the fact that I am staring at him, silently willing him to shut up. 'Anyway,' he adds, a touch sullenly, 'as I said, I'll keep an eye out and since it seems to be you she's watching, maybe you should keep an eye out too. Just a thought …' And with that he is gone.

I lock the door and see that Rosie is glaring at me, her eyes ablaze with simmering fury.

'Mum! Why did you act like that? You were really rude. He was trying to help us!'

I walk away from her but she follows me, her feet padding after me like a puppy trailing after its mother, every so often breaking into a run to keep up.

'Look, sweetheart!' I say, exasperated by the whole thing. 'As nice as he seems, we don't actually *know* him, do we? He could be anybody.'

'He's our neighbour!' she cries, her hands lifted in protest, her palms upturned and her shoulders hunched. 'Do you really think he's going to move house just so he can follow you and do mean things to you?'

'Yes actually, I do!' I shout as we sail into the kitchen. I start to bang things about, my frustration rising in great waves. I pick up a cup and put it down again then drag plates out of the dishwasher to put them away. They crash into the cupboard spinning across the surface, drowning out our words.

'Stop this, Mum,' Rosie says, her voice suddenly gentle. She reaches over and puts her hand on my arm. 'I know you said there are some people out there who hate you, but you have to realise that not everyone is bad.'

'How do you know?' I ask. I want to tell her that she has no idea how it feels to have the whole world against you, to have the whole world wanting you dead. She can't begin to imagine what it feels like. She really can't, and nor would I want her to.

'I don't know how I know,' she says softly, 'but I honestly think this Rupert guy is actually being kind. I don't think he is one of your haters, Mum. I think he is just being a general good guy.'

Something deep down in my gut tells me she's right but I can't be absolutely sure about it. In the words of Benjamin Franklin, *"In this world, nothing can be said to be certain, except death and taxes."* I have trusted people before and they have let me down. My friend, Sally, for instance. I got close to her and look what she did to me contacting Davey, telling him all about my past, even sending him newspaper clippings about the case. People are unforgiving, insular; they will turn on you at the drop of a hat. I know this to be true. But at some point, there has to be somebody out there who will help me, someone who will listen to me, perhaps given time they might even believe me. I'm just not sure if our neighbour, Rupert, is that person.

LISSY

Sleep came easy to us. After all the carry-on, both Rosie and I were exhausted. We found ourselves, at nine o'clock, dropping off in our armchairs while *Iron Man 3* played itself out on the TV. I didn't expect to crash so easily. My body was a jangle of nerves and I had the mother of all headaches, but fatigue got the better of me, and after checking and double-checking all the doors and windows for what felt like the thousandth time, we crept up the stairs and collapsed into our beds with the promise we would each wake one another should we be disturbed by the slightest noise.

'And I mean slight.' I had warned Rosie before practically crumpling on to my bed, my eyes closing after only a few seconds and letting the crushing tiredness have its way.

The house is silent when I wake. Rosie is still sleeping soundly, which is hardly surprising given the issues she has had to deal with of late. Her poor brain must be in near meltdown. The light filters into my bedroom through the horizontal blinds, small strips of pale yellow projected on to the walls and fall softly on to the dark blue duvet. My head has a slight residual soreness, the left-overs of yesterday's gargantuan headache that had me in its grip. I lie there for a while, listening to the gentle sounds of early summer outside; the low hum of nearby farm machinery, the chitter-chatter of birds as they search for food and swoop through the warm, cerulean sky. I had forgotten how it could be life when it treats you well. Is this how most people feel each and every morning when they draw their curtains back and stare outside at the expanse of cobalt blue and hear the soothing chirrup of birdsong? No worries about how they will make it through the day without somebody recognising them and following them, their minds full of ill intent?

I throw back the covers and get up, then head straight into the shower, eager to scrub away the nastiness of yesterday and rid myself of the lingering scent of fear. I lather my body and wash at my hair until it squeaks, feeling oddly relieved we had a trouble-free night.

By the time I get downstairs I am beginning to feel half-human, my skin emitting the sweet smell of honeysuckle as I head into the kitchen and prepare breakfast. I decide that today, Rosie and I will spend time in the house together, trying to heal old wounds and discussing our future. She is right, of course; we shouldn't have to spend the rest of our lives running away from crimes I didn't commit. I have no idea how we will manage to do it, but there has to be a way.

I scramble some eggs and put the kettle on to boil. By the time Rosie gets up the kitchen is filled with the heady aroma of buttered toast and fresh coffee. She sniffs the air dramatically as she saunters in the kitchen, her hair askew and a fluffy dressing gown wrapped tightly around her slim body.

'Hungry?' I ask and watch as her eyes light up.

'Starving!' She flops into a chair and fills her plate with piles of honey-coloured toast and as much egg as she can fit on without it all toppling to the floor in a messy, sticky heap.

I pour her some juice and slide the glass over thinking that, at the minute, an impartial observer would be forgiven for thinking we are a normal family.

We sit and eat, our demeanour and conversation civilised and easy, yesterday's events safely tucked away for later when we both feel ready to tackle it all. Rosie tells me about how she would love for us to visit Shakespeare's home in Stratford, and when I ask if she would like to visit the Tate Gallery in London her eyes light up and she nods so rapidly I imagine she sees stars. We've never done anything like that before taken a break and strolled around villages and cities without a care in the world. I've always been too cautious, too frightened. But that's all in the past now. I'm done with running away. I've had enough of hiding.

It's while I'm loading the dishwasher that I hear it, the familiar crunch of gravel telling me somebody is coming up the drive. I stand stock-still, praying it's the postman. It's too early for him, I know it is, but there is a small part of me that doesn't want to face up to the possibility that it's not over, that this thing will never, ever be over. All our plans for holidays and rest and relaxation were pie in the sky; silly pipe dreams. I feel my anger and resentment begin to grow as my chest tightens and a wheeze escapes from the back of my throat. I must keep it together, for Rosie's sake. I look up and listen to the dull rush of water hitting the shower tray above me and think about how excited she looked at the mention of time away, only for it to be snatched away from us. I clench my fists and take a deep breath. Is there ever going to be any end to all of this? *Is it ever going to fucking well stop?*

There is a protracted silence while I listen, my own breathing a deep, roaring echo in my head. The gravel noise has stopped. I can't work out whether this is a good thing or not and am desperately wracking my brains about what to do next when the sound of shattering glass fills the entire house. The floor seems to rock beneath me as I am overcome with a sudden bout of dizziness. I grip on to the kitchen surface until my brain decides to click into action, spurred on by a sudden surge of white-hot fury and deep resentment. Who the hell do these people think they are? Telling me how I should live my life, making me permanently on edge, turning my daughter into a nervous wreck. How dare they? *How fucking dare they?!*

I race through to the hallway and stop, staring down at my slippered-feet. Splinters of glass cover the floor, their sharp edges staring up at me menacingly, daring me to walk among them. I run back to the kitchen and come back with a pair of walking boots which I quickly yank on to my feet. I grab at the keys and am out the door and racing down the path, my senses in overdrive, my heart leaping about my chest in next to no time.

And that's when I see her. Just sitting there at the side of the road. A distant silhouette in a car. A red car. Terror bursts inside me as I slowly make my way down there, sharp bubbles of breath trapped in my chest. Each footstep feels laboured and heavy, my body weighed down with trepidation and dread as I approach the driver. I get close enough to see that whoever it is, is staring down at her phone, her head dipped and turned away from me. I lift my hand and rap on the glass. Very slowly, the head raises and turns to stare at me. And then I see her ...

ERICA

I am in the middle of clearing away our breakfast pots when I get the text. My phone buzzes and I watch as it dances about on the marble worktop, a low ache beginning to form in the bottom of my abdomen. I snatch it up, afraid Arthur will hear it from his study at the end of the hallway, and stare at the screen, horror swelling in my chest. There seems to be no end to this woman's hatred, no depths she will not plumb to get what she wants.

I read the message telling me she has decided to take things a step further. I feel like I no longer know this person. She isn't the same lady I spoke to all those months ago. She has mutated in some way, altered her persona. She is a warped individual and I fear her malicious intentions know no bounds.

I briefly consider contacting somebody about her threats but I am uncertain who to go to. If I were to report her to the police she would simply say we did it together. I would be guilty by association and I can't take that chance. I feel slightly sick as I continue putting pots away and wiping down worktops. I am trapped. This has all spiralled out of control and I do not have the energy to deal with it any more. My appointment with the consultant is at the end of this week and I need to prepare for my operation. Her demented texts are the last thing I want to be dealing with. I thought about blocking her, but then what if she does something really stupid, like contacts me here at home by ringing me on the landline? Or sends me a letter? Arthur is at home all day and has taken it upon himself to open all the post. There is no way of predicting what she will do next.

I look again at the message before peering out of the kitchen doorway. Arthur is holed up in his study, scouring the Internet for job opportunities, emailing old acquaintances to see what's out there. I imagine he'll be in there for a while. Long enough for me to do what I need to do.

I read the message again and let out a trembling sigh.

Taken two weeks off sick. Seems pointless being there now the girl has been excluded. Spending my days watching them. This thing isn't over till it's over. Which it will be soon …

A deep sense of foreboding bleeds into my bones as I type my reply.

You MUST stop this. This is pointless. Go home. Please, go home and leave them be.

I keep it brief. I doubt she will read it anyway. She's only texting me to punish me for backing out. My words will fall on deaf ears, but I send it anyway, feeling I have to do something, *anything*, to get her to see sense. I shake my head wistfully. I think Beverley stopped seeing sense a long time ago now. She is driven by blind fury. It eats away at her, day after day. Soon there will be nothing left of her; nothing but a burning ball of anger. A white-hot orb of fury and madness.

I think of Lissy and her daughter and wonder if she actually deserves any of this. Isn't it time we all moved on with our lives? Let the past be and look forward to the future. All of a sudden, mine is precious. It is finite, my years ahead in limited supply and I, for one, intend to make the most of it. I doubt Beverley cares much about hers. She and her mother don't get along that well; I know that from the conversations her mum has with my mum and the old lady is a drinker by all accounts, more than partial to the odd drop of gin. Beverley doesn't have any children to think about, and her only sister is a drug addict. She only has her husband and he works away most of the time. She doesn't have anybody to live for. When I think about that, it makes me feel quite sick. There is nobody to keep tabs on her, nobody to pull her into line and tell her how to behave. Only me.

BEVERLEY

It seemed pointless going into work when she wasn't there. A complete waste of my time. I don't want to spend my days filing and typing and listening to Shirley drone on and on and on about how bloody marvellous her children are and how beautiful her grandchildren are and how great her husband is. That isn't why I took the position. I took it so I could be near her, Lissy's daughter, and if she isn't in the building then there's no point me being there either. So, I called in sick, told them I had a stomach bug and I would be back when I felt better. I didn't give them a time frame. I may not go back at all yet. I'll just have to wait and see how everything pans out.

My phone buzzes and I sigh, annoyance running through me. I know who it will be before I even check. I haven't yet replied to any of Warren's messages and he is starting to get jittery; panicking about his emotionally fragile wife and her current mental state, hoping there isn't another incident like last time. He will never let me forget that, will he? The child was alone, wandering the streets long after he should have been home, tucked up in bed. All I did was take him back with me and look after him. Such a sweet boy he was. I told him he suited the name Greg far better than the name his parents had given him. Tears prick at my eyes. They took him from me, told me he wasn't mine, made me hand him back. And then they took me …

I should reply to Warren, I know I should, but I've been rather busy, and he is in Switzerland, also very busy with work, so he's not about to jump on the next plane to see how I am, is he? I should reply, if only to keep his worries at bay. Warren helped me out last time I was ill; convinced the police to not press charges, paid for me to spend time in an expensive institution, talked to the family of the little boy telling them it was all a simple mistake and that I was getting help. Once they all heard about my miserable childhood, the loss of my brother, they all softened to his charms and let me be. Poor Warren, having to do all that because of me. Because of *her* and what she did to our family. What she did to my little brother my Greg.

I stare at the screen. As expected it's him, my Warren, making sure I'm managing. I reply that I'm fine but have contracted a stomach bug so have been sleeping a lot and that's why I haven't answered any of his texts. He sends me lots of terms of endearment and phrases about resting up and taking it easy, followed by a stream of kisses. I sign off, telling him I'm about to have a nap, then push my phone into my pocket and grab my keys before heading out the door.

∞∞∞∞∞

The thing about being an early riser is that you get to see the best part of the day. I sit by the roadside and watch flocks of starling dip in and out of the hedgerows, foraging for food. A family of hares tear over the fields, their long bodies arched and graceful as they leap, gazelle-like, across the grass and disappear into a wall of dense shrubbery. It's quite a magnificent sight. I hope Lissy and her pathetic drip of a daughter have appreciated it so far, and not taken any of it for granted, because if I get my way the pair of them won't be around for much longer to see it.

I sit for a good while longer, and am closely monitoring her house for any signs of life behind her curtains when I see it, a darting, flickering movement in my peripheral vision. I watch, completely mesmerised as a hooded figure seems to appear out of nowhere and creep up her driveway. They are cloaked in darkness, wearing a long coat and carrying an object in their right hand. The figure lifts their arm, leans their whole body back and throws what appears to be a rock at the front door, shattering the glass into a million, tiny pieces, the noise taking my breath away as it echoes across the sleepy, morning air. Then the figure turns, face still in the shadows as they run down the driveway before turning and heading into the garden next door where they disappear behind a line of conifers. I raise my head to try to track their movements but the ridge of trees is too high to see beyond it.

I'm not sure whether I feel slighted by it all or whether I want to laugh out loud. Someone else got to her first. I'm not the only one. Somebody else has stolen my thunder.

Grabbing my phone, my hands slick with excitement and the sheer thrill of witnessing such a spectacle, I send Erica a message. I don't care that she will undoubtedly ignore me again, I have to tell somebody about this, and right now, she is the only one I've got. A sense of unfulfilled exhilaration caresses my skin, sending tingles of pleasure through me as I press the letters, my fingers trembling on the screen. I am in the middle of letting her know we are not the only ones who are on Lissy's trail when the noise filters into my brain, disturbing me, making me look up. And when I do, she is there, her face and mine separated by a pane of glass. After all these years, all the desperation and sleepless nights and breakdowns, she is here. And she is staring straight at me.

LISSY

'You!' I shriek, unsure what else it is I should say.

I yank at the door handle but it's locked. I move swiftly around the car, pulling at each door, knowing that if one is locked they all will be. Such a coward. I stare in at her and am incensed to see that she is smiling; a devious sneer that creases her face at the corners, giving her the look of somebody twice her age. In a moment of fury, I step back, lift my foot and kick her stupid vehicle with as much force as I can. I shock myself with how much strength I am able to muster up and am not surprised as I watch her wrestle with the door handle and jump out. As soon as she does, I realise my mistake. She is furious. This woman before me still believes I killed her brother and no amount of talking or trying to reason with her is going to persuade her otherwise. She steps on to the pavement, her chest sticking out slightly as she takes a few deep breaths and strides towards me.

'You have no right to smash my window,' I say, as calmly as I can, despite feeling so scared I fear I may pass out right here on the street.

She stops just inches away from me and I watch with a creeping sense of unease as she glares at me, her eyes wide, full of fire and hatred.

'And you,' she hisses, moving so close to me I can smell toothpaste on her breath, 'have no right living somewhere like this after what you did.'

'It's criminal damage,' I mutter feebly, blood rushing through my ears, hot and viscous as it swills around my head, making me dizzy.

I watch with unabated horror as she takes a step back and begins to laugh. 'You think I did that?' she croons, pointing up to the gaping hole where my window used to be, and letting out another shriek of laughter.

I nod mutely, watching as a trickle of frothy saliva gathers at the corner of her mouth.

'Listen, lady, if I was going to do anything to scare you, it would be far worse than a smashed window.' She juts her chin out in the direction of next door's driveway and flicks her gaze back to me, 'Looks like I'm not the only one bearing a grudge.'

I feel my heart dash about in my chest and place my hand up to my throat to stem the disquieting sensation that has settled there.

'Seems like one of your neighbours has got it in for you, as well,' she says breathlessly. 'I saw somebody dash up there after they hurled the stone at your door. So, if you want to pin the blame on anybody, and bring charges for criminal damage, I think you should look closer to home.'

Rupert? I try to stop my weakness from showing in front of her and bring my hands down by my sides, my legs slightly apart for balance. She is taller than I remember and her glamorous looks have been replaced by a mask of bitterness. Deep lines curve around the edges of her mouth and a mesh of fine wrinkles sit under each eye. Her shoulder-length hair is lighter than it used to be presumably to cover the grey and her clothes are expensive looking. I stare down at my baggy, grey jogging bottoms and old walking boots, caked with mud from a brief amble in the nearby woods, and wonder if she is assessing me as I am her. She will want me to look grubby, and for my face to portray years and years of angst. She wants me to show her that I have had a miserable existence and for my eyes to have a haunted aspect to them a look that tells her I am a tortured soul, that my hellish existence has no end to it.

I stay rooted to the spot. I desperately want to look up at Rupert's house, to let him know that I know what he is up to, but I refuse to let her win. She is watching my every move; every flicker, every shift, every little twitch I make is under scrutiny. I know full well what her game is.

'Well, you would say that, wouldn't you?' I reply frostily. I refuse to be drawn into her little game, this cat and mouse tactic of hers. 'And you need to leave here right now, before I call the police.' I feel my face flush as the words leave my mouth and hope she doesn't notice the tic that has taken hold in my jaw. I press my teeth together to try and stop it.

Her eyes bore into mine as she speaks, 'Go on then, do it. Here,' she says in a low drawl, 'why don't you borrow my phone? Tell them who you are and then see how long it takes them to turn up.'

The burn continues to spread over my face. I bite down harder to control the pulse in my jawbone.

'Do you not think they have better things to do than come running to your rescue? Little ole' you. I mean, Christ almighty, how important do you think you actually are?'

She moves a step closer to me and I blink hard, thinking of who would rescue me if I were to shout out for help. The farmhouse over the road is set in the middle of a field so large it would probably take me a good half hour to get to it. A car hasn't passed on the road all the time we've been standing here. And as for the other neighbours...I think most of them are elderly. I've certainly not seen anybody except Rupert while I have lived here. My stomach plummets when I think of him ... the man who is very possibly behind the breaking of my window. Disappointment engulfs me. I hoped he was better than that. And yet, why would she lie?

An almost imperceptible movement in the corner of my eye catches my attention; a swift turn as Beverley moves closer to me, and before I am able to do anything her hand is twisting my arm up my back.

'Don't say a word, OK? Because if you do, your darling daughter will never see you again. Do you get what I'm saying,

Lissy SMYTH?' She spits the last word out, accentuating its sound, dragging it out to let me know that she knows. 'Or should I say McLeod?'

We start to walk up the drive, the pain in my arm excruciating as she twists it further up my back.

'Did you really think that only changing your surname would work? Did you *honestly* think it would stop me finding you?' She stops and leans forward to stare into my eyes. 'Or is it that you just don't give a shit? Because if I was you, I would have left the country. Packed up and left, taking my tainted offspring with me, rather than hang around here where nobody wants me.'

I stop and try to pull away from her but the pain shoots up into my shoulder taking my breath away.

'Oh, what?' She laughs. 'You don't like me referring to your daughter as tainted? But she is, isn't she? She's part of you, and you, my dear, are very much tainted. I mean,' she says in a shrill, tuneless voice, 'she stole all that money, didn't she? And what about the bullying incident? All those awful names. And that poor child …'

Pain whistles through my arm and up into my neck as I grind to a halt.

'What?' She laughs again, and before I can stop myself, I bring my leg up and knee her in the back of her leg. Her hold over me lessens, but not for long.

Gripping my arm tighter, she also grabs a handful of my hair and hauls me up towards the door, pain howling through my scalp and over my shoulder.

We reach the spread of glass at our feet and stop. She pulls my face towards hers and a fleck of her spit lands on my lip as whispers into my ear, 'And in case you're wondering, I thoroughly enjoyed it, seeing your filthy child being blamed for it all. So much like you, isn't she, eh? Like mother, like daughter. All the same, your type. Wonder how she would get on in prison if I decide to alter my plans, twist stuff a bit; point the finger of blame at her for something I did? The press would have a bloody field day, wouldn't they? They'd take one look at who her mother is and their minds would pretty much be made up, wouldn't they?'

My eyes swing around wildly at her words. I need to get away from her, make a break for it. Somehow, I need to get inside and grab Rosie and get the fuck out of here, just get in the car and leave. I don't care if I have to mow this madwoman down to escape. We just need to get away from this place.

I wince as she pulls me tighter. Years of painting have left me with a weakened upper arm that no number of steroids can alleviate. I swallow down vomit as she pulls me inside, our feet crunching over the shards of broken glass.

'This is the fun part,' she hisses at me, her breath now turning rancid. I gag and try to turn away but she grabs my chin and whips it round so our faces are almost touching. 'This is the bit where our sweet little Rosie finds out what sort of woman her mother is; the bit where I tell her that her mummy dearest is a cold-blooded murderer.'

'She already knows,' I say quietly, the air suddenly still and heavy, loaded with a simmering anger.

'What?' Her voice has a slight quiver to it, before she regains her composure, pulling my head to one side as her fist tightens around my hair. 'You're lying,' she murmurs as she leans in so close to me, I feel sure she could crawl inside my skin. 'Once a liar, always a liar. Let's see, shall we?' And before I can say or do anything she drags me into the living room, my scalp burning and throbbing, my arm feeling as if it's about to pop out of its socket.

'Oh, Rosie! Come and see who your mother has invited round for tea!' Her eyes meet mine and for one awful minute I want to laugh. Saliva is running down her chin, a great glob of it sticking to her grey skin. Her eyes are wild and her hair has come loose and is falling over her face. She looks every inch the lunatic that she is.

I close my eyes and pray that Rosie has her earphones in and is listening to music, or has her TV turned up so loud she can't hear us.

'ROSIE!' Beverley's voice is a roar, so loud it makes me want to curl up and disappear from everything.

My stomach turns to water as I listen to Rosie moving above us. There is the thump of a book being dropped on the floor beside her bed, a sound I recognise only too well, then a squeak followed by the soft shuffle of feet as she climbs off her mattress. My flesh crawls and sweat coats my back as I listen to the heavy thud of my darling daughter's footfall as she pounds her way down the stairs. By the time she enters the living room I am shaking uncontrollably, my eyes wild with fear.

I am unable to look at her, too terrified at what my daughter's reaction will be.

'Mum?' Her voice is a thin warble as she stands staring at us both. Then, after a few seconds her voice again, 'You? What are *you* doing here?' she yelps incredulously as she fixes her gaze on Beverley.

Very slowly I turn to look at Rosie hoping she will pick up on it; see my signal for her to watch me. Our eyes lock, and while Beverley is busy watching my daughter, I mouth the word to her: *RUN!*

It takes a few seconds for my words to register, for the importance of them to slice through Rosie's terror. Her eyes flicker and in a second she turns and races out of the room, into the hallway and out of the door. I listen with a thumping heart as she crunches her way over the hideously sharp fragments of glass and out into the front garden.

Time slows as I wait for Beverley's reaction. For a second, she loosens her grip on my hair then, before I can brace myself for the rush of pain, she pulls me out of the room, her voice booming in my ears, 'Stop her! Tell her to stop or I swear to God I will slit your fucking throat!'

'Too late,' I cry meekly, 'she's already gone. And we both know you're not going to hurt me.' I keep my tone neutral, soothing even. I don't want to upset her or tip her completely over the edge. If I can remain calm, talk to her, perhaps I can bring her round, make her see reason. I can see that it's pointless telling her about my plight. She will never believe me, and it'll only aggravate her all the more. I need to be careful here. She is volatile and I have absolutely no idea just how far she will go with her threats. We used to be friends; I thought I knew her quite well, but we are, and always will be, perfect strangers.

'Don't pretend to know what I'm capable of, Lissy. You can't possibly know that when I'm not even certain of it myself.' She lets out a deep, throaty giggle that bounces around us. 'Anyway, she's not going to get far, is she? There's nothing round here for miles.'

'We have neighbours!' I bark, hoping Rosie has gone to one of the other houses and knocked for help. Not Rupert. Please don't let her have gone to see Rupert.

She goes silent and I can tell she is thinking about it, ruminating over the possibilities of what could happen in the event of a stranger stepping through the door with a police officer following closely behind.

I try the softly, softly approach, hoping she doesn't see through it, praying to God it doesn't rile her even more. 'The one thing I remember about you is how kind you were to me back then. You let me hang around with you when nobody else cared.'

I can hear her breath next to me, hot and ragged, and hope I'm getting through to her.

'You were the only one I had back then, Bev. Nobody bothered about me except you. Even my pa—'

'SHUT UP!' Her voice rings in my ears. 'Just shut up, will you? I'm trying to think!'

I feel her fingers pull harder on my hair and my arm gets hoisted even further up my back. I howl and blink back tears as she drags me over to the sofa and pushes me down, still keeping her fingers tightly wound around my hair. I begin to sob. It's been so long since I've cried, I'm not sure that I will ever manage to stop. Forty-odd years of unshed tears spilling out of me. I cry for the situation I find myself in and I cry for Beverley and what the passing years have done to her mind. I cry for Rosie, out there trying to get help and for the two children who, all those decades ago, were robbed of their chance to live happy and fulfilled lives. But most of all I cry because none of it was caused by me. I am not to blame. I know it now for certain. *I am not to blame …*

My neck clicks painfully as my head is yanked back and Beverley's face looms in next to mine. My nose is running and I can barely see through the stream of tears that I can't seem to control. She lets go of my hair and fumbles in her pocket. Noticing I'm watching her she yanks my arm even further up my back. An arrow of excruciating pain rips me in two. My face twists as I let out an involuntary shriek. I feel a wall of heat as she places her face next to mine and holds something up in front of us, her hand displaying a small object. For one horrible moment, I fear she is going to hit me with it, bring it smashing down on to my face. I think of the rock that was hurled through the window and try to still my battering heart that is fit to burst as it pulsates against my ribs. I try to squirm away and move my free arm but she grips me tighter. Snot and tears merge into a sticky mess all over my face as she holds the object aloft. I hear her screeching voice and a throaty cackle as she waves the object about.

'Smile!'

My pulse dances an irregular beat as I try to work out what is going on. She brings the object closer and I hear her voice once more as she nudges up even closer to me, her hot face pressed against mine. 'Come on, misery guts! SMILE!'

My mouth quivers and my teeth chatter together violently as I try to do as she asks.

'There. Now that wasn't so bad, was it?' she growls, presses a few keys and slots it back into her pocket. 'Right,' she says in a voice that sounds as if we are old friends, 'where were we? Oh, that's right. How could I forget?' And she tugs at my hair once again, pulling it tight.

My scalp aches and throbs, but it's nothing compared to the agonising, howling pain that is ripping through my spine and shoulder and spreading up into my neck. It feels like a flamethrower has been pushed under my skin.

'OK, you're going to do exactly as I say without a fight. Do we understand each other?' she shrieks as I am unceremoniously hauled to my feet.

I want to tell her that I couldn't fight her at this moment in time even if my life depended on it. The pain in my arm is like nothing I have ever felt before. I feel sure it must be broken and think of how I will ever manage to paint again after this. I nod, more tears and snot falling as I do so.

We stagger to the kitchen, my mind full of images of Rosie and Rupert, her fighting him off as he turns on her with a manic expression plastered on his face and a rock in his hand. I let out a whimper and without warning my head is slammed on to the kitchen surface, the side of my face meeting with the marble worktop. The room spins and a bellyful of vomit rises up my throat, hot and acidic. I swallow it down and try to stay upright, my legs buckling under me, an explosion of pain filling every inch of my skull.

'Stop crying and moaning! STOP IT!' Her screams silence me.

This is it. All those years of being terrified of venturing outside, of being recognised, finally culminate in this. I gulp back the tears and try to concentrate. I can't let this happen. Rosie needs me. I have to protect her from all of this. If anything happens to me she won't be able to survive all the media attention that will ensue. They will eat her alive.

I feel myself being pushed into a sitting position and stem another howl of agony as my arm catches on the high back of the kitchen chair.

'Right, this is what is going to happen.' Beverley's voice is clipped and official. It sends a wave of sickness through me as I try to figure out what she is planning on doing. 'I am going to contact every newspaper I can think of and let the entire world know where you are, so if you're thinking that this is just a minor occurrence, me finding you, if you're thinking that I'm the only one who knows you're here, then think again. By this time tomorrow the world and his wife will be after your blood. And Rosie's, obviously.' She lets her words hang there, hoping they will unnerve me.

I remain as still as I can, my blood surging and pulsing through me. And all the time I am working out how I can escape from her clutches. I need to get to Rosie. She is my priority.

'And by the time they all descend on your house, and by God they will descend, I will be gone and you'll both be here, ready for them.' She lets go of my hair and I freeze as I feel her fingers begin to stroke it strand by strand, untangling the knots and smoothing it down. 'But, of course, I can't guarantee what sort of a state you'll both be in by then. Or whether you'll even be well enough to tell them what happened.' She continues stroking and straightening, my head flopping backwards and forwards as she tugs at the tangles, freeing them up. 'Not that it matters, anyway. Even if you're well enough to name me, do you really think any court in the land is going to care what I did to you both? I doubt they'll even believe you. You're not exactly an upstanding member of the community, are you? Or a model citizen? No,' she continues, 'I can do whatever I want to you and nobody, my dear, will give a shit.'

I close my eyes. She is right. I know that, which is why I must find the strength to fight her off, to get her away from me and go and find Rosie. That's just how it is. I've always known I would be on my own in this world; that there would be so few people willing to help me if things turned sour.

'I mean, last time,' she says, her voice suddenly soft and non-threatening, 'it was quite rewarding. Knowing the only real friend you'd had since getting out of prison believed me when I followed her home and told her about you. But this,' she says with a sudden hiss, 'this is beyond anything I've ever dreamed of. It's just so fucking brilliant.'

I gasp and another sob escapes as I try to take it all in. 'It was you,' is all I can say. I feel momentarily winded, all the oxygen sucked out of my system, my lungs empty and deflated.

'Of course, it was me!' she shouts pulling my arm back again. 'But all that resulted in was you being left on your own. So what? There's plenty of lonely people out there! Hardly a fitting punishment for a crime as terrible as yours, is it?'

She begins to sing softly, a tuneless dirge that fills me with revulsion.

I can barely breathe. The room spins. It was her. All this time and it was her. I swallow hard and take a few stilted breaths. She is going to kill me. I can see that now. I think, deep down, I've always known it.

I trail my gritty eyes over the kitchen and try to think of all the positives. For one, I know this house better than she does. I have the keys. I also know all the hiding places. And I know exactly where I keep all the sharp knives. Trying to still my breathing, I shift slightly under her touch. I want her to think I'm relaxed, that she is controlling me. I also want to clear the fog in my brain. I need to stay alert, have my wits about me, and fear will only clutter my thinking. If I can free myself, get my arm back in place, I'll be able to make a run for it, lock her in the house while I grab Rosie and escape.

I am rapidly trying to go through all the possible ways of freeing myself from her clutches when I hear it, the crunch of footsteps coming up the drive. My heart leaps into my throat as I listen. More than one set of feet marching up towards the front door. Rosie? And Rupert? Just as I fear my head will burst with the tension, Beverley stops. She has heard it too.

'Looks like your daughter has decided to join us,' she croons, as her grip on my arm tightens and she leans down so that her face is next to mine. I feel her warm breath as it wafts around my face. 'Fasten your seatbelts,' she says in a sickly voice that makes me want to retch. 'The real fun is just about to begin.'

ERICA

I cry out loud and drop my phone into the sink. It spins around on the porcelain before coming to a standstill, rocking against the surface with a clatter. I grapple with it, dropping it again as I try to pick it up with trembling fingers and rapidly failing dexterity. Tears blind me as I finally manage to scoop it up and dry it off on my sweater.

Slumping down on to a nearby stool, I stare again at the screen, at the hideous image that is jumping out at me. Two faces, one sneering, lips curled and twisted with a contrived smile that is more of a grimace and the other, terrified, her face wet with tears, eyes bulging, her mouth gaping with fear. My hands shake violently as I drag my fingers over the screen to enlarge it. The image is even worse close up. A victim and her attacker here on my phone. I quickly close it and wipe my eyes with my sleeve, my arm shaking, my entire body gripped with panic. Shutting my eyes tight against it all, I take a shuddering breath while I try to think what to do. I knew Beverley was angry, unhinged even, but I had no inkling she would actually go through with something like this. My face burns with humiliation and fear. I am associated with all this. I'm a part of it whether I want to be or not. Terror and an unshakeable sense of accountability eats at my brain. I helped to create this monster, this unstoppable situation that is unfolding right in front of my eyes, and I now have no idea how to bring an end to it or what I should do next.

'Everything OK?' Arthur's voice behind me makes my head buzz.

I missed his entry into the room. I'm normally acutely alert to his movements but this time he has caught me unawares. My mind was elsewhere and now he has snuck up on me and I'm not sure I am in the right frame of mind to cover up my tracks. I'm not sure I even want to. It's been truly exhausting keeping all of this to myself for so long. And isn't this what we both wanted? Complete honesty and transparency with everything we do? It can't have been easy for Arthur, having to admit to losing such a powerful and highly paid job. But he did it, and yet here I am still clinging on to secrets that could be far more damaging than any redundancy or financial repercussions brought about by a job loss. I need to do this. I have to find the courage to own up to what I have done. I have helped to cause this trauma and now I have to try to bring an end to it.

'Well,' I reply, my voice threatening to fail me, 'I'm not sure, really.'

I watch his eyes widen, see a pulse begin to build in his temple as he tries to assess me, work out where this is all going.

'The hospital?' he says quickly. I register the look of panic in his eyes and quickly shake my head to reassure him.

'No, it's nothing to do with the hospital,' I say softly, my head dipped as I try to hide the shame I feel at what I am about to tell him.

'Then what?'

I scrutinise his face, trying to freeze frame his expression and stance; the way his shoulders drop ever so slightly when he's concentrating on something important, the azure of his eyes as he watches me, the slight tilt of his head as he waits for me to speak. These are all the things I want to remember about him before I change everything with what I am about to say; before I shatter his illusion of me when he finds out this terrible, terrible thing that I have done and what sort of a monster I really am.

I let out a deep breath, my body almost convulsing with the effort of it, and push my phone towards him, hoping the picture will somehow be enough for him, that it will explain everything to him without me having to admit to any wrongdoing in all of this. I blink away tears. It won't, I know that. Of course, I do. He will open the picture and be confronted with a horrific image of two people he has never met before, one of them sneering at the camera and the other with such an expression of fear and grief on her face that it will take his breath away. He will want to know why such a grotesque photo is on my phone, who sent it to me and what it has to do with me. And then I will have to tell him.

I watch his face as he opens the picture and his brow knits together. I swallow hard and hold my breath …

BEVERLEY

It is so near perfect, so much better than I ever imagined it could be, I almost cry. I don't, however. Tears are for the weaklings of this world; all the hopeless victims and people who enjoy sitting about wringing their hands and telling anyone who will listen their tales of woe. The ones who get crushed underfoot, they are the ones who sit about weeping. But not me. I am growing in strength, day by day, gathering muscle as I plough through with my plans, no longer an impotent bystander while the scales of justice decide to reward the criminals and punish the innocent.

I pull her arm harder and higher up her back and watch as she squirms and sobs beneath me. She deserves to be in pain and I have earned the right to watch.

I glance around the kitchen for anything I can use to hurt her even more, to show her who is in charge here, but practically every surface is bare. She is a minimalist. A place for everything and everything in its place. And I thought I liked things neat and tidy.

I am guessing all the sharp implements are hidden away somewhere and I'm in the process of mentally working out where they can be when I hear it; footsteps outside. I wonder if that's why she has a gravel drive? So nobody can creep up on her and catch her unawares? It wouldn't surprise me one little bit. She has every reason to feel scared and be constantly looking over her shoulder.

I tremble with excitement. She can't have gotten far, her daughter. No police around these parts. No need, is there? What on earth could happen in a sleepy hamlet such as this one? I'll bet Oakhill has the lowest crime rate in the whole of the country. Until now, that is.

I lean down and whisper in her ear about how excited I am at what's going to happen next. Truth be told, I have absolutely no idea what's going to happen, but if that next-door neighbour of hers is as furious at her as I am, then I think I have very possibly found myself the perfect accomplice.

The air is thick with anticipation as the footsteps grow closer, crunching over the gravel and pieces of shattered glass, tramping through the house. More than one set of feet, and they are heading our way.

My breath becomes slightly laboured as I prepare myself for whatever it is I am about to be faced with. I wanted excitement and vengeance and it doesn't get much better than this. Adrenalin fizzes through me while I wait, Lissy's hand in mine as I keep it tucked tightly up her back, giving it a good yank every so often to remind her of her predicament.

There is a second's silence, an exquisite moment of the unknown; the calm before the storm. I lower my head slightly, let out one long shuddering breath and then look up to see them standing there in front of me.

∞∞∞∞

'WHAT?' is all I can say before my voice leaves me. For what feels like an eternity, I am speechless, my body locked rigid with alarm. All I can feel is the rapid pulse of Lissy's blood as it hurtles round her body. My own heartbeat thrashes around my ears, a thick whooshing noise as it forces itself through my veins. Even my voice sounds distorted as I try to make sense of what it is I'm seeing, this sight before me. It isn't possible. The whole thing is like a warped version of reality. It defies all logic; a completely parallel universe.

'Not expecting me, then?'

I shake my head and look down to see Lissy screwing her eyes up, trying to work out who this person is that is standing in front of us, holding her daughter fast with his big, strong arms. The daughter is pale and is held in front of him. Her eyes are brimming with tears and I can't be absolutely certain, but it looks like a bruise is beginning to develop across her left cheekbone, a bloom of sepia slowly spreading over her flawless skin.

'Come on, MOVE!' he shouts to the girl as he pushes the back of her legs with his knee.

They stumble forward, and it's only then that I see she has her hands held tightly behind her back with his large fingers, while he is holding a fistful of her clothes with his other hand to push her along.

I'm not sure whether I should feel terrified or elated by his appearance. It's certainly unexpected.

'Sit!' he barks at her and she slumps awkwardly in a chair opposite her mother. Their eyes meet and the girl's chin trembles as her mother gives a weak smile and raises her free hand to reach across to touch her.

'Oh no,' I say with a smile, 'no touching. Not today.' I pull her back, lifting her arm up her back again. Just a slight push, that's all it takes to stop her in her tracks, to make her take a deep gasp and think twice before she tries to do anything stupid.

A deathly hush fills the room until he looks over to me and smiles. 'Bet you weren't expecting to see me again, were you, eh?'

I shake my head silently. I don't want to speak just yet. His appearance has left me slightly stunned and rather edgy, so I want to take some time to think about what it is I'm actually going to say.

'Please,' the young girl cries in such a pleading voice it makes my toes curl. 'Please, just let us go and we promise we won't tell a soul, will we, Mum?'

They both shake their heads vigorously, their eyes glassy and wide as saucers. I watch, mesmerised as a stream of tears cascade down their faces. Too late for tears. It's all far too late for all that emotion, all that fucking nonsense.

'You've had decades to do your crying,' I say, in a voice that sounds as if it is coming from somebody else.

'Are we not going to do any introductions, then?' Daryl asks, his solid belly swaying from side to side as he speaks.

I ignore him, my mind working overtime as I try to work out what to do next.

'Mum, he's hurt Rupert!' Rosie's voice rings out across the kitchen, but before the girl can say anything else, Daryl's hand comes down and swipes hard across the side of her face with a resounding thwack.

I feel her mother flinch and drag her arm higher before she can do or say anything. Daryl is such a fucking idiot. Doing something like that is bound to freak her out and she will possibly try to make a run for it. That's the last thing I want. I've waited far too long for this moment. She is staying here as I long as I decide to keep her.

A sobbing sound emanates from Rosie and I watch as she lifts her head, blood trickling down from her nose. There is a scarlet handprint covering the side of her face and her neck is flushed bright red.

'Leave her alone!' Lissy's voice is a squeak as I apply more pressure on her shoulder.

'Shut up,' I hiss, my patience waning rapidly. 'The more you talk, the worse things will be for the both of you.' She nods and more tears flow down her pale, skinny face. Good enough for her.

'So, what's the plan then, eh?' Daryl asks, an orb of sweat visible under his armpits, his shirt darkened with the moisture. He is smiling and for some reason this sickens me. He shouldn't be here. This is my moment, not his.

'Why were you following me, Daryl?' I bark at him and it takes a second for my question to sink in. He looks bewildered and then starts to smile.

'Follow?' He laughs loudly. 'I haven't been following you! What makes you think that?'

I try to mask my confusion. He's lying. He has to be. I have no idea why he has done it and I refuse to play games with him. He wants me to ask why he's here but I'm not going to. I won't stoop to such levels. I'm better than that.

I shake my head and turn away. A few minutes to gather my thoughts; that's all I need.

'I saw her a few weeks ago. That's how I ended up here,' Daryl says, and now I am all ears. 'Just a stroke of luck, really.' He leans over and stares at Lissy, his stomach pressing into the back of the chair, folds of fat protruding around and through the edges of the wooden slats. I exhale loudly and look away. 'Unfortunately for you, I saw you when I was dropping your neighbour off after I picked him up at the station,' he croons at her, 'you really should be more careful, you know. Standing in your front garden like that, letting everyone know where you live. Out there, watering plants like lady of the fucking manor. The likes of you should be hiding away, not flaunting yourself to the public. And you've never changed. Still a skinny little runt.'

I see Lissy's shoulders drop ever so slightly and hear a small moan escape from the back of her throat.

'He hit him, Mum. This man hit our neighbour and he's unconscious in th—'

'I've already told you to SHUT THE FUCK UP!'

I watch as both of them shrink away, fearing another beating, and I don't know if I want to laugh or feel sorry for them.

'Shut up!' I cry, furious at them all. This is my moment; my piece of utopia and they are all ruining it. I pull Lissy to her feet. 'Come on you, UP!' and nod to Daryl to do the same with the girl. He complies with a crooked smile, hoisting her upright with a rough jerk of his hand. He is only too happy to assist me; like a puppy, so eager to please, so desperate to be wanted.

'In the garage,' I say after some thought. 'We can tie them up in there.'

He grunts slightly as we drag them along, their feet slipping and twisting underneath them. I can see the girl's head as it swivels from side to side. She thinks we're going to kill them. I catch sight of her eye and wink. Let's just see how events turn out shall we? That's where the buzz lies; not knowing what's going to happen next. The unknown. It's all part of the fun.

ERICA

I watch Arthur's face, looking to see if I repulse him. I should. I repulse myself. He would have every right to leave me. I've done a terrible thing; a dreadful thing and now people's lives are at risk. If anything happens to Lissy and her daughter it will all be my fault. The blame will lie squarely at my door.

I drop my gaze, no longer able to watch him, to see the look in his eyes as he works out what to do next. The faint hum of the fridge in the corner of the room takes over everything, a distorted groaning sound that bellows in my head, a roaring reminder of this awful act that I have initiated.

'Is she mentally ill?' he says and I snap back into focus.

'I-I didn't think so, but now, well now …'

'You don't think so?' he says, a deep furrow appearing in his forehead just above the bridge of his nose. 'She has done this and you're saying you're not sure? Dear God, Erica, what were you thinking of, getting involved with somebody like this?' His voice is growing in crescendo and I don't think I can stand to see the look of horror and disappointment on his face as he glowers at me.

'You have to remember, Arthur, she had a dreadful time as a youngster, and—'

'So did you! But you haven't kidnapped somebody, have you?'

My heart feels like it's going to explode right out of my chest. 'I know, but her family didn't handle it as well as we did,' I say, my breath pulsing out of me in short, stuttering gasps. 'Her father committed suicide and her sister is a drug addict. Beverley's mother blames her for all that went on Greg's death, her dad's death, her sister's addiction. She should never have gone out and left Greg

198

with Lissy. If she had stayed in the house as she was told to then none of it would have happened.' I stop, suddenly breathless, my face hot with humiliation at the fact I am associated with all of this.

'We need to call the police. You do know that, don't you?' He is calmer now. His brain has clicked into work mode and he is planning, working out a way to resolve everything.

I am awash with relief. Arthur knows. He is here with me and he is going to sort it all out.

'I didn't know she was actually going to do anything like this, Arthur,' I say quietly. 'I'm so sorry.' I keep my eyes lowered, not wanting to see the look of disgust in his expression.

'It's fine. You're not the one involved in it. It's her, this Beverley who's done this, not you. Problem is,' he says, and my blood freezes, 'we don't know where she is, do we? How can we tell the police where to look when we don't know where she is?'

Something stirs in my brain; a memory slowly coming to life. A fragment of a thought pushing its way forward until I jump up and grab at my phone.

'Here!' I half shout, thrusting the screen in front of Arthur's face. 'She sent me her address and I meant to delete it but didn't! It's here!' I say, panic and tension rippling through me at the thought of being able to help her, to bring this whole sorry mess to an end. 'Oh God, we need to ring them as soon as possible. Oakhill is where she lives, Arthur. Oakhill in North Yorkshire ...'

I watch as Arthur punches a number into his own phone and stares at the address on the screen in front of him. My chin trembles. He gives me a smile and winks at me and it's then that I know he is in charge once again. I lean back in the chair and let the tears come.

LISSY

Daryl? What has he got to do with all of this? I feel as if I can't breathe properly. What the hell is going on here? I wince and blink back tears as Rosie and I are dragged along, our legs weak with fear. My heart breaks as I watch my daughter get assaulted and manhandled by that thug. The look on his fat, ugly face tells me he's enjoying this as well. He always was completely gross. People don't really change, do they? We are what we are, and he is, and always will be, a complete monster.

I am furious at my own powerlessness against these two maniacs. I have to do something or we will both die. I feel sure of it. A picture of Rupert flits into my thoughts. He was innocent all along and now he had been brought into this situation, become embroiled in my past. He is hurt next door. He could be bleeding to death with nobody to help him. And he is unable to help us. What a *fucking* awful mess this whole thing is.

'In there!' I hear Beverley's voice as we stumble into the back garden and head towards the side door of the garage. I meet Rosie's eyes and mouth to her to stay silent. She nods sagely, terror dilating her pupils and drawing all the colour out of her skin. A large red welt is appearing on her face and as I watch it grow and discolour. I want to launch myself at him, knock him to the floor, and tear at his skin with my nails. How dare he? *How fucking dare he?*

'Rope,' Beverley says, her voice low and croaky. Hope grows in me that she is starting to lose her nerve and has thought better of killing us. 'We need something to tie them up.'

I pray they find something, otherwise their frustration and fury will only increase, and if that happens there's no telling what they might do. In my mind, I see Daryl's hand as it hits Rosie's face, and I try to think of a way out of this. I need to do something.

'Here!' Daryl's voice echoes through the emptiness of the garage. 'No rope but some tape down here with these paintbrushes and stuff.'

'Perfect,' Beverley says, in a voice so dead and lifeless it terrifies me. A dagger of ice scrapes down my spine.

They make us sit back to back on the concrete floor and tape our hands together behind our backs before pulling off two long strips and slapping them across our mouths. He is loving this. I can see by his eyes. There is fire in them. His skin is red and he is barely able to keep still, rubbing his hands together and shifting from foot to foot as he watches Beverley apply a second strip of tape over our mouths pressing it down so hard I feel sure my teeth will crumble away. They tape our ankles together and step back, staring at us both.

I make a muffled cry but they ignore me, too high on their own excitement, too involved in their own sick plans.

'Right, we'll leave them here for now. Until I've worked out what to do next.'

I watch the way Beverley shuffles her feet across the floor, notice her awkward gait, how her head is lowered, and I realise she is unravelling fast. My stomach shifts and turns. She could go either way; lose all sense of reality and slice our throats open, or lose her nerve and soften. I have no idea which way it will go and hope that she sees sense. I shut my eyes tight and pray for a miracle.

BEVERLEY

'Some place this, isn't it?' Daryl says breezily as we head back into the house through the back door. I try to ignore him. He's ruined this whole thing; scuppered my plans and sent me off-kilter. I can't seem to think straight any more since he's shown his face.

I look around and try to see the house through his eyes but all that greets me is a huge lounge and a clinical kitchen. Everything has suddenly lost its shine, the allure all gone now I'm in here.

'She always was a skanky bitch, wasn't she? How the fuck did she end up with a place like this?' He is walking the length of the living room, his fingers trailing over the walls and along the length of the cabinet that sits halfway along the room.

I shrug, no longer interested in her financial situation. I need to work out what to do next. An idea of driving them miles away from here and dumping them in a field or a quarry somewhere really remote pops into my head and gladdens my heart. I wouldn't give them any money or water. If they make it back home then they make it back home. And if they don't … well that's just tough, isn't it? I smile to myself. It's an appealing option.

I sit on the sofa, feeling the expensive leather spread and sigh under my weight. Daryl waddles over, hitching his trousers up before sitting down next to me. I stare at him, unable to believe this is the same person I had the most terrible teenage crush on all those years ago.

'She deserved it after what she did, anyway,' he says sharply. I don't reply. He shouldn't be here. He has spoilt everything.

'Bet she thought it was you, didn't she?' he laughs.

'What was me?' I ask, not really interested in what he has to say. I need to think. Get this sorted.

'The letters and stuff.' He chuckles. I don't answer him. He'll tell me without me prompting him anyway. He is full of himself today. Never changed. But then, people don't, do they? The passing of time can enhance or lessen our traits and characteristics, but deep down the very essence of who we are never really alters.

'After I saw her in the garden that day when I dropped her neighbour off, I couldn't resist.' He guffaws as he slaps his leg. 'I mean, if she's gonna make herself that obvious then she should expect a bit of aggro, shouldn't she?'

I stare at him, unblinking. He doesn't seem to notice my dull, uninterested expression and carries on as if I am interested in what it is he's got to say.

'So, I sent her a letter saying she was a murderous old monster.' He cackles loudly as I think about the one I sent.

Getting Rosie's mobile number was a doddle. All I had to do was ask one of her friends, telling her it was to put on the system as a contact number because she was new to the school. She only had one pal anyway and she gave it to me without question. Some kids are so naive and trusting it's frightening. I had no idea Daryl was at it as well, sticking his oar in, getting involved in something that has nothing to do with him.

'And then,' he adds, 'I knocked a fox over while I was doing a drop-off in the next village. Fucking stupid thing ran right out in front of me. Nearly dented my bumper bar, it did. The idea came to me straight away. I dragged it into the boot and dumped it on her front step, right here!' He hoots with laughter, throwing his head back manically.

I say nothing, hoping he will tire of my silence and leave me alone. I need some solitude to help me think. He doesn't move for a good while and I can feel him watching me, but then I hear the creak of leather and feel his body heat close to me as he sidles along, his fingers trailing over my back. I edge away, but he moves even closer, his leg touching mine.

'We had some good times, didn't we, Bev?' He smiles at me and a waft of halitosis drifts in my direction. I close my mouth and exhale through my nose, the stench too much for me to bear. 'Some great times,' he murmurs quietly, 'the best,' he says, and places his hand on my knee. 'Until she came along, that is, and spoilt it all. Stupid fucking bitch.' His hand drops and I flinch as he moves it to the inside of my leg.

'What are you doing?' I whisper and feel a flicker of disgust as he starts to move his fingers, trailing them up the inside of my thigh.

'What am I doing, Bev?' he says huskily. 'You remember this, don't you? I'm doing what you and I did best. What we could still be doing if it wasn't for that silly old hag.'

He continues to slide his fingers upwards until he reaches the top of my thigh.

'Still hot to trot, Beverley darling, eh?' he says as he pulls my pants aside and stops before looking in my eyes, perspiration sitting around his hairline and on his top lip. 'You always were up for it, weren't you?'

'Daryl, get off me,' I whisper, the fog of anger and confusion lifting from my brain.

He laughs, a pathetic snorting chortle before leaning into me even closer. 'We both know you don't mean that, sweetheart. We both know you're up for it. Always have been, always will be. Once a goer, always a goer. The best fuck in the whole of the north.'

I lean away from him, his hand dropping between my legs. 'I'm sorry?' My voice is unrecognisable to me, like a whisper coming in from outside, something completely disconnected to me.

'Aw, come on! Don't pretend you don't know,' he says, a smirk spreading across his face. 'My mates told me all about your antics at university.'

I suddenly feel hot all over, my clothes sticking to me like cling film, perspiration coating my skin.

'What did you just say?' I gasp, my voice almost a shriek.

He pushes away from me, anger behind his eyes. 'Don't come all innocent with me, Beverley. From what I've heard, you had a fine old time at Newcastle University, shagging anything that moved. You even slept with one of my mates. He told me all about it; said you were so drunk it was like fucking a dead fish.'

I stand up, heat escaping from under me as I stagger away, fear and anger blinding me.

'You haven't denied it, though, have you?' he shouts as I lurch over to the edge of the room. I need to get away from him, away from his stench and huge stomach and greasy skin. I just need some time to think, to get my head sorted and think straight.

'But you wouldn't do it with me, would you?' he shouts after me as I continue to pace the room.

'I was only thirteen, for Christ's sake!' I bellow at him, my chest wheezing, my head throbbing as I stumble about, clinging on to the surfaces of the furniture for support.

'Yeah, well,' he mutters sullenly, 'if it hadn't been for what happened then maybe you would have hung around a bit longer, but instead you disappeared off the scene straight after. Nobody saw you. You forgot all about me, and then you went off to university and I never saw you again.'

I swing round to stare at him. 'Disappeared off the scene? I was bloody distraught, for God's sake!'

He shrugs and dips his eyes to stare at the carpet. 'She deserved it though, didn't she?'

I feel my heart crawl up my neck. 'Who?'

'Her,' he says, 'that bitch tied up in the garage. She deserved what happened to her. Getting the blame for it. After she left your house she tried it on with me, you know. Told me we could have something going. I told her where to get off, said you were the only one for me. That was just before I went to your place whe—'

'STOP!' I spin round to stare at him.

'Told you, I gave her short shrift. Told her where to get off.'

'We agreed!' I shriek at him. 'We said that we would never tell anybody you were round mine that night. We were never going to speak of it again. It was bad enough for my parents having to deal with what they had to deal with. Bad enough I spent half the night out with you,' I say, tears coursing down my face. 'But you promised you wouldn't tell anybody you were there after she left.'

'And I didn't, did I? You really think I wanted the police coming to my house when my dad had just got out of prison for handling stolen goods? Jesus, how fucking stupid do you think I am?'

I don't speak, too afraid of giving him my honest reply.

'Don't matter now, anyway, does it?' he says sullenly. 'Doesn't matter who did it or what happened. She's served her time and always was a complete fucking freak so ...'

Blood roars up my neck and swims around my head.

'What?' I hear myself say, 'what did you just say?'

He shrugs lightly, completely unruffled by my outburst.

'I said it doesn't matter who did it or what actually happened. I mean for fuck's sake, Bev, he was left with her for most of the night, wasn't he? He was up there covered with sheets and blankets when I went up.'

I try to align my thoughts, to go back to all those years ago. Daryl had come to the door and I had made the mistake of letting him in. He had practically fallen on me, pawing me and shoving his hand up my top. And at first, I liked it. He was one of the most popular lads in the school. Telling him to take a hike meant he may have dumped me and I didn't want that. I liked the status that being with him brought; all the attention and admiration at being Daryl's girlfriend gave me a real boost. But then he wouldn't stop. His hands became unmanageable, pulling at my jeans, his saliva covering my face and neck, hot and sticky. I could feel his erection pressing against me and knew he didn't plan on taking no for an answer. I was only thirteen, full of bravado, but underneath it all I was still scared. So, I pushed him away, told him he had to leave or my parents would kill us both. This infuriated him, brought out the worst in him, a raging, frustrated, young man with bulging eyes and a temper that knew no bounds. I swore at him, told him to get out.

'Yeah, when I've had a piss, OK?' he had said and disappeared upstairs.

I remember standing in the lounge, listening to the crash of my own heartbeat while he was up there, wondering if he would come down and start again, get so carried away he wouldn't stop. I made the decision there and then that nobody would know he had been round. I had been under strict instructions to not let him in when my parents were out. It was bad enough I had been out for most of the night but if they discovered he had actually been in the house … my life wouldn't have been worth living. Daryl's family were a bad lot; in and out of prison, heavy drinkers who thought nothing of fighting in the street should anyone look at them the wrong way. His older brother had only recently appeared in court, charged with aggravated assault, and as Daryl was upstairs I began to worry he would do something similar to me. When he finally came down his face was flushed and I worried he was going to do something awful to me, but he didn't. He shuffled about a bit saying he'd better be off anyway. I recall feeling so relieved that I almost pushed him out of the door, yelling at him he mustn't tell anybody he had been here.

'What are you saying, Daryl?' I mutter quietly, too afraid to voice my deepest, darkest fears out loud. 'What is it you're trying to tell me?'

He shrugs and pushes his bottom lip out. A tiny globule of spit appears at the edge of his mouth and dribbles down on to his chin, glistening on his pulpy, reddened flesh.

'All I'm saying,' he murmurs, wringing his hands tightly, 'is that she deserved it, all right? Whatever happened to her, she had it fucking coming!' He forces his bulky frame out of the seat. It wheezes gratefully, reshaping itself as he begins to pace around the room, his feet pounding across the wooden floor.

I can hardly breathe. My head throbs and my body expands with terror and rage as I analyse his words, try to sift through to the hidden meaning underneath all the anger and guff.

'What happened upstairs, Daryl?' I ask softly as I slyly put my hand in my pocket and grip my keys, running my fingers along the serrated edge. Not particularly sharp but enough to do any damage should I need to protect myself.

He doesn't answer me. I try to keep my voice as calm as I possibly can when I finally speak again, 'I mean, like you said not that it matters now, anyway. Lissy always was a mad bitch, wasn't she? Totally freaky. She deserved everything that came her way. She'd already covered him with sheets and blankets, hadn't she? Poor kid was probably already half dead when you went up there anyway …'

The world stops rotating. I watch him, waiting to see what his response is. He stops stalking around and stands in front of the window. I glance at the kitchen door as he speaks.

'I was pissed off with you, Bev. Time and time again you'd turned me down. You got any idea what it feels like to have someone like you close-up, next to you, and for them to keep telling you, *no*? For them to have you dangling on a string like a *fucking puppet*?'

I stay silent, afraid of losing the moment, scared of breaking the spell. I just want him to carry on talking, to tell me what happened. I need to hear it from him.

He remains rigid, still staring outside at the rolling hills and countryside, his eyes following a flock of skylarks as they dance and swoop across the farmer's fields in perfect motion. Such beauty in stark contrast to the ugliness here in this room.

'All I did was help him along a little bit. He saw me and squawked and I knew if it got back that I'd been in your house, all hell would break loose.'

I can't breathe. Blackness creeps into my peripheral vision, a thick cloak of deepening grey swallowing me, choking me from the inside out.

'So, I just shoved him back under that big fucking pile of material. Jesus.' He laughs in a voice that isn't really his. 'So many blankets and sheets in that cot. I pushed his face away from me. Didn't want him recognising me, telling your dad I'd been up there. If my dad knew, he would have kicked my arse. So, I held him down there, just for a minute or so till he stopped whimpering. That's all it was. Just a couple of minutes …'

I feel as if I've been kicked. Breathing feels impossible. The room swims and fire burns at my skin; huge flames searing over my flesh, melting my body. If I stand up now I feel sure my legs will fail me. I need to do something, get away from this man before he turns on me. Which he will now that I know the truth. There is no way he will let me walk away from this. Not knowing what I know. And he is too unstable to reason with, too hot-headed. If I'm going to make a move, I need to do it now.

I pretend to stretch, an exaggerated move suggesting I'm bored with the conversation, hoping he can't see the nervous twitch that has taken hold in my eye, or the tremble in my legs as I stand up. I am more than a little surprised when he makes no move to follow me. I had expected a rush to stop me, to wrestle me to the floor. Perhaps a tussle or a slap like the one he gave the girl earlier. But there is nothing. As slowly and deliberately as I can, I head into the kitchen and run the tap while I try to locate the knives. So easy. They glint at me invitingly as I open the first drawer, a whole rack of them, their edges beautifully sharp, the steel so clear and perfect I can see my face in them. I stand and stare at the blade, at my slightly distorted reflection; a surreal version of me with unseeing, pale blue eyes and ruffled hair then quickly pull one of them out and grasp it tightly in my clammy fist as I hear the floor creak behind me.

LISSY

I should feel relieved now they have left us here, but I don't. They could come back any minute and I cannot even bring myself to think about what they could do to us; what they could do to Rosie. Beverley is fast losing any shreds of sanity she had left. And as for Daryl…bile rises when I think of what he did to my baby girl, the imprint he has left on her face with his big, clammy hands. I feel my pulse begin to race and take a deep breath to calm myself. My memory of him all those years ago is of an egocentric, misogynistic thug, a man whose selfishness and nastiness knows no bounds. And by the looks of things he hasn't changed that much. Once a monster, always a monster. And to think they are both here to get back at me for crimes they're convinced I committed and all the while they are far surpassing anything I have ever done. They will be sitting there, in my house, full of self-adulation for having caught us, talking about what they should do next, thinking up new and sickening ways to punish me and my young daughter for crimes I didn't commit.

I wiggle my hands about and traipse my fingertips over Rosie's. She responds with jerky movements and a strangled sob. White-hot fury howls through me. Who the *fuck* do these people think they are? Subjecting my daughter to all of this? They have no right to be here, in our house, terrorising us.

I close my eyes and try to think. There has to be a way to get out of here. I wrack my brains, trying to remember where I put everything when we moved in here. I don't have many things stored in the garage but there must be something somewhere I can use to free us from this tape. We could shuffle about on our backsides in the hope of finding a saw, a screwdriver, *anything* that will slice through this tape and set us free.

It's while I'm thinking about the possible ways out of here that Rosie does it. She starts to bang her feet on the concrete floor; a dull, rhythmic stomp that echoes through the vast, empty space. I shake my head and pant and pull at her hands to try to stop her but I hear her muffled cries and sobs and if anything, the pounding gets louder, more insistent, a hollow, sickening reminder of our predicament. She has to stop. I must make her stop, otherwise they'll hear us and come back through, their anger at the disturbance at boiling point. And if that happens, there's no telling what they will do.

I pant hard, hot air escaping from my nostrils, and push against Rosie to tell her to cut it out. It doesn't work. She starts to moan and bang her feet even louder. And then I hear it. The sound makes my skin prickle, coats my flesh with icy perspiration and sets my heart into a frenzied tempo.

Rosie hears it too. She stops the banging and muffled noises and we both turn to stare at the garage door that leads in from the garden. Is this it? The end for me and my teenage daughter? All of our lives, running and watching over my shoulder only for it to end like this. It was all for nothing. I lower my head and stare at my feet, bound with silver duct tape, and feel the heat of my tears as they flow down my face. My whole life has been a complete waste.

The dull creak of the door opening booms in my ears. This moment in time, this waiting, this sensation I am feeling is how people must have felt as they walked to the gallows knowing that, in just a few short moments, they will be breathing their last. This is how it feels when you know your life is about to come to an abrupt end.

I inhale deeply and look up, ready to stare death in the face. I wait and watch.

Stooping and filthy, Rupert steps in, his hair matted with sticky blood and his arm hanging at a painful angle. I let out a small gasp and feel my body begin to buzz. My head shakes involuntarily and Rupert nods at me and slowly scans the garage for anything to get us out of here. He groans softly and leans into a large crate at the back of the floor space, half hidden in shadows. It only takes him a few seconds to come out with a pair of old dressmaking scissors that I haven't used for so many years I fear they won't work and will seize up when he moves them. For once the gods are with us. I feel my hands become free as he leans down between the pair of us and gently snips away at the tape. It's stubborn and doesn't come loose easily but I eventually feel my wrists fall apart from Rosie's and don't even try to stop them when more tears fall.

I swing my arms free and rub them tenderly, pain shooting up my arm after having it so viciously pushed up my back. Steeling myself, I close my eyes and rip the tape off my mouth. A searing hot wave of pain burns at my lips. Spinning round, I turn to see Rosie watching Rupert intently as he cuts the tape away from her ankles, her legs flopping apart as it falls loose. Grasping the tape at her mouth with all her fingers, Rosie tears it away, seemingly impervious to the pain. I throw myself into her arms and we sit there, slumped against one another, sobbing until there are no tears left.

I lean back, my body exhausted, and whisper to Rupert, 'Thank you. Thank you so much.'

He nods and I watch as a small trickle of blood traces its way down the side of his head, travelling over his temple and cheekbone, resting just above his jaw. Another reminder of what I have done; what I have put people through.

'I know him,' Rupert says, his voice thick with fatigue. 'He's my taxi driver.' He stares down at the floor, his dark eyes full of anger and astonishment. 'Well, I thought I knew him. Just goes to show, doesn't it? We don't really know people at all, do we?'

I feel my face grow hot and wonder what Daryl has told him about me, whether he has said that he is living next door to a murderer or whether Rupert is still ignorant as to why we are all here, tied up and bloodied on a concrete floor. I don't have time to think about it anymore as Rosie jumps up and begins to head towards the door.

'No, Rosie! Please,' I say in a voice that is so desperate it makes me feel sick. 'It's too dangerous to go out there.'

'We need to ring the police, Mum! For God's sake let's just get out of here before they come back for us!'

She's right. Of course, she is. We need to go to Rupert's house and call the police. Rupert grips my arm and hauls me up, his fingers digging into my arm. I take a sharp intake of breath and catch his eye. His hand continues to grip me too tightly as he stares down at me, his large frame suddenly a frightening sight. I look over at Rosie. She is standing in the doorway, her back to us, waiting. When I look back, Rupert is still staring at me, his pupils black as coal. My heart crawls around my chest once more as his mouth closes into a mean, tight line.

'We need to be careful,' he says, his voice a low hiss in my ear, 'he's a complete madman.'

For a second I don't know how to react. I look at his fingers clutching my arm and try to still my heart, to stop it from battering around my ribcage. Then he suddenly loosens his grip and gently places his hand on my shoulder, his look so normal once again, I wonder if I imagined it. Everything is so rushed and muddled and terrifying I no longer feel sure of anything or anyone. This isn't my life. This is a warped version of reality, the one I have dreaded for so long, and now it's here it feels completely unreal, as if it's happening to somebody else. The worst-case scenario that I have had played over and over in my head for so many years now is actually happening, and all the things I promised I would do to defend Rosie and myself, all the plans and intricate ideas I had in my brain to help keep us alive, have deserted me.

'I'll go first,' he says in a voice that no longer scares me. He has taken charge and I have never felt so relieved.

Stepping forward, he slides past Rosie and out into the glare of the late spring sunshine, into the arms of uncertainty as we duck down and creep round the back of the garage, past my house.

We're just about to make our way round to Rupert's house when Rosie stops. Her eyes are locked on our living room window. I want to shout at her that they'll see us, that she needs to step back or she'll be spotted but I'm too far back to catch her attention.

She turns to face me and I glare at her, silently mouthing to her to move, shooing her along with my outstretched arm, but she shakes her head and stays rooted to the spot. Rupert also spins round and motions for Rosie to follow him but once again she shakes her head determinedly and points in the window. I stop, too afraid to do anything. What the hell is she doing? We're so close now, so very close to escaping all of this and here she is, risking it all.

Rupert stares over at me, his skin grey, his eyes unblinking. The wound on his head is still bleeding and he is staggering. He might die. I have no idea how much blood he's lost and if we don't get to his house and make that call, get an ambulance here as soon as we can, he may well collapse. I can't let that happen. Not after he risked his life to help us. We have to get him to hospital.

'Rosie, MOVE!' My voice carries over the air, a thin trail of sound as I spit the words out through gritted teeth.

'Mum, look!' she hisses, her eyes pleading with me as she bobs her head about to indicate I should look inside.

Every part of me hopes to find them both either dead or gone. I don't for one minute expect either of those situations to have occurred and am at a loss as to what it is that has gripped Rosie. Very slowly I edge along the wall, panic surging through me at what I am about to be faced with.

I stand next to Rosie, too afraid to turn my head, too afraid to do anything. She presses her face next to mine and whispers in my ear, 'Look, Mum! Just look …'

As if in slow motion, I take a deep breath and stare in the window, my hand flying up to my mouth in horror at what I see there.

BEVERLEY

He is standing behind me when I turn with the knife in my hand. His swollen belly bobs up and down as he takes a step back. His jowls wobble about and for a second I consider running at him, sticking the blade into his portly flesh, twisting it about and watching him tremble and beg for mercy before he slumps at my feet, his huge body a bloody red mess of seeping, ripped flesh. But that would be too easy. I go through my options. He's overweight and unfit but undoubtedly stronger than me. As long as I grip the knife tightly, I can do this. I can win.

Already I can sense his terror, see the glimmer of desperation in his eyes. It sets my pulse off, makes me tremble with delight. All these years and I had it wrong. So many years hating the wrong person, so many years thinking it was her, when all this time it was him; this disgusting piece of shit with his wandering hands and filthy mind.

I step back away from him and that's when I decide, when I know what it is I have to do.

'Move,' I say, quietly at first.

'MOVE!' I bellow when he doesn't respond.

I wave the knife at him as he slowly retreats back into the lounge, enjoying the look on his face as he stumbles and panics, his limbs flailing about through the air.

'Beverley,' he says in an imploring tone, so weak and childlike it turns my stomach. 'Come on, Bev, this is madness. We can work this out.'

I shake my head at him and press the end of the knife into his gut.

'Shit! Stop it, Bev. Fucking stop this, right now!' he screeches as a small arc of blood starts to seep out of his navel.

I don't reply. I need to centre my thoughts on what I'm doing now, not get distracted or waylaid by him. This is too important a task to mess up.

We keep walking until we're in the middle of the room. I point the blade at the floor, 'Sit down.'

He looks at me imploringly. 'On the floor?'

'Yes, on the floor!' I shout. 'Where the fuck did you think I meant?'

He nods, his chin vibrating like jelly as he slumps down, the wood bouncing under my feet. I move forward and jab the knife at the side of his head. More blood appears, a spring of red that trickles down the side of his face.

He lets out a small moan and I watch as sweat covers his face.

'It was you,' I whisper, 'all these years and it was you who killed him.'

'No!' he cries, 'it wasn't really like that. I only—'

'SHUT UP!' My voice breaks and cracks with emotion as I roar over his head. 'Not another frigging word or so help me God I will kill you right now. Do you hear me?'

No answer.

'DO YOU HEAR ME?'

'Yes.' His voice is a feeble whimper.

I almost laugh at him. So weak, so utterly pathetic. No longer the hard kid around town, just a gibbering wreck of a man who can't even defend himself against a middle-aged woman.

I jab the tip of the knife at him once more, just because I can, catching his forearm and bringing another spot of blood forth. He lets out a whimper and clutches at his flesh.

'You're a maniac. You're nothing but a stupid, fucking maniac!'

And before I can do anything he is on his feet and running at me. I do my best to keep hold of the knife but it somehow slips out of my grasp and drops on to the floor with an almighty crash, spinning round and round accusingly before landing blade first, pointing at me.

'Not so fucking clever now, eh, Bev?' he shouts and grabs hold of my arm, pulling me back away from the carving knife.

He brings his hand up and smacks me across the side of my face, the pain so heavy and so sharp it takes my breath away. For a second I am stunned, too dizzy to move. I can't stay like this. I have to get to the knife before he does because I am absolutely certain he will think nothing of carving me into small pieces if he reaches it first. He killed my little brother, he killed my innocent, baby brother. He will have no qualms whatsoever about killing me.

'Don't ever do that to me again,' I scream at him, my voice stronger than I feel.

'Or what?' he cries as he brings his hand up to strike me again.

Without thinking too deeply about it, I bring my knee up and slam it into his crotch as hard as I can. I feel the impact of the soft skin between his legs as it connects with my kneecap and watch as the pain takes a couple of seconds to register. When it does, his face folds in on itself as he doubles over before falling to the floor in a slovenly heap; deep, earthy groans escaping from his slightly parted lips. Wasting no time, I snatch the knife back up and jab at him again while he is laid on the floor. Small, red spots appear all over his back, angry crimson scars, dotted all over his body; more and more of them as I attempt to summon up enough courage to plunge it deep into his flesh.

'You always were a stuck-up bitch,' he spits as he rocks from side to side, his eyes still screwed up against the waves of pain vibrating through him.

'And you always were a useless bastard,' I reply, kicking him in his belly.

He groans again and closes his eyes.

'You killed my little brother,' I pant, barely able to comprehend the words I'm saying. All these years I had this planned in my head and it was never like this. Not here with him. It wasn't meant to be this way.

There is a silence as he rolls about some more, his body finally stopping as he lies on his side, his hands tucked tightly between his knees, his eyes are narrow slits as he stares up me.

'I'm sorry.' His voice is a whisper.

I won't listen to his words. Too late. It's all too late.

'It doesn't matter now,' I reply hoarsely, 'nothing matters any more because now I'm going to kill you.'

I hold the knife aloft, fury splitting my veins, pulsing through me, burning my flesh as it traverses round my body. A furnace of anger driving me on, making me do it. I take a shuddering breath and stop, poised, thinking about everything that has happened. I stare at the face beneath me; see how the features are contorted with terror. The knife trembles in my hands. I grip it tighter as it slips about in my palm. It feels alien against my skin, the metal smooth and cool, the blade glinting as it sways about. I gasp. This isn't me, not the real me.

'Don't do this. Put it down. Please, just put the knife down.'

I shake my head. The room seems to move. Images rush past me, a blur of colours merging and fusing, seeping into my brain making me dizzy. I grip the handle tighter.

'Let me go and I won't tell anybody about this, I promise.'

I try to speak but the words won't come. They stick in my throat, hot and clunky, no way to escape. Trapped. I widen my eyes and a trickle of saliva escapes from my mouth and runs down the side of my chin.

A small whimper, 'Come on, you know this is wrong. Just let me go. Please … LET ME GO!'

The knife wobbles in my hand. It's heavy; a deadweight. I hold on to it. I have to go ahead with this. All I need to do is push, place all my weight on it and drive it home. That's all I need to do.

The air is thick with fear, the smell of it filling my nostrils; an acrid, pungent stench ripping through me, over me. Great waves of terror gliding across wet skin.

Outside, birds sing, cars drive past, life rolls on. The mundane continues. Just as it did all those years ago, as it always will. People everywhere eating, sleeping, going about their lives while others kill and die and grieve. Life offers no compassion. It is a cold, hard mistress and we are all its victims. I stand here ready to do it, to finally bring an end to it all.

A noise from behind alerts me. My heart thumps even faster. I keep my back to it. No time to reconsider. My mind is made up; has been for a long time now.

'Put it down,' the voice calls from behind me, a gentle beckoning for me to stop.

I bring the blade up, hold it high above my head and stand with my legs apart, ready. It wasn't meant to be like this. Everything is different, wrong, spoiled. Nothing is as it should be.

'Please,' the voice in front of me begs, 'please put it down. I'm sorry. I'm so sorry.'

'We're all sorry,' I murmur, before everything goes black …

ERICA

rthur puts the phone down and rubs his face wearily. 'All done,' he says, his voice gravelly with fatigue. 'And as you probably heard, they didn't take me too seriously to begin with but apparently they're on the case. Or at least that's what they said. We can only hope, can't we?'

'I thought about ringing her but she's so volatile and unpredictable I might end up making it worse,' I say, biting at a loose piece of skin on my lip. It comes away and I welcome the sting that accompanies it. Nothing compared to what Lissy is going through at the minute. And, of course, there's her daughter to think of. I fight back tears at the very idea of what is going on in that house, the terror they must feel.

'Best to leave the police to do their thing, now.' He makes to leave but then stops. 'They also said they might send somebody round here later to take a full report after they've checked the property out.'

I feel a tug of dismay at the thought of it; having to tell a perfect stranger about a secret I should never have had. Something so repulsive and grotesque I can hardly believe those thoughts and ideas ever belonged to me.

I nod and let out a deep, rattling breath, my eyes misting over.

'All over now, Erica. All behind us,' he says reassuringly. 'This Lissy woman will probably move on to another place, disappear once more and Beverley will get some sort of psychiatric help. We've done all we can now to help them. Let the police do their bit now.'

Arthur fills the kettle and busies himself getting mugs out and emptying the teapot of the old dregs. I smile and brush my hand over his as he passes me a coaster. He reciprocates, giving my fingers a squeeze. And that's when I know everything is going be all right.

LISSY

He'd be dead if it hadn't been for Rupert. After we crept in, my heart lodged firmly in my gullet at the sight before us, he had tried to coax her to put the knife down, but I could tell by the expression on her face she was beyond any kind of reasoning. Rupert saw it, too. He did what he could but she wasn't listening. She had crossed that line.

It all happened so quickly. She was standing there with the knife above her head, ready. I didn't dare breathe. Every pocket of air that exited my body felt like a monumental effort. Rosie stood, her eyes wide and glassy, her face pinched in horror at the sight before her.

We watched as Rupert shuffled forward, bit by bit, his every movement an effort, his eyes screwed up against the pain. I tried to stop him, to hold him back but he just kept on going, hobbling forward, fraction by fraction until he was so close, he could touch her.

We watched as Beverley brought the knife down, and Rupert lunged for her, grabbing her round her legs, bringing her crashing down to the ground. Her head hitting the wooden flooring, the knife spinning over Daryl's head and landing on the other side of the room.

∞∞∞∞∞

And so here I stand, next to the man who I now know did it, the person who quite happily allowed me to take the blame for something I didn't do, allowing me to go to prison for a crime he committed. And now he thinks he has the right to come here and punish me.

'Mum, you need to take this!' After the tussle, Rosie had run over and grabbed the knife and now stands with it in her hands, her thin arms shaking with fright, the welt on her face more visible than ever.

She passes it over to me, too frightened to hang on to it, its presence a sickly reminder of what we have been through. I watch as she rushes over to help Rupert, who is hanging on to his arm. Beverley emits a low moan as she attempts to sit up, her eye already ballooning where her face hit the floor.

And then there is Daryl. I stand over him, the knife still in my hands, shiny and heavy, the jagged edge glinting in the light as I wave it about and shout down at him, 'You. UP!'

He doesn't respond, his shirt peppered with spots of blood, his hands lodged between his legs as he hangs on to his crotch.

'I said, get up!'

He rocks about and pushes himself up into a sitting position, his face pasty, a film of sweat covering his pulpy flesh as he opens his mouth to speak.

'NO!' I bellow at him. 'No talking. You had your chance to talk all those years back but said nothing.'

Air escapes from my body as I watch him look up at me and smile. The room moves about violently and for a second I think I'm going to be sick.

'Doesn't matter now, does it eh, sweetheart? What's done is done. Served your time and all that ...'

I wiggle the knife about and listen to the sounds behind me as Rupert gets to his feet and Rosie scrambles about to help him, telling Beverley to stay away from her.

'It's OK, sweetheart,' I murmur, 'they're both going to stand up now, aren't you?'

No movement from either of them. I take a step back so I can view them both, watch what they plan on doing.

'I SAID GET UP!' They both stagger to their feet and I sense Rosie's ever-growing terror behind me.

'It's all right, Rosie,' I say, desperate for her to listen to me. 'Please do as I ask and do it quickly, OK?' She nods at me, fresh tears pouring down her face. 'Take Rupert and go next door. Call 999 and tell them to send the police and an ambulance.'

'But, Mum!' she cries, 'I can't leave you here with these two.'

'Yes, you can, sweetheart. I have this knife. Nothing is going to happen to me. I'm perfectly capable of looking after myself but if we don't get Rupert to a hospital as soon as we can, he might die. He's lost a lot of blood and is still bleeding.'

She stares at me then looks at Rupert, who is pale and shivering. She reaches out and places her hand over his forehead.

'He's freezing, Mum.'

'I know he is. He'll be fine if you take him and make that call. You need to go now, Rosie. Please go now!'

She is a clumsy jumble of panicky limbs as she drags Rupert along, his tall body swaying beside her as they cling to one another; a pair of damaged survivors. I watch as they lean in together for support and head back next door to Rupert's house.

'Right you two, get on your fucking feet, NOW!'

As if sensing my renewed swell of anger, they swirl about, grappling to get up, their injured bodies knocking against the wood as they finally manage to stand upright. My ears become attuned to a noise in the distance. I need to move quickly.

'Turn around with your backs to me!' I yell, my pulse throbbing in my ears.

They both do it without question, Beverley's legs buckling, her gait laboured and unsteady.

And that's when I hear it his voice, a sickly, sweet lilting tone in the eerie stillness of the lounge.

'You fucking well deserved it, anyway,' Daryl says. He turns to look at me, his face twisted into a sneer. 'I might have killed him but you set the scene, sweetheart. You set the ball rolling.' He winks at me as he speaks, 'How was prison food? Get yourself a girlfriend while you were inside? Got a bit of action going, did you, if you know what I mean?'

I do it before he has chance to do anything, to run, to scream out, to even breathe. I plunge the knife deep between his shoulder blades and force it in, pushing with all my might. So many years of anger and frustration and hurt pouring out of me, funnelling their way into the blade that I drive deep into his pale, flabby skin. He falls on to the floor, his body twitching and convulsing, blood seeping out of him, a huge pool of burgundy liquid covering the floor, spreading around him in great, pulsing waves.

Outside I hear the wail of sirens as they grow ever closer, a cacophony of noise blaring in the still spring air.

'It was self-defence,' I say to Beverley. She nods in recognition and reaches up to touch the wound on her face.

'Rosie's face, yours, Rupert's injuries, this piece of shit did them all, yes?'

She whispers her agreement, her voice brittle with exhaustion. Suddenly I feel calm, all my fear and resentment and rage disappearing bit by bit, ebbing out of me as we sit down together on the sofa and listen to the screech of tyres as a convoy of cars pull up outside.

'Self-defence,' she says quietly, lightly touching my arm as we sit and wait.

ROSIE

Isn't it funny how you think you know someone, then you feel you don't know them at all, and then everything changes and they're back to that same old person that you always knew? That's how it was with mum. The strange thing is, I always had an inkling that something wasn't quite right with her life story, but could never get it out of her. She was so good at covering up, at trying to protect me from it all. I don't blame her for any of it. She was, and is, the best mother any girl could ever have.

Since it's all happened our lives have changed beyond recognition. Knottswood Academy has welcomed me back with open arms. It was pretty embarrassing at first, my first day, having to put up with all the backward glances, the whispers in the classroom, but knowing what my mum went through in her life has given me some perspective. Having to put up with a few sly looks and a bit of gossip is nothing compared to what she has endured in her troubled life. But it's all behind us now. I have a gang of new friends, all completely engrossed by what has gone on. I've tried to keep a low profile, play it all down, but everyone is so keen on knowing every little detail that they pester me relentlessly. I don't mind so much. It's better than being on my own.

Mum has a renewed sense of purpose. She is out and about every day, visiting people; going to see *her*. I can't bring myself to do it but Mum reckons she needs all the support she can get. That's what I love about my mother; her capacity for forgiveness. I'm not sure I'm ready to take that step just yet, but Mum said she's spent so much of her life being surrounded by hatred that she has banished it from her life. Hatred is toxic, she said. The world needs more love and forgiveness; hate just eats away at people, rotting them from the inside out. She's right, of course. She is always right.

Beverley is in a home somewhere being treated for her issues. Mum reckons she's been through a lot and it's not her fault that she did what she did to us. Again, I admire Mum for digging deep and finding it within her to forgive that woman; not just forgive her but actually *help* her. She's a saint, my mother. She has also gone to see the two other mothers, the parents of Erica and Beverley. She said they need some closure, to bring an end to it all. Personally, I just think that she is enjoying being out of the house, having the freedom to go wherever she likes without having to constantly look over her shoulder, worrying about being seen and recognised. So many years being cooped up and now she can flit off whenever she wants to. It's all so brilliant for her.

I have done a bit of my own research and discovered that my grandparents are now living in separate care homes, their brains addled by alcohol. Mum was spot on. They're not worth bothering with. I've also tracked down my dad. That was a tricky one after what he did to us taking off like that, being so absolutely certain Mum was guilty and I wasn't his but at the end of the day he is still my dad and I am curious. My memories of him are so vague and foggy, I'd like to see him if only to reassure him that neither me nor Mum are the monsters he thought we were, that she is a decent person and now living the life she should have lived for many years. She is free and happy and nobody can take that away from her.

And as for Daryl? He didn't die. I don't mind admitting that I wish he had. You can't blame me for that, can you? After what he put my mother through he deserved to be put in his grave. He had a punctured lung and lost a lot of blood but he's still around, awaiting trial after admitting killing Greg. I'm not interested in the court case. We've had a gutful of it, Mum and me. And besides, the press are already snapping at our heels, offering Mum loads of cash to tell her side of the story. She told them to fuck off with their seedy stories and blood money. I jumped up and down and hugged her when I heard her say that to them. I clapped my hands and almost swept her off her feet. It was such a completely fabulous moment; one that will stay with me forever. There have been so many moments lately that it's hard to remember them all.

Anyway, enough about the rest of them, the other folk out there who pale into insignificance compared to Lissy McLeod. Did I tell you how brilliant my mum is? Not like the other mothers out there…mine is the best. One in a million…

ACKNOWLEDGEMENTS

Once again, I would like to thank my husband Richard for his continued support and for being my thesaurus and grammar check man when my brain has refused to work properly. I would like to thank each and every member of my family and friends for their encouragement and kind words. I am so lucky to have such close and supportive people around me.

Thank you to everyone at Bloodhound Books Fred Freeman, Besty Reavley, Sumaira Wilson, Alexina Golding and Sarah Hardy especially Betsy and Sumaira who have to put up with my manic, late night emails and panicky messages. One of these fine days, I will get a grip, ladies!

I must acknowledge the bloggers out there who help to get my books noticed. Your tireless efforts are the lifeblood of the publishing industry! I am eternally grateful for all that you do, promoting and reviewing. There are too many to mention individually but I think you are all utterly brilliant. A special mention to Carol Pickering for her help with proofreading. I always knew you had an eagle eye, Carol!

Last, but definitely not least, I would like to show my gratitude to the readers who have taken time out of their busy lives to read my books. Without you, we writers are nothing, so a heartfelt thank you from a fairly new author who is still finding her feet!

Made in the USA
Columbia, SC
04 December 2017